2

POISONED CHALICE

MABEL DE BELLEME
Normandy's Wicked Lady

BY
J.P. REEDMAN

COVER-Pixabay/Herne's Cave

C2021 by J.P. REEDMAN/HERNE'S CAVE

CHAPTER ONE

The day my mother was strangled, I was plucking green apples from the craggy trees in the castle orchard. My nurses had warned me to stay away, insisting that unripe apples would turn my belly and make me wail with pain upon the privy, but I was determined to ignore their feverish admonishments—as I always did. The nursemaids were a gaggle of miserable old crows, horrified if I dirtied a shoe or stained my kirtle. As for apples, I liked them...*sour*.

That is me, in truth, I supposed, dragging down a heavy branch bearing a large apple tinted with a faint reddish blush. *Sour...not sweet*. Unlike most maidens I had met, I loathed girlish fripperies, pointless needlework, tales of silly romantic exploits. Hounds and horses—those I much preferred, riding out from the castle of Alencon with the wind in my hair to watch the hunt.

My father, William, nicknamed *Talvas* because he was as hard and unyielding as the iron shield he bore, was strangely pleased when he witnessed his little daughter's unfeminine attitude. Standing with his great, sword-roughened hands on his hips, he would roar, "Ah, Mabel...my little Mab! I swear you are more like a son than a daughter. I swear by God's Beard, you are more like a son than my son!"

Such jesting talk needled my brother, Arnulf, a milksop if there ever was one, thin as a reed with close-set eyes that appeared crossed when he was angry. It also needled my mother, Hildeburg, who was very like Arnulf in both looks and mannerisms. She was the complete opposite of my sire, consumed by religious fervour and acts of charity and piety. I seldom saw her off her knees, and when she was, she was prone to scold and chide, all the while toying with her long string of gemstone rosary beads, a priceless gift from her mother.

Clackety clack, the beads would go, running between her bony fingers. "Mabel, your conduct shames me!" *Clackety-clack.* "Mabel, I am aware you have not been to Confession!" *Clackety-clack.* "Mabel, your needlework appals, and your hair is a bird's nest!" *Clackety-Clackety-Clack.*

I pushed thoughts of Mother and her beads and prayers from my mind. I had my prize. Thieved apple clutched in my small hand, I retreated to a secluded corner of the garden where I might sit and feast on it in peace. I had hardly stuffed myself behind the broken wall, tripping over the daisies and wild foxgloves to find my favourite niche, when I heard the sound of voices raised in anger.

My parents were in the orchard…and they were arguing.

"I am going to church!" Mother's voice was shrill, shrewish. "That is all there is to it, William."

"You do not need to go so often." Father's retort came, a bear's growl, deep and dangerous. "You spend too much time running errands for lazy priests or conversing about your rheumatism with that old hag who runs the convent. Of late, you are seldom at home."

"Why would I want to linger here? You shout, you bellow like a stabbed boar, you cavort with strumpets before my eyes…You even cast insults at our only son."

"Pah, Arnulf? That feeble creature…Sometimes when I see him traipsing around with a lute or psalter in his hand, I can scarcely believe he is of my seed. I was holding a sword and fighting my enemies at his age!"

"William! How dare you say such things! You impugn my honour, which is precious as a jewel to me!"

"Oh fear not, woman, I know you guard your chastity well. After all, it soon became clear after our marriage that you loathe sporting beneath the sheets! Christ's Teeth, sometimes when I've forgotten to blow out the candles at night, I've had to watch your face, screwed up in disgust at my touch. I doubt very much you'd feel much different with any other man…You would have made a better nun than wife!"

Breathing heavily, I crawled to the edge of my hiding spot and peered around the edge of the wall. "Get out of my way!" Mother was standing a few yards away, her cheeks a hectic mottled red, her right hand clasping her beloved rosary beads. "I need to go to the priory—to pray that you are reformed and forgo your evil ways! To pray that you do not go to Hell, though I dare say you will no matter what I do."

My father's own face began to turn a dusky purplish shade, the hue of a thundercloud. His earlier tone had merely been mocking, hurtful but harmless—now the storm was brewing with him, true anger that burst forth in a devastating torrent. "You insult me with your foolish talk of evil and Hell, you stupid beldam. Save for my daughter Mabel, you have brought me nought but ill. She is the only good thing to come from you…"

"Mabel!" Mother spat my name as if it were gall, making me cringe. "She's a sharp-tongued, disobedient child who needs a good thrashing. As for your love of her—hah, many times I have thought you'd prefer her as wife rather than daughter, unnatural creature that you are."

In shock at her words, I dropped my pilfered apple. It hit a stone and rolled away in the grass. I made a grab for it then suddenly recoiled, for a worm was oozing out of its damaged heart, white and wiggling in the pale sunlight dappling the orchard.

"What did you say, Hildeburg?" Father's voice had dropped low, almost a growl. Full of violent promise, it was worse than a full-blown roar. "What did you intimate about me and our daughter?"

"N-nothing," she stammered, shaking her head. She knew she had gone too far. "It was just a foolish barb, meant to wound. Now, let me pass, William; *let me pass.*"

She tried to push past father, but he grabbed her arm in fury, yanking her backwards. She had been clutching a prayerbook in one hand; it fell to the ground and the pages tore from the binding and spiralled in the wind. She struggled to free herself and snatched up the soiled and damaged book, but he kicked it violently away, causing the cover to rip free.

Mother wailed, aggrieved. "I loathe you, you devil!" She flung herself at him, nails daggered, mouth distorted by a bitter howl. The gemstone rosary, attached to her girdle, glittered in the wan light—black shining jet eyes, sombre sapphire tears, blood-red ruby droplets.

"You defy me, you goad me…*enough*!" Father stepped back, pressing his hand to his cheek. She had scored it; red oozed between his splayed fingers.

She stared, her breath making ragged, railing noises—and then she tried to flee.

He caught her roughly, spun her around until she faced him. He tore her headdress off, so that she stood, shocked, mouth hanging agape, her hair falling down in a tangle of darkness.

Darkness...so much darkness...

I thought he would strike her. He certainly had done so before. But there was a different look in his eyes; a glazed look, a redness; the very surface of his eyes shone with almost unnatural, feral light as if a demon had possessed him. Taking her torn veil, he wrapped it around his hands.

I frowned. What was he doing?

The next moment, the band was wound about my mother's throat. Father gave a strange cry, almost triumphant, as he pulled it tighter and tighter. Eye bulging in terror, Mother clutched at the restricting cloth, unable to make a sound as her air was cut off. Face filled with deadly intent, Father dragged her further into the apple-garth, well out of my view and, heart drumming, I stumbled back to lean against the ruinous wall. What had I witnessed?

I crouched in the long grasses for what seemed an eternity, dandelion spores and spiderwebs blowing past my nose in the stiff breeze. Eventually, I deemed it safe for me to leave my hiding spot. Tentatively I stepped out from my niche, trying not to breathe too hard or rustle my skirts in case I was heard.

A shadow descended over me, black and overwhelming, and a frightened gasp broke from my lips. Glancing up, I saw the face of my sire, mottled, scratch-marks and a smear of blood on his cheek. He breathed heavily, raggedly, his chest heaving. I cowered in his presence and he grabbed my arm, hauling me closer.

"What did you see? I know you were watching."

My mouth gaped as wide as that of a hooked fish. Words would not come out. Would he strike me for spying—or even do worse? William Talvas was renowned as a cruel warlord, feared by other knights and barons throughout Normandy. In war, he would take his captured enemies and blind them and their children, so that they were fit only for life in a monastery—if they survived their mutilation.

Father shook me again; my head wobbled stupidly on my neck as my teeth jolted together. "I saw you fighting mama...and the cloth around her throat. I swear I won't tell. Just please, please do not kill me or blind me because I saw. I did not mean to watch!"

Father's face pressed into mine; the stink of wine hung on his breath. His violence was always worse when he drank heavily. "Did you truly think I would hurt *you*, my only child who is worth anything. Do not be stupid, Mabel!"

My heart's frantic beating began to subside. I was safe! "Where...where is Mother?"

"You do not want to see."

"She's dead, isn't she?"

He hesitated for a moment and then, "Yes."

"I want to see her."

"No."

"Yes. I want to make sure."

He grunted. "As you wish."

He stalked into the trees and I followed. Under one of the apple trees, mother lay slumped, eyes open, glazed, lips grey and parted, tongue thrust between them. Definitely dead. A fly walked over one eyelid.

"She wanted to go to church so much...Well, now she will be buried in one for eternity," snorted Father, folding his arms. "So it comes to all who dare defy my will."

I turned to my Father, murderer of my Mother, throwing my dishevelled braid back over my shoulder. I took a deep breath. "I suppose we should get someone to collect her body and prepare it for burial. How will you explain her death? Maybe you could haul in a few stupid sots from the village tavern and blame them. Who would dare to that say that you, the great and terrible William Talvas, was lying?"

He stared at me with something akin to admiration. "Mab, I am amazed at your fortitude...and pleased. I thought there would be tears at least."

"For Mother?" I sniffed. I glanced at the body. "Father, you know we never got along. I never liked her much anyway." And with that, I stepped to her body and took her beloved gemstone rosary from her girdle.

I held it aloft, its stones flashing. I had never liked her much...but I *had* always liked those pretty beads....

Mother was buried in the local convent and the nuns sang prayers over her tomb. Father stood like a statue, clad in crimson and silver, showing no emotion, while the Abbess cast him evil glances. Arnulf, my brother, was weeping, but I kept my composure throughout the interment, even though the whole proceedings rather bored me. The church was cold, the rites dismal and drawn out, while the heavy incense made my eyes water...Well, perhaps if the smoke brought a few tears to my eyes, it would not be such a bad thing. I did not want to appear heartless, after all. People were watching.

After the funeral was over, Father and his men rode down to the village. The rest of the mourners followed, under heavy guard. A scaffold had been raised in the market square, its crossed timbers black against the brightness of the sky. Two village men, unshaven, piggish oafs, were dragged from a prison cart that had rolled down from the castle even as the nuns sang over Mother's entombed body. They gibbered like madmen at the sight of the gallows with its swinging rope. "My lord, mercy!" one screamed, clutching the bars of his cage. "We were nowhere near her ladyship when she was killed. We will swear on any holy relic you wish!"

Father refused to even glance in the prisoners' direction. He nodded to the soldiers guarding the cart to drag the men out. Stumbling, their ankles in shackles, they were driven up the scaffold's stairs. The crowd crushed against the foot of the scaffold went wild—half of them eager to see them die, the other half weeping and wailing in despair. The sound was horrific, like terrified asses braying and dogs howling...only it was men and women.

The hangman forced the prisoners onto stools and looped the nooses around both men's necks. The first one who had spoken was crying. His fellow, a great bullnecked man, looked more furious than afraid. "None of us would harm the Lady Hildeberg!" he roared. "None. She was a good woman who gave alms to the poor and sick in the village. If it's a killer you're looking for, my thought is that he came from closer to home."

Father's nostrils flared. His eyes were flint. "Hang them!"

The hangman and his assistant kicked the stools from beneath the condemned men's feet. They fell like stones, struggling, kicking and jerking as they were strangled by the rope. The crowd surged forward, some trying to mount the scaffold, while others cheered with an obscene kind of frenzy.

"Come, Mabel," ordered Father. He swung up onto the back of his ebon stallion and I clambered onto my fine rouncey, and without a backwards glance at the gallows, we hastened back to our castle.

Soon Father and I were at table having a lovely meal of mutton and *laurices*—newborn baby rabbits—with the fire crackling merrily in the centre of the hall, castle a warm, comforting glow. Arnulf strolled in, glared balefully at us both, and then stalked back out.

Father had thrown a bone after his retreating back. The dogs that always wandered around the hall grabbed it in their jaws and began to fight over it. "Those dogs," Father nodded at the growing hounds, "even they are more loyal than my spoilt brat, Arnulf."

"I would still be careful of him, father," I warned, dabbing my mouth with a napkin. "He is, after all, your son."

"Is he? I wonder sometimes." Father gnawed a shank of mutton straight to the bone. Glutinous beads of fat trembled on his beard. "But no, he must be; Hildeburg was such a bloodless, passionless creature, steeped in her piety. She'd never have cuckolded me. Never."

"Whatever the case, we must watch Arnulf," I said.

"I will leave that to you, Mabel," Father said, as he tore again at the mutton. In the flickering firelight, I could still see the marks on his face where Mother had clawed him before she died.

Sadly, I failed at my task of tailing my brother. A few days after the funeral, he took horse and rode out of Alencon—and did not return by nightfall. Neither Father nor I knew where Arnulf had gone, which filled us both with unease. The local villagers scowled and glared at us with hatred—but that was nothing new. I ignored their hard, worn faces as I journeyed about Father's demesne on my rouncey, almost, I fancied, taking my mother's place at his side. Father enjoyed my company; I was quick-witted and made him laugh, and unlike my mother, who had scorned earthly fripperies, I loved the bracelets and circlets and brocades he bestowed upon me, wearing them all at once until I looked a shimmering peacock rather than a modest young maiden.

But it was not a life of simply parading around in finery—I had an education, of that my sire made sure, although he could not read himself and signed documents with an X when he could not use his seal. "I do not wish for a dullard for a daughter," he said, patting my head with a great, calloused paw. "You will learn Latin, you will know how to write. I have acquired several monks to teach you; men terrified of women, so they will never try to breach your virtue. And if they should dare try to take any carnal liberties, by God's Finger I'll make them into eunuchs."

My tutors were Brother Laurence and Brother Giso, from the abbey of Evroul. The former was old, half-blind and smelt of rank cheese; he was my Latin teacher, while Giso, a young monk, taught me how to write in a fine calligraphic style. I liked to tease Giso; he was a tall, thin stalk of a man, with red hair like a fiery ring on his tonsured head. He was, as Father said, terrified of girls, no doubt fearing they would lead him into sin. For that reason, I would say things such as, 'Giso, my wrist is cramped. Can we not go for a walk to take the air?' He always agreed, and I would insist he come with me, as my 'honourable escort.' I would then lead him, a lamb to the slaughter, to the meads behind the castle, where the village girls and castle maids would bathe naked and unashamed, cavorting in the murky water like gross mermaids with mud and weeds trailing down their white flanks. He would stutter and stammer, his face turning the hue of his hair as he tried vainly to avert his eyes, and I would say, all innocence, "Whatever is wrong, Giso? What you see is how God made us. Surely what God made cannot be evil!" and he could scarcely argue.

Sometimes my behaviour was even worse; I'd stretch myself like a cat, and my skirts to my knees and wade in the water myself. Giso's face would go bone-white, no doubt as he envisioned himself locked in the dungeons with Father's torturers for daring to look at me...but he could not keep his eyes off my shapely calves and ankles, pale beneath the surface of the water. Yet he never dared touch, or do anything improper and of that I was secretly glad. As amusing as he was to torment, I did not want to see him killed, so innocent and silly.

Giso was more innocent than *me*, and I was but a girl of thirteen summers.

Winter had reached Alencon when the troubles started for Father and me. Outside the castle, the younger villagers were skating on the frozen moat. Opening the wooden shutters on my bedchamber window, I would doff rabbit-skin mittens, grab the icicles off the ledge below and hurl them like spears at the children below. The urchins would scream as these missiles smashed around them, and lose their balance, falling on their bottoms on the ice, sometimes even going through into the frigid water. I would laugh and laugh until I could barely breathe.

But then, on one dim afternoon just before sunset, after the last skater had vanished back to the village, I let my bored gaze wander over the winter-blasted landscape to alight on a distant clump of denuded trees where dozens of rooks flitted through the bare branches. A green hedge of dense brush grew around the tree-trunks—and, to my wonderment, it seemed to be moving as if possessed of unnatural life.

Leaning dangerously far out of the window, I squinted into the low, blinding winter sun. The castle walls and towers spun dizzyingly below, as I inched even further out of the narrow gap, onto the back of a carved grotesque with bat-wings and gaping, eroded mouth that jutted out below the window ledge. Mother would have screamed and wailed and prayed to God upon seeing me so precariously perched, but she was dead and the dead see nothing....

Clinging with one hand to the grotesque's moss-furred horns, I shaded my eyes with the other and focussed my gaze on the trees. At first, nought seemed out of the ordinary, and I began to think my imagination had merely played a cruel jest on me. Then, suddenly, the foliage sprouting around the tree boles shivered again and the shrieking rooks took off in a great dark cloud against the bloody sky, and I caught a glimpse of one horse, then another, then another, and many men in mail and on foot. Spears thrust up amidst the tangled greenery, bristling like thorns.

My heart began to thud. Father had many enemies but I had seen something ominous flutter briefly between the boughs before being swiftly furled. A banner bearing a fierce castle keep upon a sable background—the symbol of our House, the ancient House of Belleme. My brother Arnulf was out there with an army! I *knew* it was him, had suspected from the start he would not lie low forever, no matter how Father taunted him as a craven weakling. He had come to attack Alencon, to seek vengeance for my mother's murder.

I wriggled back into the chamber, my nose red and streaming, my fingers numb from the cold. Throwing open the chamber door, I fled through the dim corridors to find my father.

He was in the hall, drunk as was his usual wont, with his retainers all clustered about him, shaggy loutish men deep in their cups. A strumpet squatted upon his knee, as intoxicated as he, her paps nigh bursting out of her indecently low-cut kirtle.

Ignoring the lewd, wine-sotted stares of his men, I rushed up to the dais at the head of the room. "Lord Father!" I gasped, out of breath from my long run through the castle.

"Mab, my little Mab, this is no place for you," he slurred, as the harlot in his lap planted a wet kiss on the side of his neck. "Go back to your chamber. Whatever has you so riled can surely wait till the morrow."

"No, it cannot!" I grabbed a great lump of firewood and smashed it down in the centre of the firepit, throwing up a shower of red sparks. Father's men leapt back, as did the rangy hounds that traversed the hall, eating scraps and licking at spilt drink.

"Mabel!" roared Father, knocking the whore off his knee. She fell upon her round bottom with a harsh squawk. "Do not defy me!"

"My sire, I have seen what you, a man well-schooled in warfare, have missed!" My eyes flashed. "There are enemies without Alencon, hiding in the trees upon the distant rise beyond the river. I have seen our own banner amongst them before they hid it away. It is Arnulf, no doubt, seeking to cause trouble."

"Arnulf!" Father blinked as if the idea of his son fighting against him had truly never entered his mind despite my earlier warnings.

"That monkish fop. Pah, I'll feed his liver to the dogs if he dares come at me. But I am sure he won't. He would never dare to assail these stalwart walls...he knows my strength and the courage of my men."

"Would he not attack?" I cried. "I think he would. And many men across Normandy hate you, as you know—it would bring no surprise if every soul you ever bested in war, every man whose father or brother was blinded by you, flocked to Arnulf's banner, not out of any love for him, but to see you fall."

Father loosed a roar of laughter. "See the bold girl-child tell her Father all about the ways of fighting men! What a girl I've spawned. Fear not, my little hellion, even if Arnulf has recruited some of my enemies, we are behind stout walls here at Alencon. He will never get through them; he may hurl himself at our gates as much as he pleases." He spat in the rushes. "Now off with you...I have business to attend."

"Business!" I grabbed the wine carafe on the table before him and poured it out on the rushes. The men gathered in the hall laughed. "This is your only business it seems—drinking...and whoring. I give you good warning; why do you not listen?"

"I give *you* warning, brat!" Father heaved himself up, menacing now. "I will hear no more talk of Arnulf. Go to your chamber and bother me with your female chatter no more—if you continue to flap your tongue, I shall send you away to a convent."

"No, you would never do that. I am not stupid, sire. You hate nuns. And you know I am of more value to you if I am marriageable than locked in some dismal cloister."

"Then I'll marry you to someone rich but old as Methuselah; how would you like that, Mabel?"

The hardened warriors in the hall burst into laughter again and began making crude jests.

I stamped one foot in rage and fled out into the passageway, leaving the sounds of bawdy mirth behind. Why would Father shame me and refuse to listen, despite encouraging me to be clever and astute, unlike most other maidens? Furious, I stormed to my bedchamber, opening the window as wide as possible, despite the possibility of freezing to death or catching a deadly ague. I had a duty to protect my home.

A nursemaid slid in through the door, scolding me and trying to close the shutters but I roughly pushed her away. "Go from me, Aude," I yelled. "I do not want you here. I'll stay at the window all night if I wish. I will guard the castle if my stupid father won't!"

Aude scurried away, head bowed, and I perched in the window embrasure, straining into the darkness. Nothing stirred, save the nightbirds that played around the towers; in the far distance a fox yipped, its voice sounding almost human. Wrapping myself in a fur, I continued my vigil as the moon westered and the stars set. I began to shake and tremble despite the fur; my teeth clashed together, chattering, and goosebumps stood out white on my arms.

Finally, I could bear the almost painful cold no longer. I banged the shutters closed, and with a little mewling noise curled up before the fire brazier, flinging a handful of kindling on the flames to gain more warmth. Once I had thawed out, I crawled wearily into my bed and slept, cocooned in embroidered coverlets and warm sheepskins.

And nothing broke my sleep, no sound of drumming hooves or clashing swords...

Feeling rather foolish, I trudged into the great hall the next day with a subdued demeanour. On his seat on the dais, Father glared and muttered under his breath, but he was too rough from his night's drinking to pay me much heed. I spent the rest of the day avoiding him and sitting in boredom through my lessons with Giso, who had a cold and kept sneezing. I would have preferred to go riding or hawking but with Father in his drink-addled state that was impossible. Later, lessons out the way and Giso gone to bed with a red nose and a poultice on his chest, I sought the solitude of my chamber where I nibbled on a venison pasty I'd stolen from the kitchen and then headed to my bed. Last night's futile guard shift had wearied me, and bags hung heavy beneath my eyes.

I was asleep almost as soon as my head touched the bolster.

Midnight had not long passed when Arnulf and his followers came. How they gained entrance to the castle I do not know; I suspect he had sympathisers who must have opened the postern gate or turned a blind eye to grappling hooks thrown up along the wall.

The first thing that awakened me was the vague smell of smoke; not the usually smoky fragrance of the hall but a stronger scent that brought me to wakefulness with loud coughing. Then I heard screams from below and the warning bell over the castle gatehouse began to a frantic clanging.

Leaping up, I flung on my garments and raced from the chamber. The hallway outside was full of thick, roiling smoke, and hysterical servants who ran blindly about, screeching as they bumped into each other and the walls. Covering my mouth and nose with my long sleeve, I staggered through the smoky dimness, feeling my way along the stonework with my free hand.

When I reached the Great Hall, I saw that the hangings behind the dais were alight. Unfamiliar soldiers were rampaging through the chamber, ripping down imported tapestries, smashing and overturning tables, even carrying off Father's large oak chair with its armrests carved into dragons.

He was nowhere in sight; a sharp spear of fear ran through me.

Suddenly a large, unfamiliar man in a conical helm thundered up behind me, grabbing me by the waist. He hurled me over his shoulder, knocking the air from my lungs. "Look what I caught!" he bellowed. "It must be my lucky night."

I screamed with fury and tried to reach back to claw at his face, but his metal nose-guard prevented my fingernails from causing much damage. I drummed at him with my feet, bruising myself on the mail shirt he wore. "Bitch!" he bawled. "I will teach you, slattern…" He flung me down onto one of the collapsed tables and slowly approached me as an unpleasant grin widened across his stubbled face.

At that moment, Arnulf thrust his way in front of the hulking soldier. He looked different from the last time I had seen him—older, harder, less like a timid scribe and more like a young warrior. He wore a tabard emblazoned with the dark Tower of House Belleme, and in his fist, he held an unsheathed sword, its blade flickering orange in the flight of the flames that danced on the curtains and began to lick the ceiling.

"Back off, brute!" he shouted at my assailant. "That is my sister, Mabel. Touch her again, and I'll have your head. You hear me? Let her go. She's not for you; there is plenty of other plunder!"

The soldier, troll-like, made a disappointed grunting noise and hastily stomped away. Arnulf grabbed me by the wrist and yanked me to my feet with little tenderness. "Are you hurt?"

"No, I do not think so. Just bruised." I winced as little ripples of pain ran down my spine.

"What were you thinking of coming into here alone, you stupid girl?" Grabbing my shoulders, he shook me roughly.

"I was trying to make sure I didn't burn to death in the fire your sellswords started!" I spat, trying to break free of his unwelcome grip. "Now, let me go! I must find Father."

"You're not going near that miscreant! His evil influence is already clear to see in you. I am taking you from Alencon and placing you in a convent, where the nuns will beat the wickedness from your soul and make you a proper, biddable female!" Clutching my arm, he began to drag me from the Great Hall and the growing conflagration.

We were halfway across the smoke-clouded bailey, me dragging on his arm, protesting loudly, Arnulf admonishing me for all my sins, real or imagined, when the thundering of hooves sounded amidst the crackle of flames, the shrieks of the servants, the mirth of Arnulf's hired thugs as they looted and burned. Out of the acrid vapours, a great heavy war-horse pounded towards us, hooves hewing the muddy ground, and upon its back rode Father, teeth gritted in a rictus grin, the whites of his staring, wrathful eyes glowing in the gloom.

"Unhand her, you treacherous worm!" he shouted at Arnulf, and then he bore down upon us, swinging his huge sword in an arc.

Arnulf ducked—I had never seen him move so fast!—and the blade clove air where his head had been a mere second before. Dropping my arm, he fled like a craven, rushing back into the burning castle. "Coward!" I screamed after him. "Father will kill you…*kill you*…"

"Mabel, be silent!" Father's voice lashed me like a whip. "Get over here."

Obediently I went to him, and he wrenched me up onto the saddle. He hauled on his steed's reins, turning the beast away from the castle doors. "What are you doing?" I cried, aghast. "Aren't you going to follow Arnulf and end his treachery?"

"He's brought too many men. I had no idea the weasel had so many friends—or that I was so despised. We must flee, Mabel…"

"Flee! But that…that's *dishonourable*! He…he'll…"

"He gets the castle and the expense of repairing it. We get our lives," said Father harshly. "Now cease your wittering or I'll bind your mouth."

Father struck his spurs into his horse's flanks and it thundered away across the bailey toward the castle entrance. Men leapt out of the hazy gloom, attempting to stop him; he rode them down, and they fell screaming before his stallion's dagger-sharp hooves. Up ahead, the turreted gateway loomed, gates smashed asunder and hanging on their hinges. Men were fighting hand to hand with swords and axes, while several arches loosed arrows from the wall walk. I saw one man fall, his head split open like a ripe fruit, and it was all I could do to contain the contents of my stomach.

Father struck heels to his mount again and the animal lunged forward at even greater speed. "Stop him…that's Talvas!" I heard someone shout, and an arrow whistled through the air. Father bent low over his horse's mane, crushing me beneath him and the missile skipped harmlessly on the cobbles.

Again, we barrelled into a horde of armed men who stabbed and slashed, trying to bring the horse down. A fierce beast trained for war, it bit at them with its huge yellow teeth, ripping one attacker's arm away from his shoulder. He fell screaming, as blood spurted into the air.

A few minutes later, we had passed the shattered gates and were careering down castle hill, the freezing wintry wind blasting into our faces. Father sat upright in the saddle, and gulped in the icy air; above me, I noted his eyes, blood-red from smoke and winds, damp almost as if he wept.

But Father never wept. He mocked at tears. It could only be from the smoke…

We continued to flee, crossing the frozen moat and galloping out into the shadow-cloaked fields. I glanced back once at the castle. No one came in pursuit; though a few figures brandished their weapons menacingly in the maw of the gatehouse. Behind them, flames leapt on high, swirling up the ivy that had cocooned the great donjon, now a vision of Hell with the fire reflecting off the underbelly of the low hanging clouds.

Our home. Gone.

I turned my face into the darkness, facing the cold, bleak miles ahead. If Father did not weep; neither would I.

CHAPTER TWO

We were like homeless beggars on the road. Some of Father's retainers followed along behind us in our flight, joining with us when we stopped to rest, but many of them soon became disgruntled and peeled away under cover of darkness when they realised the direness of our plight. Arnulf had taken not only Alencon but our other strongholds such as Domfront. No one wanted to aid him; he had made many enemies over the years, all with long memories. He had insulted the Duke of Normandy by muttering loud, drunken insults about the Duke's bastard son, William, when he was a babe in arms, and had fought bitterly and bloodily with Herbert Wake-Dog, Count of Maine, over castles and lands. Besides a few greybeards and lowborn youths who had nowhere else to go, only his vassal, William Fitz Giroie, and Fitz Giroie's followers remained loyal, and as we journeyed aimlessly through Normandy and beyond, it seemed even his loyalty was becoming stretched beyond endurance.

"We will have to fare to my brother, Yves," Father grumbled one evening as we sat around a dismal watchfire in a scraggy woodland, warming our hands before the thin flames. "I cannot bear the man...but we are blood."

Uncle Yves was the Bishop of Seez. He was more than just 'blood'; he was technically our lord. As Yves was the elder son, he was the Seigneur de Belleme, and all of Father's lands were held in right of his brother. He never failed to let Father know how he could take all he owned in an eye's blink, or remove him as heir if he preferred someone else.

"Do you think he truly will help?" I wrinkled my nose. The fire popped; behind us, I heard a derisive snort from one of the men. Uncle Yves' meanness was legendary throughout Normandy.

Father shrugged. "No...but at least he might give us fresh horses and clothes. Christ's Toes, I could use some clean garments. I smell like a pig. And so do you, Mabel."

I scowled in the flames, loathing the thought that I looked—and smelt—like some street urchin, a creature of lowly birth to be mocked at and despised.

William Fitz Giroie, who was toasting a haunch of rabbit on a stick, laughed at my sire's words. I glared in his direction. Who did he think he was? He was only a vassal—how dare he laugh at me and my bitter plight?

"Your face, Mabel," said Father unkindly, grabbing Fitz Giroie's rabbit and tearing off a big mouthful. "It looks like a gargoyle's, girl. It offends me. Learn to smile before your grimaces stick forever."

Hatred boiled in my heart; not toward Father for his unfair insult, but towards William Fitz Giroie, whose unwelcome laughter had prompted the comment. I hoped he would soon leave us as our other so-called allies had done.

Still scowling, I scuttled away to a little shelter Father had made me from woven boughs, and huddled on the forest floor, wrapped in his warm woollen cloak, dreaming of sunlit future days when we might have our castles back and things would return to how they were, only *better*—with faithless Arnulf's head gaping sightlessly above the castle gates.

The next day we fared on to Seez, the seat of Uncle Yves' bishopric. Arriving at the neat little town, we were confronted by a great white-washed twin-towered gatehouse crowned by two pointed red turrets. The town guards manning it stared disdainfully down at our unimpressive party as we gathered before the iron-bound gates. They did not even seem to care we flew the flag of the House of Belleme.

"Open!" bellowed Father, staring up.

"It's after curfew, sirrah." A man in a pointed helmet leaned out of the parapet and stared down. "The bell has tolled."

"Do you not know who I am?" Father sputtered in fury.

"Can't say that I do." The guard's companions, crossbowmen all, sniggered loudly.

"See this flag, churl?" Father grabbed the Belleme flag from his erstwhile banner-bearer, a spotty-faced lad more suited for cleaning stables than serving lords, and waved it in the air at the men lurking above. "*That* is who I am. Belleme. I trust you are not such a lackwit that you do not recognise this symbol. The banner of your own lord, Bishop Yves."

The man in the pointy helm spat over the wall, still full of impertinence. "How do I know you are who you claim? You could have stolen that from anywhere. News has reached us that William Talvas' castle at Alencon has been sacked by his own son, Arnulf. You could have taken it during the looting."

"Do not play these games with me!" Father roared, standing up in his stirrups as if he would leap from his mount's back and scale the walls with his bare hands to get at the offending guard.

The guard seemed unmoved by his fury, although the sniggers from his fellows ceased and then looked one to the other, confused and uneasy. I cleared my throat. Perhaps a little female diplomacy might help the matter at hand. I fluttered my eyelashes at the guard, trying to look meek, frightened and distressed. "Good sir," I said, "please forgive my sire's rough speech…"

Father's head whipped around and he glowered at me. I ignored him, and continued, "He has been through much, including the loss of his castle through treachery. Please, I beg you, take a message to my Uncle Yves, Lord of Belleme, to let him know we are outside the town and in desperate need of his succour. Tell him that his own niece, Mabel, is with the party wearing only the clothes she stands up in and much afraid after all that has befallen."

The man hesitated, and my heart jumped. Hesitation was a positive sign. He nodded at me, then spoke urgently to someone behind him, while pointing down at me. "It shall be done," he said, after a few long minutes, "but you all must wait outside until we receive approval from his lordship the Bishop."

The wait for Uncle Yves to allow our entrance into Seez seemed eternal. Rain began to fall, turning the ground before our horse's hooves to mud. Father ground his teeth and cast ferocious looks from beneath shaggy brows jewelled with raindrops. On the parapets above, the guards were whistling, their cheerfulness irritating and perhaps deliberate. I wanted to throw something but I doubted that who help gain us entry.

At last, Master Pointy Helm leaned over from his perch. "We've had news from the castle. His lordship says we're to open the gates!"

With a groaning of hinges, the vast, iron-bound gates of Seez swung wide. Father rode through, peering up at the walls above as if contemplating going for the insolent guard who had made him wait in the rain. Unsurprisingly, the man appeared to have mysteriously vanished, and two crossbowmen replaced him, both idly fiddling with their quarrels.

"Father, I am cold; please leave it," I said, touching father's shoulder. I was no colder than I had been throughout our flight but I did not want more distractions and fighting when I might be warming my toes before a roaring fire in Uncle Yves' castle.

Father grunted and shrugged off my hand but, mercifully, turned his attention from the town watch to the streets ahead. Seez was a compact town with cobble-stoned streets snaking up towards an impressive spired cathedral and Uncle Yves's residence, the Bishop's Castle. Despite the falling rain, it was full of bustling merchants in fancy hats and rich cloaks and peasants in bright scarlet hoods herding a large flock of grubby sheep. Baaing piteously, the beasts fled before our horses, while the hirsute shepherds grumbled curses under their breath and tried to get them under control.

Normally such as they would never dare even raise eyes to us, scions of the great House of Belleme, but we looked like mere vagabonds or mercenaries, even with our wet, bedraggled flag.

Soon we reached the Bishop's Castle; sullen and squat with a wide cylinder for a keep. The sentries at its entrance moved aside, mercifully aware that we were coming, and our befouled, dripping company clattered into the courtyard. The rain began to beat down even harder, bouncing off flagstones; muck swirled by in eddies—horse turd, trampled straw, an old squashed fruit. Grooms grabbed the horses' dangling reins and led them toward the stables, while William Fitz Giroie and the meagre remnant of Father's men were guided off to…to wherever men of lower status went. I neither knew nor cared by then—all I could think of was getting warm and dry.

Father and I were greeted by Uncle Yves' Chamberlain, a hefty man who wheezed as if he were about to expire with every laboured breath. Holding a small horn lantern aloft, he led us through the long passageways of the castle to the Great Hall.

Inside, the central fire was burning merrily while dogs worried bones amidst the rushes. Uncle Yves was standing near the fire, a tall spare man where his brother was burly, who had a long, sullen, almost lachrymose face. He was splendid in vast swathes of purple silk—and on his arm danced a hawk, screeching fiercely as the bells on its jesses jangled.

"Greetings, William," he said, without even looking at Father. He was more interested in examining the hawk—despite being a bishop, he was known as a great huntsman who kept all kinds of birds of prey in his mews. "I've had word that you've been in a spot of trouble."

"You could say that," said Father gruffly. Standing by his side, I felt the tension in his burly frame and knew he was angry. But he would suppress his rage, had to—after all, he only held his lands through Yves. Yves was the elder, the Lord of Belleme. Father should inherit by all the usual laws, but inheritances were never certain…

"My lovely castle at Alencon." Yves shook his head, his expression more mournful than ever. "Burnt I hear."

"Yes."

"When I heard, I had to buy myself six new hawks to console myself. This one is called Servet. I trust he will bring cheer." He beckoned to a falconer lounging in the shadows; the man took the hawk on his gloved fist and carried it away to the castle mews.

"If you give me the men, I will take Alencon back from my treacherous whelp!" growled Father.

Yves swept toward his brother in his regal purple robes. "I have no men to give you…"

"No men? None?"

"Not a one. None would follow you; they have heard of your cruelty, your violence. You should not have killed Hildeburg, your wife, William. That was ill done and has won you no friends."

"I am lord in my own home, am I not?" Father roared. "She defied me!"

"And you murdered her," drawled Yves, eyes narrowing. "An unusually harsh punishment for an erring wife, and I heard tell the reason you killed her was that she attended church too often and chided you for your evil ways. I am a man of the church—I cannot condone such brutality, can I? How would it look to my superiors?"

"Not much worse, I would imagine, than when you torched a cathedral with your own hands."

Uncles Yves sniffed. "There is no similarity. Three murderous thieves had holed themselves up in the cathedral spire. They polluted God's House. I had to get them out…"

"By *destroying* God's House?" sneered Father.

Yves ignored him. "By cleansing it with fire."

"So you will not help me. You support Arnulf."

"If he can remain more peaceable than you, William, then yes, I do. And before you ask, no, you cannot stay with me in Seez. It would do nought for my reputation."

Father ground his teeth. "Fair enough, then, *brother*. But what about the girl?" He nodded in my direction. "I cannot be dragging her around the countryside any longer. *Her* reputation would soon be in tatters and she'd be a burden besides."

I winced at his words. How I hated to be referred to as a burden! I wasn't like other weak women, screeching and fainting!

"Ah, yes, the girl…my niece Mabel." Yves walked in a circle around me, looking me up and down. "I will pray tonight and see if the Lord will offer me a solution. I'll confer with Mabel on the morrow—but on her own, not with you, William."

"So I take it you are not throwing me out of the castle tonight?"

"No, I'm not such a bad host as that. You can join your men in the stable loft or the servants' quarters. I will have food sent. As for Mabel, she may stay here in the castle, since she is a maid of tender years."

Father turned and began to stalk toward the door. "Father, don't leave me!" I cried, clutching at his cloak.

"Let go, child, stop scrabbling at me like a rat. You have the best of the deal. Stay here with Yves…at least for now."

He swept past me and away into the passageways beyond the hall. Yves glanced at me again. "One of my servants will take you to a room where you may sleep. Bread and cheese will be brought from the kitchens. I will see about clothes—you are in rags, most unbecoming for a girl of your rank. A bath too—you definitely need a bath."

I gazed down at my tattered skirts, the edges caked with mud. Leaves stuck out from my braids, making me look like a wild woman of the woods. Yes, I definitely needed a bath and fresh clothes.

"Thank you for your hospitality, Uncle Yves!" I said, dropping a low curtsey.

I felt honoured indeed getting such hospitality from the old skinflint.

The next morning after Mass, Yves called me to the Great Hall. I was much more presentable—my hair combed through and a loose leaf-green robe (pilfered from who knows where) hanging over a kirtle brought at dawn by a sullen-faced washer-woman. My shoes had been cleaned by a servant; they were ruined and ugly but at least no longer showering chunks of mud.

"Have you broken your fast, child?" asked Yves. He was dandling another hawk, kissing its hooded head as one might kiss a beloved child. *Weird old man*, I thought.

"Yes, Uncle Yves," I said. "A servant brought some sops. Thank you for your concern."

"Good, you will be ready to face the day then. I am taking you out into the town of Seez."

If I had thought I was going to have a pleasant excursion visiting haberdashers and goldsmiths, I was sorely mistaken. After a brief visit to a tailor, where Uncle Yves demanded a 'simple gown, plain, in the most maidenly of colours—made swiftly, even if not prettily', he dragged me onwards to the Cathedral that dominated the little town, its tall peaks overwhelming the rather modest castle.

Yves guided me into the incense-laden darkness, the flutter of low-burning cressets. A mournful-face statue of Our Lady stood on a wooden plinth ringed by tall candles that dripped red like blood.

"This is a most holy place," said Yves. "It was founded by a saint, Latiun, many centuries ago."

"How very…interesting," I said. Although not eschewing the church or God, I was far more interested in secular matters than saints and holy history. Best not tell the Bishop that, however.

"Most famous son of the church in Seez was Adelin, though, also known to some as Adalhelm."

"Who was he?" I asked, trying not to sound bored.

"A Bishop of Seez, like me. He had promised to write the life-story of a great and holy abbess called Opportuna, whose relics lay within the cathedral...but he procrastinated and time passed, and then the Northmen came, riding their dragon-headed ships up the river."

I grew more attentive. Although we all spoke of the Northmen—Vikings—as cruel heathens, almost all of us had at least partial ancestry from those tall, fair-haired warriors. Secretly, many admired them for their boldness in battle where they would become consumed by a terrible battle-rage they called 'going berserk'. "What did the Northmen do to him?"

"They put him in bonds and took blessed Adelin as a slave! Bound in the belly of a long-ship, they carried him down the Seine, heading for the sea and their homelands in distant Denmark. But as they reached the Somme, near a town at St Valery, God sent a mighty storm and their ship ran aground. They then stole some horses and decided to cross the nearby river, but the waves reared like giants and the horses were swept away in the swell. The captive Adelin was dragged into the waves too, sure of his doom—but then the waters parted, growing suddenly still, and he managed to swim ashore. Looking back, he swore he saw the cowled figure of the holy Opportuna standing in the flood, calming the waves. He vowed to return home and write the book he had promised. And he did. *Vita et miracula Sanctae Opportunae*."

I wondered what was the point of Uncle Yves' story. He must have seen the mystified look on my face, for he said snappishly. "I thought you might have an interest in female saints, such as Opportuna; your mother, God assoil her, was a most pious woman, was she not?"

"Yes...but I still do not understand."

"You cannot continue as you are, riding about the countryside with William. I thought a life in a convent might suit you; possibly you could rise to take the position of abbess—with a little help from me. Blessed Opportunata dwelt not far away, in the *Monasteriolum* near Almenèches. The house of nuns there has fallen into sore disrepair. Perhaps you, with my monetary assistance, could re-found the nunnery, to great acclaim."

"A nun!" I cried, horrified at the thought.

"Why not? It is an honourable profession pleasing to the Lord. Carry on in my brother's company, and you will have no home, no husband...and a harlot's reputation."

"How dare you, uncle! I am no harlot."

"I believe you, but if you ride in the company of men who are little more than brigands, other men will soon believe you are and treat you accordingly."

"I refuse to become a withered old nun," I spat, still enraged at Yves' presumption. "Locked away from the world, on my knees until the floor beneath wore into grooves! I will *never* agree. Father himself would never agree."

I grabbed one of the nearby lit candles and hurled it down at his feet, splattering red wax—a childish move, sure enough, but I was consumed by white-hot rage at his outlandish suggestion. Leave my Father to be packed into a convent with a gaggle of awful old women? It was an outrage! Father had spoken of disinheriting Arnulf, even if he managed to hang on to Alencon castle; if he did so, that would make me his heir and, eventually, one of the richest women in Normandy. If I was locked up in an abbey, anything my Father had would go to some other scion of the House of Belleme. I glared at Yves, wondering what distant cousin or dubious friend he might want to bestow my rightful inheritance upon.

Unlike Father, Yves remained calm in the face of my insolence. Instead, he went pale, his lips drawn into cruel, disapproving lines, his eyes steely as a storm-tossed sky. "So, you have made your choice. You will trail along behind William like some bedraggled camp follower. So be it. We will return to the castle and you will give him the happy news."

He swept from the cathedral and I followed, sullen and mutinous, still brooding on the inappropriateness of his suggestion. Once we were back at the Bishop's Castle, he sent me straight to my assigned chamber like a naughty child.

A few hours later, Father strode into the room, cloaked, hooded. "We ride on, Mabel. My brother has no sympathy for my plight. I guess Yves cares not for the honour of his House. He would see us as beggars on the road."

"It is even worse than that!" I said. "He tried to gull me into becoming a nun!"

Father flung back his head and bellowed with laughter; ear-splitting though the sound was, it was good to hear him laugh again. "A nun—you? Never! Do not worry, Mab; when I can I'll find you a fitting husband. We will rise again. Yves may not have aided me, but you will note he has not disinherited me. He waits to see how Arnulf will play out as lord. You and I both know sooner or later he will prove a failure. But now, we must go. I will not remain under a roof where I am not welcome."

I glanced down at my makeshift garments, thrown together by the servants. "Uncles Yves ordered a proper kirtle and gown…"

Reaching beneath his cloak, he pulled out a bundle tied with twine and threw it to me. "For you—a farewell gift from Yves. He got the tailor to hurry; I guess he had already paid the man and would not waste his precious coin. Get dressed and meet me in the courtyard."

Dressed in my bland but properly-fitted new gown, I hurried to the courtyard. I wished Yves had stretched his finances to pay for more sturdy shoes, perhaps lined with fur to keep my toes warm…but one dare not hope for too much with misers like Yves.

Father was already mounted, a bear-like shape looming in his saddle. He held the reins of a grey mare which he tossed to me. He looked a bit more cheerful as I vaulted effortlessly onto my mount's back, and he shouted to the rag-tag band of men waiting to depart with us—"My daughter! She can ride like a man, eh? I trained my girl better than anyone else—to be useful, rather than just a vessel to bear children. Although, I've no doubt she'll be good at that one day. Look at those hips!"

The men began to whistle and cheer, and my cheeks began to burn. I cast Father an annoyed glance and immediately he waved a hand at his followers. "Enough! Even I speak too freely. No more talk of the Lady Mabel!"

The men fell silent at once…but then I noticed William Fitz Giroie, leaning forward on the pommel of his saddle, still grinning as he gave me the eye.

My lips tightened almost imperceptibly and I whipped my head away, breaking the unwelcome eye contact. By Jesu's Toes, one day I would wipe the smirk from the insufferable man's face...

We travelled throughout Normandy searching for anyone who might espouse our cause. Most castles were shut to us; towns regarded us with suspicion, even barricading the gates at times as if they thought we were eastern marauders come to sack and destroy. Father cursed them all, shaking his mighty fist, but as winter began to approach, worry started to consume me. Could we survive as we were through the cold months?

Problems began to grow between Fitz Giroie and Father too, and I found out that Giroie was neither loyal nor much beloved of my sire. One night, as I lay rolled in sheepskin in a woodman's hut our company had commandeered, I heard shouting outside. Sleepy-eyed, I awoke and reached into my furs for a small, lethal dagger Father had given me—and taught me how to use.

Outside the hut, Fitz Giroie and Father were standing almost face to face, both men crimson with anger, their stance full of open aggression. Fitz Giroie was only a vassal, and it shocked me to see him so disrespectful to his overlord.

"So you would leave me now?" cried Father. "Miscreant! Knave! I forgave you your sins, man...and now you abandon me."

Fitz Giroie's voice was steel. "I have tried to make amends and hold faith with you...but I have had enough of this futile wandering life. I have my own lands, my own holdings; why should I die, frozen in the snows, when winter comes. You brought this on yourself, *my lord*..."

Father made a lunge for him but slipped on some slimy toadstool sprouting from the forest floor. With a wild yell, he toppled backwards, and as he thrashed and bellowed on the ground, William Fitz Giroie raced for the horses, flung himself onto the back of his mount and galloped away into the forest.

"Shall we go after him?" asked another man, reaching for a crossbow.

Father staggered to his feet, showering left-mulch, moss and crushed toadstool. "No, there is no point. He's a good fighter; he might kill you, and I'd be down more men and horses. I will deal with him later...when I am settled again. When I have regained my stature in the eyes of men."

I made to slide back into the hut and not appear an eavesdropper, but Father noticed me and trudged in my direction. "So we have lost Giroie," he said. "No great loss!"

"Are no men loyal?" I cried with passion, my hands knotting. "If I was a man and could swing a sword, I would ride out against such traitors...and kill them all. I'd present you with Fitz Giroie's head as a gift!"

He patted my shoulder heavily, his touch more like a blow. "You are a good girl, as I have said before. Too bad you were not born a boy! As for William Fitz Giroie, his behaviour is not truthfully a surprise. He was never as honourable as his sire, who assisted your grandsire against our old enemy, Herbert Wake-dog, Count of Maine. William helped me to...*gain* some lands but then thought only of enriching himself, turning his coat like a whore turns her clients!" He laughed, the tone vaguely bitter. "He also served Geoffrey de Mayenne, and held one of his castles, Montaigu, against me in de Mayenne's name."

"That was ill done. What did you do?"

"I captured Geoffrey. Put him in chains. Dragged him out like a dog on a leash to show Fitz Giroie. I told him de Mayenne would never be freed in one piece unless he destroyed his castle, stone by stone. He did it."

"Well, at least he obeyed you."

"Yes, but it was a hollow triumph. I let Geoffrey go, and what did he do—he promptly rewarded Fitz Giroie with a new castle at St Cenery."

"You should have never let him serve you again," I said hotly. "No doubt he was sitting in his precious castle, laughing at you!"

"Keep your enemies near, it is said," murmured Father. "And I hate to admit it, but I needed him at times. Even now, his leaving grieves me—what a rag-tag band we are left with now. I have heard whispers...in the night. Some would abandon me; some would murder me…and as for you…" He gazed down at me, eyes black and hard as chips of jet.

My head thumped. I knew what he spoke. I had seen the covert looks, heard the mutter obscenities masked by coughs and laughter. "What shall we do?"

A wide grin split his reddish-dark beard. "You and I shall ride away—on the morrow when we can slip away from this lot. I still may have some friends elsewhere, I think. A marriage always makes plenty of friends…and allies!"

"Marriage!" I cried. "For me?"

"Don't shout it all over the place, Mab! Yes, a marriage…but *not* for you. Not yet. For me. A marriage to give me new lands, new respectability…"

I wondered what woman would wish to marry him after hearing the rumours of him strangling Mother. But then, most women did not have the freedom to reject an unwelcome suitor; their fathers or male guardians had say over most aspects of their lives

"Tomorrow then," I said to Father. "I am with you."

"Tomorrow. Ride near me and obey my every command. Understand? Failure to act in time may see us both dead."

I nodded, understanding perfectly. I fingered my carefully concealed little dagger, wondering if I would need to use it…

The next day we rode toward a humble little village with a poor church shunted to the side of a wide, central road deeply rutted by cart-wheels. Suspicious peasants glowered as we trotted past; doors were slammed shut. I supposed the villagers thought we were a party of brigands out to rob them. One of our remaining men eyed the church and mumbled about 'might have some plate', but Father fixed him in a stern glare and said, "You do it and I'll hang you from the nearest tree."

At the end of the village stood a pitiful inn with a drab brown frontage that almost looked as if it was made of mud. Its thatching was green and mouldering jutting down to nearly touch the ground. The door hung open, half-torn from its hinges, and the caterwauling of pipes sounded from within.

"We stop here," ordered Father, and the raggle-taggle band looked pleased by the thought of ale and shelter. Rain was drizzling from the sombre, puff-bellied clouds, and they were hard-drinking men anyways, eager for ale and a brawl.

As we neared the inn, the innkeeper ran out, a bald, florid-faced man with cheeks marred by some childhood pox. "We won't be having any trouble here!" he said in a shrill voice that belied his size.

"We do not want trouble," Father assured. "Just some ale…and beds, even if in your stable."

"Can we afford even that much?" I leaned over and whispered in his ear. I knew his belt-purse was nigh empty.

"No," he slurred back out the corner of his mouth, "but soon it will not be our worry."

The horses were soon stabled and the men either making beds in the loft or heading into the inn. The piping became wilder and someone began beating on a tinny drum. I saw two of the innkeeper's men rolling a massive wine keg from a cellar into the main taproom of the dismal tavern.

"Do we have to go in?" I wrinkled my nose. The smell of an ashy fire, stale drink, dogs and men's sweat drifted from beneath the warped, worm-eaten wooden lintel over the door.

"Just for a little, Mab. We must let the drink do its worst, make them stupid…or fall down in a stupor."

We entered the common room, which was equally as unsavoury as the inn's squalid exterior. Grubby benches stretched around tables full of knife marks and smeared food. Local drunkards were slobbering over wooden mugs and eating from bowls like pigs at a trough. Everything was brown, floor, walls, the clothing of almost all the residents. The piper may have had a green tunic, but it was stained so badly, it was hard to tell. A woman tousling with one of the men looked brown too; clotted rat-hued hair, filthy skin, teeth like rotted pegs.

Father and I retreated to the furthest corner. I was aware the eyes of local men were upon me but ignored them. Father ordered some ale and gave me a mouthful from his tankard. "No food, though," he said, "It's rank. I don't want you to get the flux before we flee."

The men began to get raucous. Our lot were scratching in their purses for coins to pay for the bitter, evil-tasting brew the innkeeper offered. And then it started. A weedy man at the back, stinking in his boiled leather and visibly drunk, found he had no coin to pay for yet another drink. "That's his fault!" he slurred, pointing at Father. "He owes us pay, all of us. We've followed him through thick and thin, and what do we get—nought but a hard march to nowhere without even enough money to pay for this rank horse-piss."

"Come here and say that to my face, Eubo, you slack-jawed moron." Father rose from his bench, hand clutching at his dagger-hilt.

A knife appeared in Eubo's hand; I noticed he was missing a finger from some past fray. "I've been looking for a chance to have at you!" he sneered. "Too long following a blustering old windbag."

"You sit down, oaf!" The innkeeper pushed Eubo back towards his bench. "We don't put up with fighting here. You're off your head with the drink."

"Hardly!" shot back Eubo, shaking him off. "That week horse-piss is fit only for women! Maybe that's to your taste, though—after all, when you speak you sound just like a eunuch!"

"Don't you be insulting my ale or me!" yelled the innkeeper, his high-pitched voice cracking with rage. His florid face darkened to purple. "Bouves, Drugo, disarm this man and sling him out. See that he leaves!"

Two hulking younger men bearing a strong resemblance to the innkeeper and who I supposed were his sons (making the jibe about him being a eunuch even more anger-inducing), descended on Eubo with cudgels. They were bigger and sober, but Eubo was a sellsword and a fighting man since beard first sprouted on his chin. He roared at them and struck out with his knife, cutting one of the burly youths on the forearm. Blood spurted and the man began to howl and do an amusing little dance of pain.

Chaos ensued. The innkeeper grabbed a great dinted old sword from a hook near the fire and rushed into the fray. The tavern regulars erupted in fury, throwing over the bench and sending pewter mugs flying. The sorry remnants of Father's men also leapt up, some rushing to Eubo's side, others joining the ranks of his opponents—

Eubo was an unpopular fellow; I'd heard whispers that he was a common thief.

As bodies flailed and blood and drink flew, Father grabbed my arm and hauled me from the taproom, out through the corridor and into the descending night. "Keep on walking, Mab. If anyone questions, I will tell them you are frightened by the brawl and I am escorting you out of harm's way. Agree with me."

We hustled through the smoky air to the stables. Behind us, men screamed and cursed, crockery crashed, dogs barked furiously. In the stables, we were glad to see no ostlers—there had all run pell-mell towards the sound of fighting.

Hurriedly Father found the horse-tack and saddled up my steed and his own. He helped me up into the saddle and made to mount, but a shout rang through the stable. Glancing up, we saw the face of one of his mercenaries, peering down from the hay-strewn loft. "What the hell are you doing, Talvas!" he shouted. "You're leaving aren't you…leaving us in the lurch with no pay!"

Drawing his sword, the man flung himself toward the ladder that led down from the loft to the horse stalls. Father was on the other side of me, half onto the back of his steed. Filled with sudden fury, I struck my heels against my horse's flanks, sending the beast jolting forward, nearly unseating me with its forward lunge. Recovering my balance, I grasped one side of the ladder and pulled with all my might. I felt as if my shoulder would tear from my body, but then the ladder came away, juddering in mid-air, the sellsword clinging to it for dear life. Then it went over and down, throwing him heavily onto the floor. His head hit a flagstone with a crack and dark blood seeped from his ear.

"Well done, well done!" cried Father, revelling in the sight of our fallen foe. "You surprise and please me yet again, Mab! Now, ride, ride as you've never ridden before…and don't look back. A new life awaits us!"

Together we thundered out across the courtyard and away into the night. Behind us, the tavern's thatching had somehow caught alight and flames twisted into the darkness. *Let the past burn and all those disloyal to William Talvas and his daughter!* I thought bitterly, bent low over the mane of my steed. *Let them all burn in Hell…*

CHAPTER THREE

We were near the Castle of the Beaumont family, and feeling a little safer with the vast grey pile almost within bowshot. Hiding in a little coppice outside the surrounding town, Father had me shave him with my dagger and cut his hair as best I could. I endeavoured to be careful; one wrong cut and I feared I'd be beaten or worse. Father had already slapped my hand when I'd accidentally nicked his cheek.

"We must present ourselves well to Raoul de Beaumont," he said. "So, no high and mighty antics from you, eh?"

"Me? I know how to behave," I muttered, casting clumps of hair and bristly beard onto our pitiful watchfire. All hair must be burnt, lest witches or sorcerers took hold of it for use in their spells. The acrid fragrance of it burning curled into my nostrils.

"Yes, I am sure you do. Keep it up." He removed up an armband he always wore, bronze, studded with cabochons; he polished the bronze and gazed at his reflection, satisfied. "The Beaumonts may have some kinsman who might be available to marry you too. But my needs must come first. A new wife and a family to support me in my unlawful exile."

I scowled, not liking this talk of marriage. I did not know the Beaumonts, had never met one. This Lord Raoul however, was of the House of Belleme through his mother, Godchilde, a distant, long-dead cousin.

Pleased with his new, tidier appearance, Father kicked dirt over the fire, stomped on it with his heavy leather boots and headed toward the horses. "Curfew should be over and the town gates open," he said. "Time to renew my acquaintance with dear Cousin Raoul."

We rode into the town around Castle Beaumont without incident. The sun had just risen, casting a deep golden light over the timbered houses. Chickens clucked about the cobblestones; in the marketplace, a holy man with gnarled dirty feet and a bird's nest beard thundered and raved about God's wrath, while the townsfolk, clad in brown and russet and green, ignored him and went about their morning tasks.

We were ignored too, for the most part, although a few stall-keepers gave us a glare when we did not pause to examine their wares. They hated us not only because we were foreign but also because they deemed us poor. Which we were, with Arnulf and his allies holding Alencon, Domfront and other castles and lands of ours.

Reaching the castle gates, Father spoke brusquely to the sentries. A page was dispatched to the keep, and before long we were permitted entrance. Our mounts were taken, and a steward in a red woollen gown and an impressive bunch of keys jingling at his belt led us into the Great Hall.

On a small, wooden dais, sat Raoul de Beaumont and his wife, Hildegarde of Anjou. Raoul was about Father's age, with a clean-shaven, square-jawed face and dark hair shaved up the neck. He wore a floor-length green tunic embroidered with chevrons and herringbone patterns around neckline and cuffs; a sapphire studded golden chain hung from his neck. His belt was made of thick silver links, and on a loop hung a sword in a pearlescent sheath. At his side, Lady Hildegarde was a lean woman with a small oval face, straight nose and determined mouth. She wore a white wimple decorated with seed-pearls over dark braids, and her robes were sea-blue, as rich as her husband's, also patterned in the same chevrons.

"William!" Lord de Beaumont rose from his seat and descended from the dais, clasping Father in a short, hard embrace. "Glad am I to see you after all these years. I have heard unsettling rumours…."

Father let out a deep, heartfelt sigh and stared ruefully at the floor. He was as skilled as any mummer in his act, and I curbed a smile to see his pretence. "Such rumours are true, my old friend, my partner of many battles. My son, Arnulf, the greedy, treacherous whelp, has driven me out of my lands with nought but the clothes on my back…and my little daughter, Mabel."

I curtseyed, casting de Beaumont what I hoped would pass as a winsome, appealing smile.

"Ah…the girl…" Raoul rubbed his square chin and gazed at me thoughtfully in a way that made me squirm. Then he turned back to

Father. "Have you no thought of taking back your lands? What of Seigneur Yves, your brother, the Bishop."

Father shrugged, feigning a look of sad helplessness. "Yves, you know Yves surely—like most Bishops, ranting about God but as mean as the worst miser. We never got on. He was bookish, while I was blooded by thirteen. He supports Arnulf, who is regrettably similar in temperament to him."

"You have vassals to aid you, surely?"

"Had. They abandoned me. You know how it is, Raoul, old companion—I held the allegiance only through fear. They were never true friends, just enemies forced to follow by circumstance. All enemies. But you know what they say—a man who makes no enemies, makes nothing at all."

A wry little smile moved Raoul's lips. "Hm, true enough, but now you have nothing at all, my *friend*..."

A small flash of anger darkened Father's eyes, hastily hidden. "If you want me to leave you castle, Raoul, I will understand. But I promise that if I am permitted to stay, I shall forever be your right-hand man and fight your battles with ardour. And if ever Arnulf should be removed...Well, I promise your lands will flow with milk and honey in gratitude."

Brow furrowed in concentration, Raoul returned to his seat on the dais. Hildegarde glanced over at her husband and reached to touch his arms. "He is your kinsman, Raoul...and, there is always trouble brewing, where an extra sword-arm might come in useful." She turned from Raoul and gazed solemnly down at Father. "You want a new start, do you not, William Talvas? A new life...a new marriage..."

Father was caught unawares by her shrewd perception of his desires. Reddening, he blustered, "Well, that would come in good time and I would be grateful of it. A man needs a wife."

"Did you not have one, my lord?" Her voice was silken and yet steel. She was still smiling, oh so gracious. "What was her name...oh, Hildeburg, was it not? I could not help but remember her. So close to my own name."

Father's hands clenched and unclenched. Had Hildegarde been alone and speaking in such a taunting manner to him, she might have shared a similar fate to my unlamented mother, not just a similar name!

"I—I did," Father managed to control his temper. "A most religious woman, known for her piety. Never saw her much as she was always praying or aiding poor men or lepers. She died."

"Did she now?" said Hildegarde. "What a pity. I am sure it was a great shock to little Mabel."

I jumped, not expecting Lady de Beaumont to mention me. My eyes widened. This Hildegarde was not the meek, docile wife I had expected. It was as if she knew everything that had happened at Alencon, and was baiting us!

"We will meet tomorrow and discuss the future then," said Lord Raoul. "You are my kinsman, William, yet there are hard questions that must be asked."

"I will answer them." Father sounded sincere. "I will not disappoint you."

"No, my lord Talvas, you will not," said the Angevin woman, Hildegarde, inclining her head. "Bring the child with you, too. She is old enough to speak for herself and to answer questions."

Father's nostrils flared slightly but he nodded his acquiescence. "Mabel will be with me. After all, at present, she is my heir. Arnulf is a traitor and when and if I can remove him from my castles, they shall, one day, go to my daughter."

Raoul and Hildegarde de Beaumont lounged in their private solar. The noon-bell tolled outside, its clangour dulled by the thick walls. Servants brought in food and drink; meat pies and savouries, roundels of cheese, wine in tall, fluted goblets. After we had partaken of our hosts' generosity, Raoul had the platters cleared away and dismissed the servants so that we were alone in the well-lit chamber with its high, painted walls and fresh rushes thick on the floor.

"Now…" de Beaumont said, and there was a harshness in his voice that was not there yesterday, "what do you want from me, William? No dancing around—just tell me, what do you want?"

Father spread his hands out on his knees and gazed at the floor as if ashamed. "I am now scarce more than a pauper; you can see that.

I have a daughter who needs protection so that one day she might make a great marriage. I need to rebuild my wealth and status, robbed from me by Arnulf. I am a widower—I need a fitting new marriage to aid in the recovery of my status in the world."

"A marriage. You think I can help you with that? I have no daughters, just my son, Raoul."

"You have sisters, do you not?"

"Emmeline is long wed…

"Was there not another sister…a widow? The one who married Sire Tesseli of Montreveau?"

"Yes, Haberga…but I have heard it is in her mind to become a nun in her widowhood."

Annoyance passed over Father's face. "Can she not be persuaded otherwise?"

"Why should she not go to the Church?" asked Hildegarde, leaning forward in her chair. "And why should we persuade her to marry you, William Talvas? Your reputation is fearsome and your coffers are now empty. Tell us truly—what happened to your first wife? We heard the tales—that she was strangled…by your hand."

My ears burned and I cast a surreptitious glance at Father. His visage was filled with feigned indignation. "She was strangled, indeed…but not by my hand. The local townsfolk hated me; they were always trying to destroy my property. The murderers have long been put to silence."

Raoul stared at the table before him in silence for a long while, toying with a great gold ring with a lion carved on the bezel as he contemplated the situation. "If I were to press your suit with Haberga, what gain would I have from it? Little…unless as part of the marriage-alliance you swear to me to make me your lord. Then I would see you not only to wed my sister but a holder of adjacent lands presently held by Haberga. However…I would want a share of the revenues gleaned from those lands. If I am to show you kindness, you must show me the same."

Father hesitated then nodded. "I will swear to you, Raoul. I will fight for you. My treasury, once there's something in it again, will be open to you."

I was surprised Father's usual rage had been kept so close in check, and a cold wave swept over me as reality dawn—he was virtually begging. Until now, our plight had seemed more of…unfortunate adventure than a possibly permanent situation. In my silly childish head, I had somehow imagined that my Father's noble blood would carry him through, that after much tutting and eye-rolling, Uncle Yves would send troops to trounce Arnulf, or that a smiling Raoul would see him set up as an equal, a brother-in-arms. But none of that was going to happen. Yves was keeping the purse closed, and Father would have to agree to be a vassal of de Beaumont, his inferior.

"I am glad you are being so gracious, William," said Lord Raoul, making a steeple of his long, ring-clad hands. "But there is one more thing I desire from you…something Hildegarde spoke of last night when she and I talked in private."

"And what is that?" Father's voice was so low it was almost a grunt.

"We want your daughter Mabel as our ward, with the right to make her marriage."

Father went red and I thought he might shout. I grasped the rim of the table in shock and gazed desperately at my sire. He ignored me.

Then he rose and stalked toward Raoul, who remained seated. My breath hissed through my teeth—was he going to strike him, ruin the tentative alliance they had made? Across from me, Lady Hildegarde went white. Raoul did not move, just tilted his head upward to meet my sire's angry gaze.

I saw a muscle flicker in Father's cheek. Then, clumsily, he sank to one knee before de Beaumont. "I swear to be your man, Raoul de Beaumont, and to be a good husband to your sister, Haberga, or any other kinswoman you may choose for me if she is unwilling to wed. And yes, you may have the right of my daughter Mabel's marriage—but, by God's Nails, I beg you make it a worthy—and profitable—union."

CHAPTER FOUR

I was furious thinking about two strangers arranging my future marriage but dared not speak of it to Father. Angrily, I mulled over ideas of running away—none very realistic. In my heart, I knew if I did flee, I'd be found dead in a ditch within the week. I even contemplated fleeing to Arnulf and begging him for mercy, but no doubt he would soon have me wed to one of *his* favourites, or sent to a convent, so my position would not have improved one jot. I would just have to hope that Raoul and Hildegarde's choice of husband would not be too repulsive.

Over the next few months, Hildegarde drew me into her inner circle and employed me as one of her tiring women. It was a comedown for me to serve in such a manner, but she was kind enough though keen-eyed—nought I got up to was ever missed by Hildegarde. When my behaviour was satisfactory, she rewarded me with silk gowns and cloaks lined with fur, which definitely was an incentive that curbed my worst excesses—I now resembled a noblewoman again rather than a scruffy street urchin.

Raoul had, by some miracle, managed to persuade his sister Haberga to give up her idea of becoming a nun and marry Father. She arrived around Midsummer, a rather stout woman with the same square jaw as her brother. It looked fine on a man but gave her a pugnacious, angry look. But Father was not marrying her for looks. He was marrying to become part of the de Beaumont family—Raoul was a Viscount, after all.

I saw Father's mouth droop at the sight of Haberga but he quickly replaced his disappointed expression with a great wide grin. He swept up to her, bowed, and kissed her hand like some modern courtier, while Hildegarde's ladies sniggered and nudged each other. Haberga looked slightly dismayed by the unexpected attention but managed a crooked smile of her own.

Soon the wedding took place at one of Haberga's small holdings where she planned to live with Father—a surprise, for I expected the happy occasion to be celebrated before the castle's chapel doors or at the town church. Father had requested my attendance, but on the day I was to set out, I realised I was on my own, thrust into a covered litter by my guardians who then announced their intentions to stay behind in their castle, sending along a paltry gift or two for the unblushing bride rather than attending the celebrations. Hildegarde had looked both nervous and yet resigned as I settled into my litter, telling me to mind my manners and to 'keep out of the way.' At the very end, she leaned forward into the draperies of the litter and murmured next to my ear, "Mabel, do you have your dagger on your person?"

"W-what?" I stammered, not realising she had known about my pointed 'little friend'.

"I know you carry a knife with you wherever you go," she said. "Believe me, child, there is nought I do not know of the goings-on inside my castle. So—do you have it?"

"I carry it almost always," I said, unapologetic. "Even to the privy."

To my surprise, she nodded. "Good. I hope you know how to use it. I expect you do, though…being a Belleme."

"Do you think there will be some kind of trouble at the wedding?" I asked. "Is that why you and Lord Raoul are not going, even though the bride is his Lordship's sister?"

Hildegarde shrugged slightly. "Maybe, maybe not. Guests are going…whom Raoul does not trust. Raoul and Haberga were never close anyway, and it is not as if she is a virgin bride."

"Guest? Who?"

"Never you mind, child—you ask too many questions for a young girl! Just remember my words. If anything goes amiss at the nuptials, keep well out of the way—and keep the weapon I gave you close to hand."

Haberga's castle was small and rather mean after our fine home at Alencon, now under my horrid brother Arnulf's hand. Nonetheless, the farms and vills around would give Father an income and the opportunity to build his own army again and gain allies through which he might be able to oust Arnulf.

Arriving in my litter, I clambered stiffly out into the muddy courtyard, a fine cloth thrown down before my feet by a menial to preserve my shoes. As I was led toward my apartments by a steward, I observed the men crowding into the far side of the bailey. To my startlement, I noticed the banner of William Fitz Giroie, who had left Father and me to fend for ourselves after we were driven from Alencon. Fitz Giroie, who I loathed above all men for what he had done. I even hated him more than Arnulf, for he disrespected me more than my brother. Had Father decided to make peace with him? It seemed unlikely, given the circumstances. I wondered why he was here.

And then I felt my dagger cold against my thigh where I had bound it with a strip of linen. A chill—or was it a thrill?—rippled through my slender frame. Could Hildegarde had had foreknowledge that William Fitz Giroie was attending the celebrations? Is that why Raoul failed to attend his sister's wedding?

I entered the castle corridors, my mind awhirl with possibilities…and, turning one dark corner, almost bumped straight into William de Giroie and his ugly henchmen. He halted, grinning. He had lost a front tooth since last we met, and his breath hung rancid in the enclosed space, smelling of onions and cheap wine. "Oh, so it's the Lady Mabel de Belleme. I scarcely recognise you, milady. Last I saw you were covered in muck, like a pig in the sty."

"Last I saw of you was your craven arse as you galloped away into the woods," I shot back. "Why are you here?"

"I've come for the great wedding, of course. I was invited. Lord Talvas thinks it's is a time to bury the axe…"

"In your skull," I said.

Fitz Giroie's companions roared with mirth at my quip, clapping him on the shoulders. "She's a feisty one, Will!"

"I think she should give me the kiss of peace," leered Fitz Giroie. "Or maybe, now that I am back in favour with her sire, I should ask she join one of my sons in marriage…"

"I'd refuse and so would my Father, let alone my guardian, Viscount de Beaumont" I said. "Now let me past…or I'll tell my sire you were abusing me and you'll end up at war with him again."

He stepped aside with a mocking bow, and I swept past him, head held high. In my little room, cold and chill with rats tapping in the ceiling, I did not sleep all night, thinking that he, that awful turncoat who had abandoned us to penury, slept and schemed within the same four walls.

Shortly before noon the next day, the wedding was held before the doors of the ancient little castle chapel. Father appeared at ease, almost dashing in a furred tunic, while Haberga, although still dull as a wet day, was slightly improved by her expensive blue gown and jewelled headdress.

After the priest had finished droning out the interminable marriage rite, the wedding party processed to the candle-lit Great Hall and a great, drunken feast was held in the newlyweds' honour. Even I was filled with good cheer as I downed sweet and heady honey-mead and stuffed myself to the gills on venison pie, rabbit in pear jelly, and eels bathed in creamy sauces full of imported spice. I kept my eyes off Father and his bride and made sure I never gazed in the direction of Fitz Giroie who was, mercifully, far down the trestle table, well below the salt.

At the end of the evening, all the men in the hall gathered around Father, shouting out bawdily, as he pulled his un-blushing bride from her canopied seat and led her away to the bedchamber. These guests followed along behind the new couple towing a bevy of minstrels and a Fool behind them.

Being a woman, this masculine part of the ceremony—the bedding—was forbidden to my eyes, for which I was eternally grateful. I did not wish to behold any of the uncouth antics—Haberga unwrapped like a grotesque fleshy present in the marriage bed while Father strutted about, proud in his masculinity, and the menfolk stole glances at the bride's teats and arse, which they would later discuss while deep in their cups. Despite my youth, I was no mindless innocent; I knew exactly what went, having heard the gossipy chatter of Hildegarde's tiring women.

Instead, I took my leave and sought my bedchamber, thankful that Father had seen fit to let me have it to myself, rather than share with one of the other wedding guests. A scrawny girl sent by Haberga arrived to help me unlace my dress, and clad only in my kirtle I slipped into the bed. Soon I had fallen into a light sleep, as the bagpipes wheezed from somewhere in the castle and men roared, belched and bellowed.

Sometime in the dead of the night, it all went silent. In fact, too silent. An owl hooted somewhere in the gloom, bringing me from uneasy drowsing to full wakefulness.

An owl? Or was it? It sounded odd, out of place. I glanced out the narrow window-slit. Saw nothing. No bird flew through the gloom despite the closeness of the cry. A feeling of apprehension washed over me. In my mind's eye, I kept seeing an image of William Fitz Giroie's gloating face with its missing front tooth. Was he up to something, treacherous to the last?

Sliding out of bed, I yanked on a robe and picked up my dagger. I knew Father would be furious to think of me creeping around the castle in the dark, armed like a brigand, but that was too bad. If Fitz Giroie was up to any foul tricks, I wanted to know, and Father would doubtless be too busy taking his conjugal rights… I made a sick face at the thought.

A little cat-like shadow, I swept through the chilly halls where the torches had burnt to stubs, plunging them into fuggy gloom. Reaching the door that led to the courtyard, I quietly lifted the bar and exited. Night-furled, I slunk along the stony side of a tower. Over to my left, I heard the owl hoot again, louder than before. I smirked. Owl, indeed. The noise came from the ground, not from the towers of the castle. It was some kind of signal made by a man.

I pressed forward through the gloom, my eyes growing accustomed to the murk. Suddenly, a hand grabbed me by the hair, almost yanking me off my feet. I struggled and attempted to scream but a hairy hand clamped over my mouth. My fingers scrabbled for my knife but they were struck away.

"Mabel, *stop!*" hissed a familiar voice at my ear.

Father! I ceased to battle and went limp and he released me. "What in the name of Christ are you doing out here?" he snapped in a low tone.

"I could ask the same of you!" I retorted, shaking from the shock of being unexpectedly grabbed. "I thought you would be humping your ugly bride."

He hit me. Not very hard, but enough to drop me to my knees. I felt my face. He'd avoided my nose and teeth, which was good; I would not be marred in my looks.

"I am out on men's business, Mabel." Reaching down, he hauled me to my feet. "Dangerous business. No business for a little girl. Settling scores."

"William Fitz Giroie," I said. "It's him you're after; I know it is."

"Yes. Time to make him pay for abandoning me. The fool...he should never have come here, invitation or no. Mabel, I should send you back to your bedchamber, but as you are my heir, and will need to be as tough as any man, I bid you come with me. But if you screech or cry at anything you witness tonight, I swear I will beat you black and blue!"

"I am brave; you know that. I won't cry. Not at anything!"

"Yes, I believe you." He gently rumpled the hair he had tugged so viciously just minutes before.

Moving off into the darkness, Father beckoned me to follow close on his heels. Now I spied other shapes in the darkness. A man behind a bush in the garden, another crouched in a niche in the wall, several squatting on a staircase, a couple kneeling on top of the wall separating inner bailey from outer. Father's men.

He held up a hand for me to halt, then pulled me down onto the wet earth beside him. In the distance, came the singing of merry, drunk men.

The only light was from the fingernail-paring moon; the torches in their brackets set around the courtyard were out, as were the fire braziers near the gate. I assumed this was deliberate. It certainly made the courtyard and inner bailey as black as the pits of hell...

Out of the night staggered William Fitz Giroie and his band of oafs, all drunk and leaning on each other as they sang a lewd ditty about a harlot from Harfleur. "Well, a fine feast it has been at my old lord's expense," chuckled Fitz Giroie. "Old fat fool. He must be desperate to get enough men to oust his son. I will play him like a fiddle...but now..." he yawned, his mouth a black cavern. "Now we must find our beds and sleep..."

Father suddenly sprang up and gave a shrill whistle. Fitz Giroie whipped around in surprise, almost overbalancing, and shouted, "To arms, men. Attack!"

But it was too late. Father's soldiers huddled on the wall leapt up, firing their crossbows. They instantly took down five of Fitz Giroie's men. Bodies fell, blood gleamed black in the dimness. Fitz Giroie's retainers began to shout, gathering around their lord in an attempt to get into some kind of battle formation. However, they were all inebriated and crashed drunkenly into each other. I found it all quite comical, especially when they reached for their swords and remembered they had been required to leave them in their lodgings during the feast. They only had their eating knives, no better, perhaps less lethal, than mine.

Several more of Father's men sprang into play, confronting their confused, drunk foes. A sword clattered against a knife; a man's hand was sliced off at the wrist. Wailing, he fell into his knees—but the sound was cut off as Father's man struck off his head. It bounced like a ball, the eyes starting from their sockets in frozen terror, terrible to gaze upon in the wan blue moonlight. Another enemy whirled about, tackling the soldier who ran up behind him as he attempted to leap upon his back. The two men fell together, rolled in the grass for a bit, then a blade shone pale and Fitz Giroie's man lay still.

The carnage continued until William was on his own. He dropped into a crouch, breath white in the frigid air, his lips drawn back in a snarl. "You...you treacherous bastard!" he howled at Father."

"Only returning the favour," said Father dryly.

Fitz Giroie gave an enraged cry and lunged at his adversary with his knife, aiming for his throat.

Two soldiers loomed from the darkness and caught his arm in mid-swing. A knee went into his belly and he went down. He was quickly disarmed, the dagger clattering onto the blood-splattered flagstones. I thought it might end there in the courtyard, with Father running him through with his sword, but my sire made another motion with his hand. "Bind him. Then bring him to the dungeon."

A black hood was thrust over Fitz Giroie's head, muffling his shouts. His arms were yanked back and bound with thick rope. He was dragged into the castle and hustled down the spiral stairs that led to the dungeons many feet below the earth.

Father reached over and grasped my hand. "You came outside. You will witness my justice. Are you afraid?"

"No," I said, fierce and determined. "I have nothing to fear."

He led me to the stairs. Down, down they spiralled into the bowels of the castle, slimy and green. The air reeked of urine and mould and even worse things. At the bottom of the stairs, a light bloomed, tentative, wavering. One of Father's minions had lit a torch and was holding it aloft. I was glad; I did not want to slip on the slime and look foolish before all.

At the bottom of the stairs, I found myself in a vaulted chamber, the stonework ancient and eroded. Water dripped somewhere in a lightless corner. Six cells with doors faced me, and an oubliette, a lightless shaft covered by a rusty iron grille, yawned in the filthy floor.

William Fitz Giroie was pushed to his knees and the hood torn from his head. Furious, he gazed up at Father and his men. "Unhand me!" he shouted. "This will not go unpunished! All men know you for what you are, Talvas."

"Do they? And what have they ever dared do about it?" Father laughed. Grabbing Fitz Giroie's head, he wrenched it back by the hair. "I should slit your throat this minute and let my dogs lick your blood."

Still defiant, Fitz Giroie spat into Father's face; the spittle crawled down his cheek like a slug's pale leavings. "Dogs? Well, I see you've brought your little bitch with you, that much is true!"

With a shock of anger, I realised he was talking about me. "How dare you?" I lunged forward and slapped him across the face.

Father pushed me back, shaking his head, but suddenly an unpleasant grin split his thick beard. "*I* won't hurt you, Fitz Giroie," he said, "but I cannot say the same for Lady Mabel, whom you have slandered. Daughter, what do you think would be a fitting punishment for this miscreant?"

I shrugged, not knowing what answer I was expected to make.

"Put his eyes out," said Father, suddenly abrupt. "If he likes not the sight of you, let him see nought ever again. He can keep his miserable life...but only as a half-man." He leaned over, laughing into Fitz Giroie's face. Don't fear, old friend; the monks will probably take you in. If you survive."

I lifted my little dagger, still unblooded, the gift Father gave me for my protection.

Fitz Giroie caught sight of its gleam in the shadows and hooted with strained, uneasy mirth. "Stop this nonsense, Talvas. Tell the child to put down that knife. Let me go. The past is the past. I'll even help you removed Arnulf from Alencon."

"Mabel?"

I took a tentative step towards Fitz Giroie, holding the dagger out before me.

"You would not dare." William Fitz Giroie fixed me with a steely glare as if trying to impede my approach with just a commanding look. I wanted to laugh but did not think it appropriate. This was serious business.

I lifted my weapon, paused.

"Do you think I am afraid? You wield that thing like a sewing needle—and that's what you should be doing, sewing like a normal maid. But you're not normal are you, you vile little whore..."

"Mabel!" Father's voice, harsh and strident, was a prompt.

I descended on Fitz Giroie and the reeking dungeon was filled with his screams...

CHAPTER FIVE

The wedding festivities were, without a doubt, over. William Fitz Giroie was in the oubliette, alive or dead I did not know, and Father, smiling contentedly, kissed me on the cheek and sent me back to the de Beaumonts in my litter.

Upon reaching Castle Beaumont, I was escorted into the presence of Lady Hildegarde and her ladies, and fed and watered in her private solar. She must have had some idea what had taken place at the wedding but she mentioned nought of any particulars and instead chattered on about Father's nuptials as if they were a marvellous thing, a cause for protracted celebration.

Her Ladyship was in high spirits, more than a little bit tipsy from a large goblet of wine, when she glanced over at me, smiling knowingly, and said, "Well, I heard that the wedding was most...*successful* for your Father."

Was that a reference to William de Giroie's fate? "Yes," I said gruffly, staring moodily into my own goblet. "My Father is a happy man."

"And so should he be," she tittered. "Such a fine, strong fellow. I believe Haberga likes your Father more than she lets on, Mabel. Perhaps by this time next year, you will have a new brother or sister."

"I do not want another one." I smacked my cup down on the table with a noisy bang. "Arnulf is more than enough. I do not want some squalling, pink, troublesome creature..."

"Oh, so jealous!" shrilled Hildegarde, as her women giggled behind their hands. "You shouldn't be so unkind about little babies, Mabel—in a few years, no doubt you shall bear many of your own."

"Unless you become a nun," said one of the other women, Ingunde. "Isn't that what you told us your Uncle Ives wanted? I can picture you as a nun, all in black...scowling at all us sinners."

Ingunde was taunting me, and I knew it. I had no liking for any of Hildegarde's women and the feeling was mutual. I thought to myself that I would endeavour to get my own back shortly—a dead mouse under Ingunde's pallet, or even better, sewn into the hem of her voluminous skirts...

Hildegarde must have seen my expression of pique. "Oh come, Ingunde, leave her be. I do not think Mabel enjoys our type of amusement…"

No, Mabel certainly does not…

The gaggle of hens quieted and I started yawning and stretching, letting them all know how tired and stiff I was from my long journey. Hildegard began to yawn, too, and she rose and beckoned for us women to follow. "Come now, our little Mabel has returned safely. It is time to bed down so that we may awake early to wash our faces in the beautifying morning dew!"

We entered Hildegarde's bedchamber, and the candles were snuffed out. I crawled onto my humble pallet near the foot of her Ladyship's bed, while around me the other women stretched out, whispering inanities to each other before their heads dipped down and they began snoring quietly.

Mind racing, I stayed awake, remembering the screams of William de Giroie in the deep dark dungeon. Such bloody memories I found oddly less revolting than the snores and breathy gasps of my slumbering companions.

As if Lady Hildegarde had spoken prophecy, within a few months I received the news that Haberga was with child. Father was full of paternal pride, boasting of his virility with Raoul and other men. Haberga was smug and precious; Hildegarde told me that Haberga had borne no children in her first marriage and her first husband had chided her for being barren. Now, she had one last chance to have a son to carry on her noble bloodline and was glad that she had eschewed the veil to wed Father.

Whenever I saw Haberga sweeping along to chapel, leaving offerings in gratitude for her newfound fruitfulness, I wanted to tell her she had best not become over-pious…lest she found Father's fingers round her scraggy neck. But I would never go that far. Father loved me, in his own strange way, but he had would have no qualms about thrashing me if he thought I overstepped the mark with his new wife.

When the time came, to my horror, Haberga gave birth to a boy in Castle Beaumont where Haburga had stayed to be attended by the best midwives and Hildegarde and her ladies. I was brought to the castle nursery to see my little half-brother. My stomach churned. He was bawling, his face purple-red and crumpled, looking like a great slug in his swaddling. He smelt of milk and fresh shite.

"Would you like to hold your brother, milady?" the porcine wetnurse asked nervously.

"Christ's Nails, no!" I exclaimed, backing away. "I—I have seen more than enough." I whirled around on my heel and nearly crashed into Father's expanding belly. He caught me by the shoulders, pinioning me against the wall.

"Visiting little Oliver, Mabel? Why are you leaving so soon?"

"I did my duty—I saw him," I glowered. "What more do you want? He's only my half-brother; he'll probably grow up as bad as Arnulf, if not worse."

"Ah...so thorny. A rose with a thorn, my Mab."

"I'm not a rose, and now I am just your useless daughter, to be discarded in Oliver's favour."

"What makes you believe that?"

"Because it is the way of things. The male takes precedence. Always."

Father's jaw jutted out pugnaciously. "Must he? Mabel, I did not expect to have another child so late in my life. I always thought of you as my heir, even before Arnulf rebelled. I still do, Mabel. You, of all my children, are the true heir of House Belleme. You may be a woman, but you are cast in my mould."

Eyes wide, I stared at him, hardly able to believe what I was hearing. Then I launched myself at him, in an uncharacteristic display of love and gratitude. "Thank you, Father...I will make you proud of me, I promise."

"You are so much like me." Red-faced, he pushed me away, a little embarrassed by my over-enthusiasm. "Hence I will always favour you. But in order for you to take charge of the Belleme inheritance one day, you must have a strong-armed husband to defend you and keep unruly retainers and vassals in their place."

I glowered, folding my arms defensively. Marriage again; it always came back to marriage.

Father ignored my look of displeasure. "Now that I am settled in with de Beaumont as my brother-by-marriage, we will have to work on a good match for you. Raoul will choose wisely, for it is beneficial to him money-wise. I won't gain anything from your union, save for having a stout son-by-marriage to support my causes, but I doubt Raoul would object to my advice in the matter."

"If you must pursue a match, make sure my husband is not old!" I warned. "Or warty. Or smelly."

He chuckled into his beard, which had grown shaggy again in the months since he had wed Haberga de Beaumont. "I think that can be managed, but no promises, Mab. If you are indeed wed to some doddering old fool, think on this—a little fall with a crack to the pate, a deathly stupor after drinking his favourite wine…" He shrugged. "Such things happen to men in their dotage."

Taking his meaning, I grinned. He pinched my cheek. We were truly two of a kind. I alone was true blood of his blood; the boys, my brothers, were just pale and feeble imitations.

Over the next year, Father lived happily with Haberga. He kept his temper in check and endeavoured to be a good lord to those who toiled on Harbega's dower lands. The grub that was my brother Oliver thrived, growing into a moon-faced creature with tawny curls and huge bulbous eyes. Behind Father's back, I called him 'Frogspawn'. I hadn't realised before, but Haberga with her broad face and wide, long mouth also resemble a great, sallow-faced frog, just like her google-eyed spawn.

Lords with their retinues would arrive at Castle Beaumont, and Hildegarde would bid me dress in my finest gown, with my dark nut-brown hair hanging loose like a fall of shining silk, and parade before them as the supped at Raoul's table. Older now and much wiser, I knew the looks of lechery or desire cast in my direction. I was not the most beautiful girl in France by any means, but I was different in temperament to most maidens, and numerous men showed interest in me, sometimes honourable, more often not. I think they saw me as some wild creature they could break and tame like a colt. Fools, all.

I toyed with some, had them meet me in the castle's rose gardens, where they would try for a kiss or more. I always found a way to disappoint or disparage them. A sudden motion of my foot, tipping them into the fishpond, or leading them around the side of a tower—under one of the chutes leading from the castle privy. I was nimble and knew when to jump away; my hot-handed suitors were not so lucky. One fellow, fat and curly-headed, a chevron blazoned on his tabard, reacted with wrath at a dousing of piss from above, and unlike most of his fellows, who had glared at me but retreated, clinging to their dignity, he erupted into a rage worthy of Father.

"You planned that, you cock-teasing little bitch!" he shouted, as dung trailed down his spoiled tabard. "What kind of an abnormal witch are you!"

"One who doesn't like jumped up lordlings with groping fingers!" I spat back at him. "Or fat lordlings. Or lordlings who smell of chamber pots."

Crazy-eyed with anger, he had lunged at me then; most maids would have wilted in terror, but not I. Dancing out of his way, I fled through the gardens, shrieking with laughter that inflamed his ire even more. He charged after me like a raging bull, trampling the flowers and herbs in their beds.

He was stopped when Father, visiting with Haberga and Frogspawn, suddenly stepped through an archway in the encircling garden wall. His eyes grew black with wrath as he saw me being pursued by a fat, reeking man almost twice my size.

"Help me, sire!" I cried. "This brute tried to molest me!"

My pursuer slowed down abruptly as he saw Father. "I-I did not!" he cried. "Believe me, my lord. The girl, she deceived…"

"The 'girl' is my daughter, the Lady Mabel de Belleme," Father growled. "How dare you speak ill of her in my presence!" The man tried to run but Father was on him. His fist flew, landing square on fat-belly's chin. My tormentor dropped into a flowerbed, blood running from his nose.

Father peered down at him. "Was it true what he said, Mabel?"

"No," I said, "well, yes. It was clear from the start he wanted to ravish me...so I decided to punish him."

Father chucked me under the chin—not terribly gently—my teeth clacked together. "Just be careful, Mabel. One time one of these fellows might catch you."

"No chance of that," I said with childish arrogance, tossing back my glossy mane of hair.

He frowned. "If a warrior had your attitude, he might find himself killed through his arrogance and over-confidence. You might fight a different kind of battle, Mab—but I bid you not be over-bold in such exploits, either."

I stopped tormenting the would-be suitors for a while, in case any news of my exploits were passed on to Father by Lord Raoul or Hildegarde. Instead, I concentrated on riding, hawking, and going on pilgrimages—I was not much bothered with venerating saints' relics, however, I enjoyed visiting strange new places and seeing different churches, castles and landmarks.

Father and Raoul met frequently to discuss men's matters—skirmishes and frays, outlaws in the woods, tithes and rents, taxes, and other such dull subjects. Rather frequently, the pair of them mentioned Roger, Seigneur of Montgomery, and his son who was now Seigneur in his stead, even though his father yet lived. I vaguely remembered old Lord Montgomery coming to Alencon when I was very small; a broad man with eagle features and piercing blue eyes. His wife was Lady Josceline, haughty and cold, with skin like marble and pale red hair; they had five sons—Hugh, Robert, Roger, William and Gilbert. The Montgomery brood had travelled with their parents once or twice, but I had avoided them. Squabbling and fighting as young boys do, they had made too much noise, and they had the doggy smell of their slobbering hounds.

They seemed a fractious brood; Lord Roger had been a supporter of Robert Duke of Normandy but upon his death had fallen afoul of Robert's heir, young Duke William, who was a close friend to Lord Roger's namesake son. Indeed, he had raised a rebellion against the young Duke, which failed, and at present he was in exile in Paris. Duke William had seen the younger Roger take his father's place, with guardians to assist him since he, like the Duke himself was not of full legal age.

Then one day the talk of Father and Lord Raoul took on a different complexion. A man of lesser rank but wearing the Montgomery colours had arrived at Castle Beaumont. I had been called to appear in the Great Hall with Lady Hildegarde; we shared bread and wine with the newcomer, and then musicians came in, and the rest of Hildegarde's ladies, and we danced prettily in a circle. Once we were done, Raoul dismissed us with a smile, and the three men closeted themselves away in Lord Raoul's private solar for hours, while I sat gnawing my nails outside the door wondering what they devised.

I soon learnt. As I skulked near the Hall late in the evening, I heard them discussing me over a meal of roast capons and dumplings. "Your daughter is a comely girl and a fine dancer," said the emissary, a man called Hugues, carving off a chicken leg and waving it on his dagger for emphasis. "Have you any offers on a marriage for her?"

Marriage again! I shuddered.

"Raoul and I have spoken of it often," said Father. "However, we have come to an agreement—for the kindness he has shown me and mine, Raoul holds Mabel's wardship and hence shall arrange and benefit from Mabel's marriage."

"Well, I have a proposal. The Lord Roger de Montgomery needs a wife. He is a keen youth and intelligent, and I predict he will have a fine future ahead. He's in high favour with young William, the new Duke of Normandy."

"The Bastard." Father emitted a belch. "His father tupped a Tanner's daughter. Arlotte…or should that be Harlotte?" He chuckled at his ribald joke.

Hugues cleared his throat. "For all that his birth may be irregular, William proves himself daily as a leader and a good lord."

"Even though he chased old Seigneur Roger off his lands and handed them to his friend?"

"The elder Roger was, alas, a traitor." Hugues reddened. "I served him well in the past, but his choices were unwise. Duke William may be of young age but he is not a man to cross."

"Aye, I have heard those reports too." Raoul looked thoughtful. "And also that the Duke is proving himself as a warrior and more. If your boy Roger is rising within William's sphere, mayhap he would indeed be a fitting match for Mabel."

"I would have him see her first, however. Roger is quite *particular*...Lady Mabel is winsome enough from what I have seen, but I know of your current...*difficulties*...Lord William. I speak of your loss of castles and lands to your son, Arnulf. What will Mabel bring to Lord Roger's benefit?"

"One day she will be heir to Belleme and all its lands when I and my brother Yves die," barked Father, banging a fist on the table and making goblets and trenchers jump. "And if someone can prise out my wretched son Arnulf from Alencon that is rightfully hers too."

"Ah, that is good to know." Hugues stroked his long, bristly chin. "The fact you will bestow the Honour of Belleme is exceedingly positive. Such wealth would indeed make her a fitting bride for my young lord."

"We will talk more of this matter tomorrow," said Raoul, clearly excited at the prospect of wedding me off to this Roger de Montgomery. Christ, I could not remember which one he was out of the squabbling brood who had visited Alencon so long ago. "Now that you know she is truly a great heiress, I am sure she will be most acceptable to your Roger. Send for the lad. Get him here to look upon his prospective bride."

I raced away down the corridor, crashing into servants as I sought the gardens and the cleansing early evening air. I had known I would be married soon but I was shocked that I would only be found 'acceptable' if Roger of Montgomery came to look me over like a beast on the block! What if he was scornful and horrible and rejected me through spite? How dare Raoul, how dare Father put me through such an ordeal! They should have told Hugues to make a decision on Roger's behalf then and there or be on his way.

Slumping down beneath a flowering bush, I hid my face on my knees. A knot of sorrow mingled with anger burned in my breast, but no tears would come.

I never cried over anything. *Never*. I would not begin now.

CHAPTER SIX

I was determined to hate this arrogant Roger, and determined to make him hate me in turn...but then he arrived at Castle Beaumont, accompanied by his younger brothers.

I was dazzled. He was tall as a spear, with wavy black hair, and fine, though haughty, features. A true aristocrat's visage. And his eyes--they were an intense sky-blue, striking and as sharp as a lance.

Lady Hildegarde nudged me as he entered the Great Hall. "What do you think, Mabel?"

"I-I think he...he is very comely and noble to behold," I stammered, embarrassed that a warm flush was already creeping up my cheeks.

"I thought you might," said Hildegarde. "So now, I hope, we will have less of your sour looks and tantrums. After all, he is quite a particular young man, as the emissary Hugues reported—and he won't want to wind up with a shrewish wife, even if she is the heir to the Belleme lands."

Later that evening, a banquet was held in honour of young Robert de Montgomery's arrival. Minstrels played, tumblers turned cartwheels before Lord Raoul and Lady Hildegarde on their dais. Servants brought brass basins with water full of bay leaves for us to lave our hands like the civilised nobles we were. White bread was laid before the lord and lady—and Roger—while the rest of us were given rye. After this, cooked livers of chickens were brought out stewed in garlic, followed by braun bathed in pungent mustard.

Sitting in a fine leaf-green gown with silver holding back my locks, I made eyes at Roger and ate daintily, like a true lady, dabbing carefully at my lips, upon which Hildegarde and her women had applied a dab of paint. Roger never looked at me. Not once.

Later, after our final sweet course of *cressees* sprinkled with ginger, a new troupe of musicians emerged and the dancing began. As I had expected, Hildegarde had arranged it so that I danced with Roger. I was a fair enough dancer and tried to do my very best to impress him. Roger, however, was so much taller than I, that our glances never met; in fact, he appeared to be staring straight over the top of my head. His expression was one of boredom and pique.

A cold chill ran through me. Despite my first opposition to the idea of marriage, and my annoyance about his fussiness, I had now set my heart upon him...but it seemed he liked me not...

He liked me not...

I could not bear the thought, especially as the pipes, flutes and tabor wailed into nothingness and he meandered away to chat with his brothers. I might as well have been invisible.

Shock at his diffidence to my charms turned to sadness—but only for a moment. Anger filled me instead. How dare he? Why should he look down on a daughter of the House of Belleme? I was not piggish, nor was I overly bony in figure; my teeth were pearly, my cheeks full of bloom, my hair was thick and lustrous, falling free to show my maidenly status. I was shorter than the average woman, true, but that was scarcely classed as a defect—my diminutive height gave the illusion that I would need to be cossetted and protected, which some men found appealing.

For the next hour, I ogled the object of my new-found affections. He did not glance over even once, talking with his pimply-faced younger brothers—and with the daughter of one of the local knights, a gangling girl with bushy corn-hued hair, who had the most annoying moon-mazed giggle as she flirted and primped before Roger. I wanted to rip out those fashionable blonde curls and send her flying on her round rump...but I knew a woman of my status could not brawl on the hall floor like an ale-wife in a tavern.

But I had to get him away from her...*had to*! Roger must learn that we were meant to be, our union smiled on by the both de Beaumonts and my sire. Beckoning to one of the nearby musicians, I whispered the name of a swift-moving dance in his ear. The musician, a rabbit-faced man with a nervous twitching visage, began to shake his head, "Milady, Lord Raoul said nought of more dancing...The servers are starting to clear the tables."

"Well, *I* say otherwise. It is for a...a surprise!" I said, eyes flashing fire. "Are you, a humble minstrel, going to refuse the daughter of a mighty lord?"

"N-no, milady," he stammered, turning crimson. I could see his hands shaking. "My little company will play the dance you require."

He gestured to his fellows, who looked surprised. One began to argue, waving his fiddle about, but the first man shrugged and nervously glanced over his shoulder at me. I smiled a smile that was pure poison. He quickly turned back to convincing—or coercing—his companions.

A bagpipe began to wail, soon joined by timbrel, rebec, fiddle and drum. I saw Lord Raoul and Lady Hildegarde crane their heads around, startled by this musical intrusion. Roger stopped talked to the blonde-haired wench and his gaggle of carbuncle-ridden brothers.

Graceful as a feather—or so I hoped, I swept out onto the floor. I flicked my hair, twirled the hem of my gown—picked out to impress by Hildegarde. My sleeves glittered with tiny sewn-on white gems, vivid against the deep blue-green of the fine imported silk—which smelt of the dried orange peels stored with it to give it a sweet fragrance. I tiptoed around the firepit to stand before Roger de Montgomery, holding my hand out in invitation.

He stared at it as if it was a withered hag's palsied paw. His two brothers clutched each other's arms and went purple, holding back ill-concealed mirth.

A rush of blood sprang to my own face—but it was not from any urge to laugh. "My lord Roger?" I tried to keep my voice light, feminine, undemanding...and yet seductive.

He glanced around, noticing that we were now the focus of attention. The knights and lords gathered around the trestle tables began to laugh and roar, pounding their cups on the wooden tabletops. "Dance with the maid, lad!" someone shouted. "If you won't, I will!"

I glanced at the noisy knight, a fat fellow whose bottom was spilling over the edge of his seat. I most certainly didn't want his greasy hands touching me or my lovely blue-green gown. "Please, Roger..." I looked into Roger's eyes, trying to make our glances meet. They did for a moment, and his gaze was full of embarrassment and resentment...but also, a hint of resignation.

I took his hand and pulled him towards me. We began to dance; I had asked the musicians to play a quick country air, but I suddenly realised it would be difficult to perform because there was only the two of us on the floor. A muffled roll of laughter came from the watchers. Roger stared down as if he hoped the floor would open up and swallow him. He was shuffling about like an old greybeard. Over his shoulders, I spotted his brothers almost falling over pressing their sleeves to their mouths to keep from laughing out loud.

Desperation gripped me. I was looking the fool, looking the worst thing a woman can look before the man she wants—undesirable and desperate. A brilliant smile pasted to my face, I attempted to draw Roger into the dance again. His hand was clammy, sweating. I refused to let go and instead twirled around him, pulling at his arm. He winced as I jolted his shoulder roughly.

The laughter in the hall was no longer muffled. Open guffaws filled the smoky air. Glancing at the dais, even Lady Hildegarde was wiping tears of mirth from her eyes. Lord Raoul's shoulders were heaving as he clutched the arms of his fine wooden chair.

This was not working! Far from making me seem irresistible, I looked gauche, clumsy and stupid. *Stupid*...in front of all these people.

I stop dancing instantly, dropping Roger's limp hand. My hands curled into tight fists at my sides as I glared at everyone in the hall. "Be silent!" I cried—and to my joy, silence fell.

But only for a moment. "Hear the vixen cry!" the fat knight bellowed, wine running down the deep lines slashed on either side of his mouth as he slurped a great draught, and then the Hall was filled with uproar again. Roger was backing away, creeping towards his two brothers.

I staggered towards him. "You—how dare you humiliate me!" He nipped around behind the three other boys, Robert, Hugh and Gilbert. "Coward! Coward!" My voice rose in a shriek.

"Do you want me to defend you, Rodge?" asked Gilbert in a sarcastic tone, eyeing his brother.

"I hate you!" I cried, and grasping an ewer from the table I threw its contents over the four lads, who yelled and shouted in startled surprise. Then, grasping my spattered skirts, I rushed from the Great Hall.

Even more laughter, horrible and hurtful, followed me.

"We will just have to find someone else for you," said Lady Hildegarde in a matter-of-fact tone. She was sitting in her solar, working on her embroidery; a blanket for the newborn babe of one of her sons.

"I do not want anyone else!" I stomped my foot. "I want Roger."

Her eyebrows lifted. "All this drama. When we first mentioned him, you were not very interested at all."

"I changed my mind. I won't marry anyone else."

"Oh, won't you? That leaves joining Holy Orders, and I do not think any convent would take a girl such as you."

"What is that supposed to mean?"

"Don't be impertinent," said Hildegard, her face mild, but an edge in her voice. "Go and find something useful to do."

Red-faced and irritated, I shuffled off. Servants fled before my stony visage. I disappeared into the herb garden with the intent of picking some herbs to sweeten Hildegard's bedchamber. Maybe they would sweeten her mood too.

Kneeling, I began to pluck lavender. Bees buzzed about my head; I whacked at them with my hand, uncaring if I got stung. And then a shadow fell over me, blotting out the wavering sunlight. Dropping my plucked bloom in a cloud of purple, I stared up, squinting against the bright sky.

It was Gilbert, Roger's youngest brother, wearing a sheepish grin on his spotty young face. He said nothing, and neither did I until I finally found my tongue and barked, "Is there something you want? Can you not see I'm busy?"

He shuffled nervously on the knotted grass. "My brother Roger has sent me."

"Oh? And why is that? To mock me even more? To chide me for making him look foolish at the feast?"

"No...no, nothing like that. He wants to apologise."

"He...*what*?" I leapt up, almost falling over in my haste. "What did you say?"

"He was churlish, and he soon realised it."

I was smug then. "I am glad to hear it. Where is he now?"

"He is currying his horse in the stables."

"He's not... *leaving* already," I cried, horrified.

Gilbert shrugged. "I think the time of our departure home will depend on getting a few matters sorted in the next day or two."

"Take me to him, Gilbert. I beg you, take me to him."

The stable was dark and dim, smelling of horses, manure, leather and straw. I spotted Roger at the far end in the stall of a tall grey courser. A brush was in his hand and he ran it through the beast's thick, dark mane. A delicious shudder passed through me, as I imagined him running those long, strong fingers through my flowing mane.

Gilbert coughed to alert his brother, then discretely vanished from the stable. The grooms were notably absent too. I was alone with Roger de Montgomery.

"I believe you have something to say to me," I said. "Or so Gilbert told me."

He put his brush aside and exited the stall. His horse whickered and pressed its nose against his shoulder, seeking treats as he departed.

"Yes... I did not behave as I should to a lady of good birth and the ward of Lord and Lady de Beaumont."

"Indeed," I said. "I only wanted a dance, especially as..." I hesitated, then the words flooded out in a rush: "Especially as it was Lady Hildegarde's intention we should wed. But her ladyship and your man Hugues said you were... *particular*, and I'd have to please you. And it seemed I did no such thing." I hesitated, emotion overcoming me in an embarrassing wave. "Am I truly so loathsome to behold that you must treat me as if I were a worm, a dung-beetle to be crushed beneath your shoe?"

Shocked, he gazed at me. "I-I never thought of you as a dung-beetle, I assure you!"

"Prove it!" I said.

He did. He kissed me, quickly, impertinently on the mouth.

I liked it, I liked it very much but I knew it was improper to show it.

"That was unchivalrous, sir!" I cried, leaping back...but not *too* far back. "You did that just to outrage my morals. Your brothers are probably peering through knots in the wall, laughing!"

"There are not, I swear it!" he cried, looking wounded. "And I did not do it to shame you! Mabel, I *want* to marry you!"

"Y-you do?" I stammered. I had not expected that!

"Yes! I...I have even spoken to Lord Raoul."

"When?"

"This morning. We spoke of many issues, but I promise you were foremost on my mind."

"Prove it!"

He kissed me again, longer this time. "Will you agree to have me?"

"I will!" The words trembled off my lips. I clutched his hand in mine. "I promise to be your lawful wedded wife and stand beside you in all things. Between us, we will make the Houses of Belleme and Montgomery great!"

"We will!" he said, his fingers entwining with mine.

And so the agreement was made, and I got what I wanted—Roger de Montgomery.

It was only by chance that the next day, after Roger and his brothers had departed for home, that I overheard, or rather, eavesdropped, on Lord Raoul and Hildegarde in their solar while coming in with a basket of roses for her ladyship's bedchamber.

"The boy wasn't all that keen," Raoul said to his wife, "that was clear for all to see, hence Mabel's ridiculous dance...but I offered him some more lands, and he came round. He has a good business head on him. I believe he knows how to pick the winning side."

A mixture of shock and anger rushed over me. *Lands!* Roger only wanted lands! I was just...*useful*, nothing more. Frustrated but knowing I dared not make a sound for fear of revealing myself, I grasped a handful of the pale pink roses in my basket and tore their petals asunder. Thorns gouged my flesh, drawing blood. It almost felt *good*...and the sudden pain calmed me, brought me to reality.

The lands did not matter. I still got what I desired. The details did not matter. Marriage was always a bargain, after all.

I began to kick at the fallen roses, showering pale petals in the dark of the corridor. No, the details of our union mattered nothing at all...The only thing that did was that Roger was forever mine.

CHAPTER SEVEN

Montgomery Castle was large and many-towered, which I appreciated very much, for it gave the impression of wealth and might. It reminded me of Alencon, which I prayed would fall into my hands in due time—taken by force if need be.

I entered the bailey in my litter to great acclamation and cheering; above, the spring sun shone and banners flapped on the spikes of every turret.

Roger's youngest brother Gilbert handed me out of my litter, gazed at me with merry, dancing eyes. "I told you Roger liked you, Lady Mabel…my sister," he said.

I cast him a wan smile. I knew Roger liked fine lands and castles even more…but never mind. What was done was done, and after today I would be Lady of Montgomery and a married woman, my rank in the world rising with my marriage and the melding of our Houses.

Gilbert escorted me into the Great Hall. Green rushes lay on the floor and flowers had been strewn amongst them to sweeten the air. Candles glimmered, their wax casting off a sweet tallowy odour. Lord Roger sat upon the dais, looking like a prince out of ancient legend with his glossy black hair and startling, sky-blue eyes.

My heart fluttered furiously, despite myself. Despite the extra lands that had sealed the marriage deal.

Head bowed modestly, I stood before him clad in blue for the Virgin, a glimmering veil bound by a band of silver dotted with star-shaped sapphires set on my head. I curtseyed as elegantly as I could, stretching out my voluminous skirts and the dangling sleeves lined with saffron-hued cloth so that all could see I was a lady of quality, despite my Father's rather chequered reputation.

"I heard she once ran wild with an outlaw band along with her old sire," I had heard some scullery girl whisper as I had mounted the steps to the keep. "They say she had a wolf for a pet and dressed like a man...even spent the night lying on the forest floor with strange men all around her."

In the future, I would have to quash such silly stories with harsh punishment, if need be. Gossip of my grievous time in exile was not to be endured; it must die a death...even if it meant the speaker must die too.

Roger smiled down at me; I fancied his smile had some genuine warmth, even a hint of desire. I felt colour rise to my cheeks and I smiled back.

Foremost in a vast procession, we were led through the nearby town of Montgomery to the large sandstone church. Overhead clouds were chasing each other across the firmament. Mounted soldiers followed us, and crowds of nobles; beyond them came the well-wishers, crowds of them, filling the side alleys and the gutters.

The church was small and old, its stones blackened with time. It had been founded by Saint-Vigor, Bishop of the city of Bayeux. The west door stood open, its rounded arches carved with beaked faces and twined monsters with goggling eyes, the remnants of our forebears lost in time, the men of the North.

A priest appeared from the vestry, his cope and his hairless head agleam in the burgeoning sunlight, giving him a surreal saintly look. Outside the doors, Roger and I stood together as the cleric spoke the words that would join us, now and forever. He had a thick accent I did not know well and could barely follow him; I merely nodded and mumbled my responses. I lost interest halfway through and pretended to cast my maidenly gaze towards heaven; in fact, I was scrutinising the carvings running along the roofline with their horns and claws and serrated grinning teeth.

At last, the ceremony was done. The crowds of onlookers cheered and horns blared out, ringing through the streets of the town. Man and wife, Roger and I handed our coins to the poor before we trailed slowly back to the castle on its swollen earth mound. I felt quite proud to walk at his side, arm entwined with his, our hands clasped; I still found him as handsome as when we first met and had thrust the problem of his desiring my lands more than me from my mind.

Back within the Castle's Great Hall, a wedding banquet had been prepared. Roger and I sat at the top table under a canopy of fine azure-blue cloth embroidered with three golden Fleur de Lis, our jewelled chalices before us, our chairs draped in deep red furs. The platters were brought in, one by one as we partook of goslings and pigeons, leverets and roe deer, sturgeon and eels, wedges of blue-veined cheese, quivering jellies in green and red, bowls of stodgy clotted cream topped by fennels seeds.

Between the courses there was music, dancing and other entertainments, such as juggling and a short play. During the second or third break, a trumpet blared brazenly, overwhelming the singing and sound or rebec and lute. All the celebrants craned their heads towards the hall doors in nervous anticipation.

Frowning, I glanced at my husband. Who would dare to interrupt our nuptials in such an abrupt manner? Roger seemed unconcerned, although his gaze was fixed on the door. "Is there trouble?" I asked bluntly. I had visions of my brother Arnulf bursting in to try to cause trouble because I was set to inherit the Belleme lands, but it was a nonsensical worry—no one had heard much from Arnulf at all. Rumour came that he was sickly and preferred to hide in Alencon with piles of books, like a monk. He had not even wed to produce an heir that might help him hold his ill-gotten lands. Father had been right—Arnulf was only half a man...

The trumpet shouted out again, ringing up to the rafters with their faint, carved figures of ancient monsters—wolves that ate the sun and wyrms that devoured their own tails.

Into the Hall marched a young man, tall, with well-made limbs, thickset rather than slender. His colouring was high, made even ruddier by the lash of the wind outside. His face was round rather than long but held no trace of fleshiness or the softness as one often sees in those with less angular, defined features. Blue-grey eyes, deep-set, stared from under thick red-brown brows that matched his close-cropped bowl of hair.

All around, lords, ladies and servants began to fall into a frenzy of bowing or curtseying. I grew quite confused, for I had no idea who this tall boy was; I'd never seen him before in my life.

Roger's eyes lit up and he leapt from the dais and approached the newcomer, going down on one knee in the sweet rushes.

"None of that is needed, Roger." The husky lad grasped my new husband's shoulders in hands like great hams, calloused from, I guessed, hard training with weapons. "You are my dearest friend and it is my honour to be here on this blessed day. The day of your wedding."

"No doubt it will be yours next, my Lord Duke...William," grinned Roger. "I pray I am there, too...and my wife, Mabel alongside me."

I knew the identity of the man now. It was the Duke of Normandy himself, young William the Bastard.

He moved towards me, strutting and assured, and I gracefully moved from my chair to curtsey. He motioned for me to rise. "Let me look at you, Lady Mabel. Let me see my good friend's chosen bride."

If it had been any other man, I would have spat in rage like a wildcat to be looked over in such a manner, but I dared not show any displeasure to the young Duke, who had, it was reputed, a fiery temper. Besides that, some quality about him quelled my ire—a sense of sternness tempered by justice. He was not making some jest at my expense. A powerful aura surrounded him and I felt drawn to him. *A mighty man in the ascendant*, I thought. A future commander, with the air of kingliness hanging heavily about him...

Blushing prettily, I rose and he took my hand and gazed into my face. His grey-blue eyes searched mine, solemn. "You are from House Belleme, are you not?" he said.

I nodded.

"Your sire liked me not. He insulted me in my cradle, I am told."

I was shocked that he mentioned an event from so long ago, and for the first time in my life, inwardly cursed my father for his rough tongue. "My Lord, I pray you forgive him. He insults everyone. Prudence is not his best trait."

William looked surprised and then he placed his hands on his hips and gave a roar of mirth. "A clear-spoken woman, with no tears or pretty ways, Roger. Refreshingly different to most."

The Duke joined us at the high table, his seat set between us, and the feast resumed. He talked of many matters with Roger and danced with me on more than one occasion. He was not as handsome as Roger, not by a long chalk, but something was entrancing about a man who exuded such power, such authority, especially in youth. I began to wish the de Beaumonts had cast their eyes towards him as a husband, but I supposed, realistically, that Father's loose words and fall in fortunes would have put paid to such an idea.

The banquet came to an end with a performance from a company of tumblers and acrobats. Dressed in daringly scanty garb, they circled the central firepit like wraiths, lit by the deep red glow of the flames, leaping over each other's backs and perching on their fellows' shoulders. Long, trailing scarves were wafted through the flames, catching alight; they whirled them around themselves, coming dangerously close to the guests, and skipped with them as if they were burning ropes. One man in a carved demon mask, horned and painted scarlet, lifted a brand on high and blew a huge flame from his mouth that mercifully dispersed in the air before it reached the old rafters high above. The women in the wedding party shrieked in fear and a few guests rushed towards the door, tripping over their own feet in fear of being burned.

Roger clapped his hands for a halt. "Enough! It is time for me and my Lady to depart for our chambers…The feasting is done!"

The women in the hall, including two girls, Marie and Erembourg chosen to be my tiring-maids, began fluttering around me like brightly-jewelled butterflies as I stepped from the dais, face flushed from the heat of the room, head spinning from the wine I had consumed. They danced me away from the chamber in a ring of linked arms and billowing sleeves and guided me up the spiralled stone steps to the Lord's apartments

The bedchamber was well-prepared. Candelabras cast flickering shadows and a brazier burned for warmth. The bed linens were strewn with pressed flowers and bags of herbs.

The women clustered around me, untying my gown and removing it. I stood in my kirtle and then that, too, was whisked away, and I stood, naked as a nymph in a tale of the Greeks, the flames casting an orange blush on my bare flesh. The women modestly lowered their eyes and began to wash me with cloths dipped in rose-scented water. Then, ablutions finished, I was led to the bed where I climbed under the coverlet, which was drawn up to my bare shoulders.

I was ready to receive my groom.

In the hallway beyond, I heard footsteps and the sound of drunken male laughter. I gritted my teeth. It was customary for the men in a wedding party to accompany the bridegroom to the marital bed with many a ribald jest. I was not unduly coy or prudish, but such intimate intrusion would be difficult to endure.

First into the room was the castle chaplain, his robes sweeping over the floor, the firelight making a halo of his sparse hair. He stood alongside the bed and mumbled Latin words of blessing as he sprinkled the cover—and me—with holy water, and then backed silently out of the room, still mumbling prayers.

Into the bridal chamber marched Roger's closest friends, well sotted after hours of drinking, their faces red and merry...and eager. While singing rude songs about harlots and dairymaids and cuckolded husbands, they peeled off Roger's raiment. Duke William was foremost amongst them, grinning widely, as he yanked off William's belt, waved it like a flag and hurled it across the chamber.

One of my attending ladies, Marie, poured out two chalices of spiced wine and carried them to the bedside. Roger pulled back the cover and climbed in beside me. All the men were staring, grinning lasciviously at my nakedness, even the Duke of Normandy himself. My cheeks burned but only a little. This was an age-old custom and the men's behaviour meant nought to me. They would forget a brief glimpse of bare flesh once they'd downed a few more flagons of wine.

The cups at the bedside were placed into our hands and we drank and toasted each other, and then, with many lewd noises, gestures and laughter, both men and women vacated the bedchamber and left us in peace.

"You are not afraid, my dearest?" asked Roger, as he pulled the coverlet tightly over us.

I shook my head. "Why should I be? You are not a beast, I take it? You are my husband who has sworn to cherish me…and if you do not, my Father will kill you!"

He laughed, but a little shakily. "I hope it will never come to that!"

"Then treat me with all honour, for all our lives together. And if you must lie with some mistress while on campaign, so be it…just never tell me of it, and bring no bastards to our house."

"I swear that will never happen! No mistresses…and no bastards."

His hands were questing now, stroking, playing. A fire was kindled in my belly, down below, deeper, fiercer and more primal than anything I'd ever experienced. "I will give you many fine sons, I promise you that," I said fiercely, although I knew that God alone could bless a union with many babes.

He made a deep, satisfied grunting noise, as he dragged me to him, and rolled atop me amidst the rumpled sheets with their scatters of petals and holy water.

Duke William stayed at Castle Montgomery for a week. He and Roger went hunting in the nearby forest, bringing back deer, and once a small wild boar. They also hunted with hawks and on those occasions, I was allowed to accompany the men. I was even given my own hawk, a grey peregrine falcon I named Sanguine. I loved to see her dive and soar, returning to me with her prey, her claws beaded with jewel-like blood as they clamped on my gloved wrist.

The Duke watched me with interest, a wry smile on his lips. I basked in his admiration while keeping careful not to seem overly interested. "It is good to see a woman active and not soft," he said. "I trust one day I will find a wife that will suit my taste in such matters."

"It is good to be married," said Roger with a roguish grin, "in many, many ways."

"I am sure," the Duke grinned back, his gaze skimming approvingly over my trim, slight form.

Then, just as suddenly, I was forgotten, and the two young men began to talk of more serious subjects, just as if I had suddenly become invisible. "I cannot wait to come of age," said William. "I itch for power, to lead men into the field. But as it is, I am pursued by my enemies instead…"

"Enemies like my foolish sire." Roger hung his head, ashamed.

"He is in Paris and at least has ceased to cause trouble. Others I fear far more. They would assassinate me, Roger. Over the years, they have killed all my guardians—Alan, Duke of Brittany, Gilbert of Brionne, poor Turchetil, and faithful Osbern, who fought off an attacker in my very bedchamber. The man skewered him before my eyes, Roger, although the guards arrived in time to save me."

Roger groaned. "I beg you, do not remind me—it was my own father who was behind the death of poor Osbern. The man was mad! Why he was nicknamed 'the Good' I shall never know. He was never 'good' to me or my brothers. When his favourite amongst us, Will, was killed in a riding accident, we all became poor seconds to be abused."

William nodded and continued, brow like thunder, "After Osbern was so brazenly murdered, my Uncle Walter even hid me in a peasant's hut for a time…but I grew tired of hiding. Tired. I will hide no more. I am young but I am a child no longer."

"Soon you will reach your majority, as I shall," said Roger, "then you can make your enemies fear you—and I shall stand at your side, sword ready."

"I would ride with you to battle if I could," I interjected, hating being left out of the conversation. William and Roger both turned in my direction, wide-eyed in surprise.

Then William laughed. "Oh, the Lady Mabel has spirit! But no, the battlefield is not the place for gentle-born ladies. I cannot imagine one enjoying the fray, enduring the bloody strike…Although…" He looked intently at me, "I once heard a strange rumour about your Father's wedding feast to Haberga de Beaumont…"

My face flamed then. It was, of course, a secret how I had participated in the blinding of the treacherous Fitz Giroie

"William Fitz Giroie had his eyes put out after the feast, did he not?" asked Duke William, leaning forward over his horse's withers until his countenance hung close to mine, disconcertingly so.

"My father and he had a long feud," I muttered. "He was a traitor, I assure you, your Grace."

"Well, he is a monk now. At the Abbey of Bec."

"Oh, so he survived?" I gasped, startled. I had been certain, after seeing the blood and hearing his tortured screams as he was thrust into the oubliette that he surely would have died.

"Yes, assuredly he lives, Lady. I know, for I have recently seen his sons, Arnold d'Eschafour and William of Montreuil—and they swear to take revenge for his mutilation. I tell you this, Lady, that you might warn your sire, for their vengeance will be terrible."

"I will send him a message," I said, uncomfortably. What, if anything, did Fitz Giroie's sons know of my part in their father's destruction? I did not want to bring renewed fighting to the door of my new home, marring my marriage and destroying the life I had envisioned.

Overhead, the clouds had darkened; a thin rain began to fall and a chill wind shrieked out of the north making the pines on the nearby ridge bend and wave.

"Time for us to go," said Roger, staring at the sky as black clouds scudded in the rising gale.

Duke William nodded. "Yes, and I must think about setting back out on the road. It does no good to stay in one place for long."

The Duke departed and I set to finding a swift messenger to send to Father. Even as my courier rode away from the gates of the Montgomery stronghold, I felt a sense of prescience.

The sons of Fitz Giroie. We were fools to harm the father when his sons were grown men with their own supporters.

A week later the courier returned, haggard and rain-lashed, mud caking the fetlocks of his weary steed. "My lady, grave news!" he cried, staggering to greet me as I met him at the foot of the stone steps into the keep. "The Fitz Giroies have attacked Lord Talvas' castle...."

"Is he dead?" I rushed to him and grabbed his arm. "Do not hesitate; tell me what I must know!"

His mouth gaped like that of a hooked fish. I wanted to slap him he looked so stupid, so incompetent. "N-no, my Lady. He has escaped, along with the Lady Haberga. None know where he has departed. The Fitz Giroies now sit in his hall, drink his ale and eat his food. They have pilfered the contents of his treasury too, or so 'tis said."

Angrily I folded my arms. "So...he is set wandering again, just as when Arnulf drove us from Alencon. Father...Father is becoming a fool with age. He should have ransomed William Fitz Giroie instead of getting me to...instead of having him blinded. Or he should have made sure his bloody sons were there and killed the lot of them!"

The man jolted back, obviously shocked by my harsh, but true, words.

"Go clean yourself up," I ordered him. "You look a disgrace...but that aside, you did well. I thank you; I shall see a handsome purse is yours."

"M-my Lady, thank...thank you!" he stammered, bowing until he nearly fell over.

I whirled around, storming up the stairs to the keep. At the top, Roger appeared, brow creased in concern. "Mabel, I overheard; this is ill news. Where do you think Lord Talvas will go now?"

My fists clenched. "Roger, I do not care. As long as it's not here. My sire has been a fool, a terrible fool."

"He is still your sire and my father-by-marriage," said Roger, trying to soothe my temper, his hand on my arm, caressing. "It is your duty as a daughter to aid him if he should ask it. I know well, from many tales, that he was a harsh, fierce man...but I know too that you loved him once. You followed him through thick and thin when you could have stayed behind with your brother Arnulf. In the case of William Fitz Giroie, he let his passion for vengeance overwhelm common sense, and now he has reaped the whirlwind in the Giroie sons... He made a mistake...."

"Yes, he did, husband," I said, my eyes narrowing. "He made one mistake. He cut off the scorpion's head but there is still a sting in its tail. The sons—he should have killed them; he should have killed them all."

Wishing to speak no more to Roger, I pulled free of his grasp and stormed away to my private apartments, where I threw out my tiring ladies with many curses and shouts, and then, grabbing my dagger from its hidden spot beneath my feather-filled mattress, stabbed it over and over into the bolster, pretending it was the Giroies or Arnulf…even my rash father.

At length, I toppled back exhausted. I'd torn off my wimple and my long hair lay in snarls all over the coverlet. As I lay there, breathing heavily, I heard the chamber door creak open. I pulled myself into a sitting position, ready to shout at a maid if one had dared to enter my presence when I desired solitude, but I saw it was Roger, face solemn and concerned.

"Mabel…wife, you must not take on like this. The bolster…"

"…is ruined," I placed my hand over the slits where stuffing poked out in ripped tufts. "But I do not care. About it, or my damned father. He cannot come here, bringing his troubles, bringing Haberga and the Frog, he cannot…"

Roger looked perplexed. He moved to the bed, sat on the edge. "Why not? I do not understand?"

"You would not—you are a man," I wailed, the words suddenly breaking from my lips; accompanied, at the same time, by a flood of hot tears. He gaped at me, astonished for he knew I never cried—I had told him so myself.

Yet here I was, awash with tears, unable to help myself.

"Christ's Teeth, what is wrong, Mabel?" he cried.

"Oh, Roger!" The words tumbled out between sobs that I struggled to contain. "Haven't you guessed? I am with child!"

Father arrived at Castle Montgomery with Haberga and Frogspawn, all their earthly possessions thrown into two paltry waggons. I scowled and glowered and spent most of my time hiding in my chambers. The Frog ran rampant through the castle, screeching, as his nurses ran after him. Roger was embarrassed, caught between my wishes and feeling the need to show politeness to his father-by-marriage.

Finally, Father caught me in the garden where I had been sitting under a canopy with my tiring women. It was early; I was avoiding the heat of the day and also avoiding my sire, who seldom rose before noon unless on some kind of urgent business.

Today, his business was with me. "Go, all of you," he shouted at my maids, who fled, looking terrified, into the furthest recesses of the garden, where they clustered like sheep, whispering behind their hands.

"Why did you do that?" I asked.

"I do not want that gaggle of geese to hear our conversation," he said. "I must speak with you, Mabel."

I said nothing. He slumped on the stone bench beside me; I gave him a sideways glance that was not altogether friendly. He had grown fat, his paunch hanging over his belt, and more strands of grey stippled his bristly hair. He smelt of stale sweat which turned my belly, already over-sensitive due to the coming child.

"You have heard what happened to my new lands," he said. "All stolen by the Fitz Giroies."

"Yes, you acted imprudently back at your wedding. You should have taken them all, not just the father. What were you thinking?"

You are old...old and growing decrepit. You just want to drink, whore and eat yourself into a stupor. You have lost your edge, father mine...

He gave me a hard look. "You played your part that night, Mabel."

"I was but a young girl, led astray," I steeled my face to blankness, forcing down my rage. "I had no choice."

"Hah! You loved it. You are blood of my blood." He tried to envelop me in a great bear-like hug. Crossly, I elbowed him away.

"Enough! I am not the child I was. I am wed now...and you cannot stay here. Not now, not until the Fitz Giroies are gone...*dead*. I do not want them coming to Montgomery while I am heavy with child."

Anger turned his eyes yellow, wolfish. "I made you my heir...I can unmake you!"

"And give it all the Fro...I mean, Oliver?" I raised my eyebrows. "I think my husband might have something to say about that. He expects me to receive the Belleme inheritance in the future. If he thinks he is being denied..." I shrugged. "All I will say is that he is good friends with the young Duke and many other powerful nobles besides."

Father ground his teeth; spittle whitened his moustache. "So, after all I did for you, you cast me forth, unwanted, with threats. Ungrateful whelp."

He looked truly distressed and I softened slightly. Only slightly. "I beg you try to understand. I want...*need*...peace. One day, I will finish the Fitz Giroie spawn...if someone else has not finished them first."

He sagged forward; the sun raked down his cheeks, showing the scars and wrinkles of age and hard living. "You area good girl, Mabel," he murmured, as he had said to me so many times throughout my life. "I find it so hard to see you as a chatelaine in your own right. Yes, of course, you do not want to birth your babe amidst tumult. I will go, on the morrow, taking Haberga and Oliver with me."

"Your wife is a de Beaumont," I said, attempting cheerfulness, "I am sure Lord Raoul wants to see his dear sister again."

Father harrumphed, but the next day, true to his word, he departed with unhappy wife, squalling Frogspawn, and his sad-looking carts. Impassively I watched the sorry procession leave from the topmost tower of Castle Montgomery.

I allowed myself a relieved sigh as I descended into the apartments, walking through the lit corridors on Roger's arm, my hand supporting my growing belly. I would deal with the Fitz Giroie family one day, to be sure.

But not now.

But the Fitz Giroie brothers came to deal with me, or rather, with Father. Five months from the day my sire had left Montgomery with his gloomy wife and raggle-taggle knights, they arrived at the gates of the castle.

Outraged by their audacity, Roger stood on the battlements surrounded by his best warriors, who had once served his errant father but now had transferred their loyalties to his son and Duke William. Below, on a large, bay war-horse sat Arnold d'Eschafour, the elder of William Fitz Giroie's two sons, born of his first wife, Hilltrude, and beside him was the glum, lumbering shape of his half-brother, William of Montreuil, by his second wife Emma. Arnold was the fiery one, shouting abuse up at the walls as his men raced back and forth on their steeds, waving torches like a pack of brigands ready to storm the walls.

"What do you want?" Roger called down, although he knew well. "Why do you attack my demesne. The Duke of Normandy will hear of this calumny!"

"The Duke is a beardless boy not yet come into his full patrimony—same as you!" Arnold d'Eschafour called up from the back of his mount. He was the worst of the two brothers, with a reputation for violence and hotheadedness. "We want the miscreant William Talvas."

"What makes you think he is here?" Roger yelled back, leaning over the breastwork. "William Talvas de Belleme does not dwell within these walls. Disperse, or it will not go well for you."

"I do not believe you!" shouted Arnold, eyes black in his thin white face, so like his father's unpleasant visage. "Talvas' whelp, your bitch-wife, is his daughter—and she was always at his side in all his evils. Bring her out! Bring him out!"

"He is not here. I have told you."

"Maybe we should burn the place and take the Talvas bitch and make her...*talk*," Arnold grinned. "How would you like that, Montgomery?"

I had been hiding below the breastwork, listening to the exchange. Roger had told me to keep to my chambers, but when was I ever the wilting female? With child or not, I felt desperate to hear what was said...and now anger blazed within me, hot as fire, out of control.

Clutching at the crenels of the great stone gatehouse, I leapt up and spat in Arnold and William's direction. "The 'Talvas bitch' is here, you reivers, you grunting pigs! How dare you come to Montgomery? I am not my father, and he is not here, as my husband told you!"

Arnold's face flushed; the quieter brother, William, looked slightly shame-faced. "Where is he then? Speak, woman!" Arnold bellowed.

"How do I know? I am not my father's keeper. He may even have left Normandy for all I know!"

William de Montreuil grabbed his brother's arm. "Arnold..." I heard him mutter. "I do not think he is here. We waste our time. I think she speaks truth."

Arnold tore his arm away and rounded on him in fury. "Truth? Do you think that trull even knows what truth is? Remember what the rumours said...about how she helped Talvas put out our sire's eyes?"

"But our father would not talk of it...ever. Those words never came from his lips, only the mouths of gossips."

"That's because he was ashamed, you fool! Ashamed that he did not see into Talvas's treacherous heart...ashamed that a mere girl mutilated him..."

"My father's not here!" I called down again, leaning further than was safe between two crenelations. "Just leave!"

In that instant, Arnold saw his chance and snatched a crossbow from his lap, where it had lain hidden by a fold of his midnight cloak. Raising it with an almost unnatural speed, he fired.

"Mabel, get down!" Roger flung himself onto me, driving me heavily onto the stone walkway. The crossbow quarrel soared overhead, flashing silver in the twilight, then hit a wall behind and bounced off, falling with a clatter.

I rolled on the ground, clutching my belly, as Roger sprang up, beckoning wildly to his archers standing on the parapets. "Loose, loose!"

A warning volley of dark-fletched arrows landed amidst my enemies, and hastily they began to draw their horses back. Staggering to my feet, I gazed out from the wall and saw the two brothers bickering wildly. It was clear the younger was telling the elder that they should leave.

A cramp needled my belly and I winced. "Roger..." I called for my husband. "Help me!"

He ran to me, assisting me to safety. "Keep the gate!" he cried to his soldiers and then he half-carried me down the stairs to my chambers. I was trembling by then and pains twisted my guts. My women flocked around me, twittering, making me feel even worse, helpless and small…but I did not even have the strength to drive them away.

"What can I do?" Roger's voice was high and strained.

"Just go back to the wall!" I gasped. "You can do nothing for me. Just drive Fitz Giroie's sons away from our home."

He raced out of the chamber and the door shut. The tiring women clustered around, laving the sweat from my brow. "Oh Lady, we feel so helpless," Marie said. "We cannot safely go into the village to get the midwife with those ruffians outside…but I…I have had children…"

"It cannot be coming," I gasped in terror. "It is two months too soon."

The women glanced at each other, pale and full of despair.

By the morning, the Fitz Giroie brothers had departed Montgomery. William had eventually persuaded Arnold of the futility of battering against stalwart gates that would never yield.

That was not all that was gone.

So too was my babe. Gone from my womb, gone from this world in less than an hour.

We called him Roger, after his father.

My husband was bowed with grief as we sent our son's tiny coffined body to the monks at the nearby abbey, but in my heart, I burned for revenge and stood watching the interment, cold as ice.

What good were tears? Blood would be paid with blood.

CHAPTER EIGHT

After being sent away from Castle Montgomery, Father had taken refuge with the de Beaumonts, making himself a rather unwelcome guest there, too, although tolerated because of Raoul's blood-tie to Haberga. Roger and I visited once upon invitation; trouble was brewing again between young Duke William and his opponents, and Roger was seeking to persuade the de Beaumonts to side with William and provide some soldiers.

Father, fatter than ever and puffing like a blacksmith's bellows, stalked out to meet me. "Mabel, joyous am I to see you, daughter!" He tried to catch me in a hot, sweaty embrace but I pushed him away.

"You've been drinking."

"You have gone cold on me. I heard you sent the Fitz Giroie boys packing."

I glared at him; if daggers could only have flown from my eyes, then he would surely have collapsed dead on the floorboards. "Yes, I did...and did you also hear what else happened when those ruffians rode up to my gates, bringing the troubles you wrought?"

He shook his head, looking perplexed.

"I was with child, do you not remember? I lost it the next day."

"Ah..." His great paw patted at me in a gesture he thought was comforting. "Ah, yes, women feel those matters deeply. It was...*unfortunate*. I am sure Roger is a sprightly lad and can get another babe on you soon enough."

My lip curled dangerously. "I am, in fact, with child again...but that does not mean I do not mourn the lost one. It was a boy."

"A great shame." He hung his head. "I have won back a few of Haberga's lands with de Beaumont's help, Mabel. The Fitz Giroies were truly not interested in them, only in getting revenge upon me. The one called William has now gone crusading, and the other one, for all his loose tongue, is not so fierce without his brother at his back."

"He is the one I want..." I murmured, under my breath.

"What did you say?" asked Father. "Look, girl, I can make it up to you—I'll send you his severed head as a gift to hang in your hall."

"Oh, Father, speak not so—you've done enough! Just retire on the lands you got back with Haberga and Oliver, and do not trouble me more. If I ever get hold of Arnold d'Eschafour, I will wreak my own revenge upon him…"

I walked away from him then, head held high. At my back, I heard him sigh. "You are a hard-headed wench, Mabel, but that is why I want you as my heir. Even though you will no longer speak to your poor, aged father…."

The next year, troubles broke out across Normandy. Guy of Burgundy, Nigel, Viscount of the Cotentin, and Ranulf, Viscount of the Vexsin fomented a serious rebellion, during which they tried to capture Duke William, no doubt to mutilate him and make him unfit to rule—or worse. At Valognes they sought to take him, but under the cover of night, he managed to elude his enemies and ride like the wind to the court of King Henry of France, who favoured his claim to the Duchy.

Roger was distressed, stalking around the castle like a beast trapped in a cage. I was less concerned about William's fate; I had now borne a living child, who we named Robert, after Duke William's sire. He was small but with a lusty set of lungs, and it amused me to see the Talvas temper flare in him when the nurse was not quick enough with the pap. He would strike the air with clenched red hands, his eyes squinted and his mouth gaping in an ear-piercing scream.

"You will be a devil in battle one day, won't you," I said to him as I dandled him on my lap, the hefty nursemaid from the village seated on a stool at my side. In response, he let up another piercing scream and threw up on my skirts.

One of my tiring women cleared the mess away and I shoved the babe back at his wetnurse, where he returned to greedy suckling. I went to find my errant husband, who had ceased his stalking and gone to brood on the battlements.

I found him leaning against a parapet, arms folded, lips drawn in a grim line. "It will be war, Mabel," he said. "The Duke must make an end, or he will never be allowed to rule in peace. As his main supporters, any fall in his fortunes will also reflect on us."

I nodded. "I feared that. What will you do?"

Scowling, he kicked at the stonework with the toe of his boot. "As he is with King Henry, there is not much I can do but wait. But I'll summon the levies. Wait I must for news, but I'll wait in readiness."

I slid my arms around him under the billow of his cloak. "Will it always be like this? I suppose it will. It has always been so since the dawn of time. Men must battle each other and women must battle in childbed."

He grunted, but I felt his hands clasp my waist. "We need more sons," I said, "and some daughters too. An army of them to make good alliances. Roger...maybe this is not a good time, but the midwife has confirmed it, I am with child again."

"Again?" He looked startled. "It has been six months only..."

I shrugged. "I am content. It is God's command that we populate the earth, is it not?"

His grip on my waist, still flat, tightened. "Yes, but I worry for you. For your health. Many women die...and you, you are so small in size. Almost like a child."

I rolled my eyes. "Well, I am not a child...and believe me, you will discover I am far tougher than I look."

"I have already discovered that, my sweet."

"My sweet...You mock me with silly terms of endearment."

"I shall call you my little warrior instead, then."

"I heard that Arnold d'Eschafour calls me the Termagant of Talvas and the Bitch of Belleme."

"Does he? The bastard. I will make him pay one day."

"No...*I* will," I said.

He laughed, and I was glad his heart had lightened a little. He needed to think of other than his friend, away with the French King. Fretting would sap his strength; instead, he must build towards a secure future...in the circle of winners. I hoped with King Henry's aid that the winner would indeed be Duke William—but if not, Roger must learn to bow to another and bide his time...

In January, as snow blew about the castle keep and the land lay under a white blanket, I gave birth to my third son, Hugh. He had russet hair and unlike his brother Robert, who howled the nursery down nearly every night, he slept peacefully like an angel.

Roger was well pleased with little Hugh...but not pleased with the news spreading across Normandy. He sat before the fire in our solar, chewing his lip in frustration. "They say 25,000 men have been raised, Mabel. 25,000! Disloyal curs."

"It is a great host," I said uneasily, sipping at my wine. I wondered if I might suggest that he look at the grievances of the Norman lords and see if he agreed with any of them. I did not want him to throw his life away on a lost cause, even if that made him as disloyal as the others.

"I have heard William has but 5000 men, and that includes those I will bring to him when the time comes," he murmured. "The rebels include not only Guy of Burgundy and Viscount Nigel, but Grimoald Plessis, Ranulph of the Bessin, and Hamon Dentatus, all seasoned warriors with large groups of followers."

"Roger..." I began, but as if anticipating what I might say, he rose from his seat, his cloak flowing, his cheeks flushed with passion.

"No matter what, I will support my friend, the Duke. Normandy is his by right. It is time for the young to take precedence and drive out the old...*and make them kneel*!" His last words were full of steely fury, and gazing up into his face, still only bearing the vague fluff of beard on lip and chin, I could see the man he would become in a few years, strong and stalwart and hard as steel.

Seeing such determination, such ardour, lightened my worry somewhat. He was right. He was young and so was Duke William, and where they lacked experience, they had heart and the vigour of youth. And King Henry's support, of course. My idea of encouraging him to hang back and see how the wind blew evaporated like the mist over the river at dawn. He would see my concerns as unworthy...and maybe they were a little unworthy. Cautious, but not noble.

"Make them kneel?" I asked, setting down my wine goblet and clasping his hand. "You must do more than that. You must take their heads and set them upon the battlements!"

In summer, Roger marched to meet with the Duke's army. I asked if I might ride alongside him and watch the battle from the safe distance but he stared at me as if I had gone mad and forbade it utterly. He needed to concentrate on battle plans so I did not press the matter but made him promise to send a messenger with any news, either good or ill. He swore he would.

The days stretched out long and hot. The moat stank as it dried up in the heat and the servants reeked of unwashed sweat. I gave them time off from their duties, for their very presence nauseated me—I found myself with child again. Perhaps it was a godsend after all that Roger had forbidden me to ride with the army. My one delight was to sit in the garden beneath the flowering trellises and drink cool wines brought up from the castle cellars and eat lush grapes that would drench my dry mouth.

I was sitting thus one even time, listening to a lutanist play an air from Provence, when I heard in the distance the sentry at the gates cry out a challenge. This was followed by a creaking of wheels as the great iron portcullis was raised.

"Hush!" I raised my hand, and the lutanist's hands fell from the strings of his instrument.

I rose, my saffron-hue silk gown belling in the hot summer breeze. "Someone is here, and the curfew is gone. The guards have opened the gates."

My tiring women, lounging on the grass, their knees making green patches on their light summer dresses, leapt up at once, silent as they always were until spoken to. I made sure of that. They might chatter amongst themselves when I was away from them, but I would not join in their conversations about their dull husbands and children.

Beckoning for them to follow for proprieties sake, I headed toward the courtyard, and was met by a page halfway there, who bowed and stuttered, "My Lady Mabel, it is a courier from the wars...from Lord Roger."

"Well, boy, don't keep him standing there; bring him to me," I ordered, clothing my nervousness with a stern demeanour.

The boy loped off, the sun haloing his shock of cropped reddish hair, and I tapped my foot nervously on the ground. Would this news be grim? Was I, God forfend, a widow? I swallowed, keeping down emotions I seldom felt, the emotions I sought to control at all times—fear. If the worst came to the worst, I would soon be disposed of as wife to another powerful man, and I wanted none but Roger...

A figure came into view and I squinted against the sun's brightness. A squire, Tancred, in knightly training—I had noted him about the castle before but scarce paid him any attention. Now his presence, the words he was set to impart, meant everything to me.

"My Lady." Smelling of horses and dust, he approached and knelt.

"Up, get to your feet." My voice rasped in my dry throat. "What tidings do you bring?"

"Good ones, my Lady," he stammered. "Duke William and my Lord de Montgomery have won a great victory at the field of Val es Dunes."

"Near Caen."

"Yes, my Lady. Near Caen."

"And they prevailed despite the greater number of their foes." Grateful mirth bubbled up, close to hysteria, but I fought back the urge to laugh—and weep. I was the daughter of Talvas the Hard Shield.

"Aye, Lady Mabel. For all their men and all their supposed experience in warfare, the rebels had no discipline at all. They were so unruly, full of petty squabbles with each other, that one of the nobles, Ralph de Tesson, turned his coat and rode to bend the knee before King Henry and the Duke."

"Were many of the rebels slain? The instigators of this mischief?"

"Hamon Dentatus fell, my Lady. He broke through the King's bodyguard and struck at the belly of his steed, causing his Grace's destrier to fall and the King with him. However, even as he galloped at Henry with sword upraised, the bodyguard managed to rally—and Hamo was hacked down without striking a blow to his Grace."

My laughter burst forth then. I had met Hamon Dentatus years ago at Alencon, a fat, bell-shaped lord, bigger in belly than shoulder, who shaved the sides of his turnip-shaped head but wore a long, dirty braid down the back like some rank heathen. He loved to tell all and sundry how the name Dentatus had been given him because he was born with teeth—and then he would show us his mouth. Most of his teeth were in fact yellow and rotten, but he had filed several of them into long sharp spikes, as it was said our ancestors, the men of the North, did to frighten their foes. I was not sad to hear such an oaf had perished.

"There were skirmishes for a while thereafter, and sometimes Henry and Duke William's armies prevailed and sometimes their foes gained ground. But at last, the ranks of the rebels broke and they fled...and William and his allies rode them down."

"So soon Roger shall return!" I said happily, clasping my hands together.

"Not quite yet, my Lady Mabel. Lord Roger has been bidden to stand at the King's side in support of the Duke. In October all parties involved in the dispute shall gather in Caen to negotiate the terms of a truce. Lord Roger must needs be there."

"October!" I groaned. "So long away, and nought for me to do here except stew and listen to the chatter of my dull maids."

Tancred gave a little smile, which I thought impertinent, him being but a squire, but I forgot my pique at his next words. "It is not all bad news, my Lady Mabel. Lord Roger has asked that you travel to join him and the Duke at Caen."

I was carried in a litter on the long journey to Caen. My belly had grown round and I could not ride, so it was deemed the best way to travel, although I felt both indolent and confined behind the heavy draperies. I had food and drink aplenty, and one of my tiring women played upon a dulcimer, but nonetheless it was a laborious and risky trek over a countryside still full of rebels hiding after the battle.

I was glad to reach Caen, which had a stalwart wall and fearsome gate topped by the spiked heads of slain enemies of the Dukes of Normandy. Once beyond its black iron portcullis, I felt much safer, and even more so when we reached the town's small castle, with timber palisades on steep ramparts surrounding a round stone tower like a fierce warning finger. Caen had only recently become a central place of governance to the Dukes, so it was not as heavily walled or castellated as some towns like Rouen or Falaise—yet. Roger had told me that William had plans to make it the grandest, most impregnable and most important town in the region.

A chamberlain emerged to give greetings and usher me to the castle apartments, my maids in tow. Ere long, Roger came to join me, and I told the women to go to the kitchens or the gardens for a while. I was eager to have him to myself after so long apart and was grateful that his friendship with William was secure enough that we should have been granted our own private bedchamber in the castle.

When he arrived, Roger was washed, shorn, shaven (not that he had much yet to shave but what little there was scraped away) and dressed in newly-laundered tunic and chausses A new air of maturity wreathed him as he clutched me in his embrace and tried to swing me around.

"Be careful," I warned him. "Look at me."

He stared at my belly in wonder. "I cannot believe another babe is so far on the way. Yes, yes…you must not suffer my rough handling, you must rest." Solicitously, he placed an arm around my shoulders and guided me to the large bed in the corner. "We have oranges from Spain here," he grinned. "Or rather the Duke does. Would you like one? I am sure I can convince William to let you have a few."

"Oh, yes," I said longingly, remembering the rare times I had tasted oranges, felt their tangy juices tickling my tongue. And the lemons—the lemons were a bit too bitter for my palate, but their scent was heavenly…

But then I shook my head. Knowledge came before food. Even with a babe kicking in my belly, I would never present myself as a weak, cossetted woman. "Oranges can come later…first, business. What is to happen here in Caen?"

He sat beside me on the bed, face full of memories—and fire—as he recalled the recent battle of Val-es-Dunes, his first foray into armed warfare. "A truce will be called and a treaty made. William is calling it 'The Treaty of God.' The nobles of Normandy are at last willing to bend the knees and accept him as their rightful overlord...except for Guy of Brionne, William's cousin." A shadow crossed his face. "I believe he wants the Duchy for himself, the covetous swine."

"I do not know this Guy." I shook my head.

"Nor would you want to. He fled into the east when his wing broke asunder before Will's cavalry and he is now holed up behind the walls of a mighty fortress. He will not emerge to treat, and taunts William by saying he can hold off besiegers for years."

"He might be lying," I said thoughtfully.

"Maybe, but the captain of the soldiers William sent to lay the siege have deemed Guy's castle truly impregnable, with no flaws in wall or tower, nor is there any easy way of poisoning the well. With Guy at Brionne, it cuts off William's route to access large portions of his Duchy."

"And that will be a problem."

"Yes, and one that will be addressed, and I do not think many men will rally to Guy's cause. May he rot in his castle after his defeat at Val-es-Dunes! Oh, Mab, that was a fray to be remembered...You should have seen us ride forth on our chargers, a wall of stout horseflesh. We were like avenging angels assailing the foe, galloping down upon them, our swords in hand, the wind at our backs, the sun shining on our helms! As the enemy ranks broke asunder before our charge, we drove the fleeing soldiers into the River Orne near Athis Fort, where many drowned, trampled by their fellows and their own horses as they were swept away on the river's swell. The waters ran red with blood, and down at the mill of Barbillon, the corpses were piled high, bloating and breaking out with foul gasses, after they piled up against the mill wheel."

"The miller must have been horrified."

Roger smirked. "Only by the smell. He had his lads out to strip the bodies and take what he could, even cutting rings from fingers, I'm told. He'll be a wealthy man now for putting up with a bit of stench. The monks from the nearby abbey carted the bodies off for decent burial in the end."

"A glorious victory, then," I smiled, "with the Duke showing that no mercy will be shown to traitors."

Roger nodded. "He is destined for greatness, Mab, I feel it deep in here…" He thumped his chest. "And I want to be part of that success."

"And I, too," I said, "wherever it might lead." I clasped his hands. "So, shall we drink to your victories? Call the pages—let us have more wine!"

Grim-faced, the nobles of Normandy arrived at Caen, grumbling men with their retainers in tow. I had known their type all my life and it amused me to see their pique at having to swear allegiance to one so young as William—and a bastard besides. But their forces had been soundly defeated at Val-es-Dunes and although there was seditious talk, as there always is, none made another move to unseat the youthful warlord.

At the beginning of October, the Truce of God was agreed. No fighting was to take place on Feast Days or Sundays, God's Day of Rest, nor could warfare commence on Thursday owing to Christ's Ascension, Friday, day of the Passion, or Saturday, upon which day blessed Jesu was resurrected. Permanent peace would extend to churches, peasants working the fields, womenfolk, merchants and pilgrims.

The Treaty thrashed out, the nobles fared back to their castles, still grumbling but, for the most part, resigned, although I had no doubt a few traitors lurked amongst them, waiting for an opportunity.

Duke William seemed pleased by the outcome of the gathering, and he had Roger and I break bread with him in his private closet then tour around Caen, the men riding upon their fine horses, caparisoned in gold and green, me lying in my litter, draped in furs.

Happily, the Duke spoke of his plans. "Sometime in the future, when I have the wealth I need, I am going to commence building work in Caen. It will be my capital once complete. The walls shall be stouter than those of any town in Normandy, and I shall raise a formidable castle that no enemy would dare attack—one thrice the size of the one there now. 'There dwells Duke William' my foes will cry, and they will snarl like angry dogs yet turn their faces away, for they know they cannot move against me."

"A city of martial men, then," I said. We had stopped to pray in the town's spacious but old-fashioned abbey and now stood in the Abbot's gardens, enjoying his largesse in the form of rich wines, fruit pies, savoury tarts and clean white bread laded with slabs of yellow cheese. "But surely you do not intend for eternal warfare? Life must have more than battle."

The Duke nodded. "Indeed. I also want the town to prosper, and for great churches and abbeys to rise to the glory of God, who has seen fit to give me victory over my enemies. Of course…" he grinned over at me, "there must be a gentler touch in Caen too—no, all of Normandy—someone to nurture, someone the common man and woman can plead to for mercy and compassion. I need a wife."

"And have you any in mind, my Lord Duke? Forgive me if I seem overbold in my questions, but that is the kind of woman I am. My sire always encouraged me to speak my mind, right or wrong."

William's countenance grew serious and for a moment I feared I had caused great offence, but then he heaved a sigh and gazed over my shoulder into the far distance. "Yes, there is a woman who has caught my eye, Lady Mabel. Very beautiful, breathtakingly beautiful in fact. Hair like moonlight, eyes the green of grass, skin like untouched snow…her name is Matilda."

"You sound…*sad* when you speak of her," I said.

He held my gaze now, with that intense look that made me shiver to my very core. "I have spoken to her father, but I do not think anything will come of my suit. Her sire is Count Baldwin of Flanders, and even though I am a Duke, I fear he is not enamoured of the fact that I was born out of wedlock. Added to that, Matilda and I fall afoul of the laws of consanguinity."

I waved my hand dismissively. "Laws of consanguinity? I would not worry over that, your Grace. You know the Pope loves money. A dispensation can be bought."

He smirked. "That is true, Lady Mabel…but what if Lady Matilda should refuse to consider me because of my illegitimacy."

"She would be a fool," I answered, narrowing my eyes, "a stuck-up fool. I will speak frankly—if I were you and truly desired this Matilda above all others, I would ride out and take her whether she be willing or no."

"Mabel!" gasped, Robert, clearly appalled. "His Grace cannot do such a scandalous thing!"

I shrugged. "He is Duke and a man of war. Not so many generations back, our ancestors sailed dragon-headed ships up the river in Normandy and took the land—and its women—and made the great Norman race! Why should we not still do so when it will bring benefit? It is better, sometimes, to be feared than loved."

"We can...can no longer do such acts!" Roger barked, his cheeks flaming. "That was long ago. We...we are now *civilised*! Jesu, Mabel, you blow cold and hot—moments ago, you were talking of their being more to life than battle!"

"This would be a different kind of war. The one that is played between the sexes!"

William released a roar of mirth and slapped his thigh. "Well, no matter what is right or wrong, the two of you have made me laugh—and think. Maybe, just maybe, Lady Matilda *will* get a rough wooing...but I might try the way of a loving swain first. However, dalliances must wait—I must mull over the situation with Guy of Brionne who refuses to surrender his castle. Tonight, Roger, I want you to sit in council at my right-hand side."

My husband took the Duke's hand in a tight grip of friendship. I was glad. As long as William was able to hold on to the Duchy and did not fall to the knife of some assassin, it could be highly beneficial to the Houses of Montgomery and Belleme. At the moment, House Belleme was floundering: Yves unmarried, since he was a churchman; Arnulf, although disinherited, clinging grimly to Alencon; Father dwelling on his wife's lands and accepting generosity from the long-suffering de Beaumonts. But with Roger in William's favour and my own future claim to the Honour of Belleme uncontested, I envisioned great things for all of us in near the future.

CHAPTER NINE

"Mabel, Mabel, news from Duke William!" I started as Roger's heavy footsteps pounded outside the castle nursery. I was paying my daily visit to our children, checking that they were fed and dressed properly as befitting their station. The nursemaids could be such slatterns sometimes, and I would not have such slack ways evident, not where my children were concerned.

There were now five of them, Robert, Hugh, Roger, Mabille and Emma. Emma was but a babe in swaddling, a tiny thing with a sharp nose like a bird's beak and wide dark eyes. She was not the prettiest child I'd borne, and I was already envisioning a future as an abbess for her...

Roger's cry filled my ears again, as the door of the nursery banged open. "Wife, did you not hear me?"

"I think the whole castle heard you," I said dryly, as I rearranged the embroidered blanket in Emma's cradle. "Whatever is it, Roger? You are upsetting the infants." I gestured to the youngest two, Roger and Mabille, whose faces had puckered up in fright, fearful due to their sire's shouting.

"Duke William is to be married," said Roger, "and, best news of all, we are invited to the wedding feast."

"Ah, so he has chosen a bride at last. Was it the Count of Flanders's daughter, whom he so admired?"

"It is. Matilda of Flanders, a great prize."

"So, Pope Leo issued a dispensation, as I said he would, despite their consanguinity."

Roger cleared his throat, looking a little uncomfortable. "No...but I am sure it will be dealt with in time."

I raised my eyebrows. "Hmm, and the other problem, the reluctant bride?"

"She is reluctant no longer, but it is a strange tale. I think William must have listened to you back in Caen. He asked Count Baldwin for his daughter's hand and was refused, not just by Matilda's sire but by Matilde herself, who mocked his lowly birth and asked if his mother would attend the wedding with a tanner's dyes upon her hands, a grave insult, for although Arlotte was indeed a tanner's daughter, Robert unabashedly kept her at his side in great comfort for years until he wed her to Herluin de Conteville. Humble she may have been by birth, but she became a great Lady by the will of Duke Robert."

"I have heard Duke William is particularly fond of his mother— and does not take jibes about his birth well."

"Yes, and he did not take Matilda's scorn well at all. For a few days after his proposal was refused, he stewed, grinding his teeth in rage, unable to sleep or eat. Then word reached him that Matilda was riding out in Bruges with her women to make offerings at one of the town's abbeys. Like a madman he rode to confront her, driving his steed through the crowds that had gathered to see the beautiful daughter of the Count of Flanders…"

"And what did he do when he found her?" I leaned forward in eager excitement.

"William grabbed her by her long, silver-gold braids and yanked her from her steed while her ladies-in-waiting screamed and wept. He threw her to the ground, trampling on her ornate gown, ripping her veil away and tearing the jewels from her neck. When she tried to strike out at him, he caught her arm and flung her face-down in a deep, muddy puddle on the roadside. 'You are not so proud now, are you, Lady?' he shouted as he flung himself back onto his mount. 'You are now just another dirty whore in the gutter, just as you believe my mother is.'"

My mouth hung open in shock. I had offered advice on a 'rough wooing', but had thought more of seduction or abduction, which was not so uncommon in many quarters, although the priests frowned upon it. I did not foresee the Duke smiting the woman he was smitten with, and throwing her down to wallow in mud like a pig!

I grasped my husband's forearms. "You are jesting, surely— because if William treated Matilda of Flanders so harshly, surely she would not ever have then agreed to marry him? Striking a maiden in her father's own city, and she the daughter of a Count? That could cause a war rather than an alliance."

He shrugged. "Strange as it sounds, it is true. William will wed Matilda and Count Baldwin has agreed to the match. After the Duke rode away, leaving her sprawled in the mud, she gathered her dignity and hastened back returned to her sire's castle. Sure enough, he was outraged by what had occurred and wanted reparations for William's violent act. But Matilda said no—that she has changed her mind; she would marry the Duke of Normandy and none other. And so William will wed her at the Castle of Eu, the residents of his good friend Count Robert."

"I shall have to have a new gown!" I remarked, moving away from him and rifling through a casket brimming with jewels. "Now what can I wear to impress? I cannot be seen as some gauche creature from the provinces! Not in front of the new Duchess."

"I thought you scorned the fripperies of your fellow women," laughed Roger, putting his hands on his hips. "That is what you always told me!"

"Did I? Well, it is mostly true. I hate silly, soft, chattering creatures that faint at the sight of a drop of blood. A proper woman should gladly defend her lord's castle, with sword in hand if need be. But not when she is attending an important wedding. At such an event, is far more important to be seen than heard…"

"You…and Matilda of Flanders." Roger rolled his eyes. "I will never understand women. Never."

High on a craggy rock, the mighty Castle at Eu reverberated to the sound of merrymaking. Roger and I sat on a bench not far from the high table, where the bride and groom reclined under a starred canopy held up on three red posts swirled with silken banners. William wore a jewel-festooned white mantle stitched with golden crosses and flowers and a metal helmet, polished to a high sheen and covered in scrollwork prayers. On his right-hand side, facing us, set his mother Arlotte and her husband, Herluin the Viscount of Conteville, and next to them sat Matilda's parents, the Count and Countess of Flanders, while on the dais was his cousin, Robert, Count of Eu, whose castle was the scene of the wedding.

Matilda of Flanders, seated on William's left, was indeed as lovely as I had heard, and I forced down an unseemly spurt of jealousy. There was no need for such foolishness; we both had the men we needed and there was no competition between us.

The new duchess was petite, smaller than I by the breadth of a single finger, and her hair was an unusual silver-gold, starlight and sunlight. Her tresses were thick, wound in intricate braids, coiled around her head and above her ears, or falling to her waist beneath a diaphanous veil that shimmered as she moved her head. A gold circlet inlaid with ruby crosses crowned her, and her wedding dress was deep blue like the ocean's heart with colourful embroideries swirling on hem and sleeves. She wore a mantle similar to William's, heavy with gemstones that flared in the flickering torchlight.

"Duchess Matilda is a most comely bride," I heard Roger sigh. "Do you not think so, Mabel?"

"I am hardly the judge of other women's comeliness," I said, displeased. "And you should not speak so of your lord's newly-wedded wife. Men are ever eager to cause trouble—you do not want wicked rumours to arise and cause trouble in your friendship with William."

"Are you jealous, Mab?" he teased.

"Are you trying to make me so? How unworthy." My cheeks felt hot. I had made a great effort for the Duke's wedding. I had ordered a gown made of silvers imported from the east—it cost a small fortune. The colour was purple, not too deep of course, for purple was a royal colour, but more the colour of rich twilight. Added to that was a gold-wired girdle, inlaid with amethyst cabochons that showed off a waist still small despite five children, six if one countered the one who lived less than an hour. As a married woman, my hair had to stay covered, but my wimple was of soft fine cloth, bleached and held in place by an engraved silver headpiece.

Roger, who had imbibed a few too many cups of the Duke's wine, laughed. "I would not dare," he said, "It would be too dangerous to do so. If I so much as gazed at another woman with lust, I am sure I'd find a knife between my shoulder blades…or between my legs."

He was making me cross. "You are playing the ass, husband!" I warned, toying with my eating knife.

He answered that by taking another long draught of wine, tilting his head back until the rich red liquid spilt from the corners of his mouth. It was not exactly an edifying sight, and my ire was raised even further. "I need to use the privy!" I snapped, and I hauled myself off the bench and hastened for the door.

In the dark of the privy, I sat for a while with the cold stone walls around me, not desiring to return to a smoky hall, roaring men, insipid jugglers and fools, and a drunken husband. The smell of the meat was turning my belly—not that it was any better smelling in here, although at least the piss and ordure fell a long way into the river below, so it was not the worst garderobe I'd ever seen. I mused upon my queasiness, wondering if I might be pregnant again. Roger and I enjoyed ardent bed-sports, even on days the church held as too holy for carnality, so it was quite likely my brood would grow some more.

At length, I decided it was time to move. I adjusted my gown and slipped into the hallway—and almost bumped straight into Duchess Matilda approaching from the opposite direction. Ringed by torchlight, she looked like an earthbound angel in her glimmering white mantle.

"Your Grace." I dropped a curtsey.

She beckoned me to rise. "You are the wife of my husband's friend, Robert de Montgomery, are you not? Mabel Talvas de Belleme?"

"Yes, your Grace."

"Roger was alarmed at your long absence from the table. You are well?"

"I am well, my thanks for your concern…Surely, my husband did not send you to find me, your Grace?"

"No, but I offered. I know it is my wedding feast but the night is stretching on all too slowly to its conclusion." She cast me a cat-like smile, sultry-eyed and long-lashed, the corners of her full red mouth curling. "I am grown tired of toasts and small talk. My veils and hair reek of smoke. I would rather be alone with my lord to finalise the marriage, so that no one may set us apart. Even if the Pope continues denying us a dispensation, once consummated it would become harder to deny that our marriage is a true one, and if a babe was on the way…"

I nodded, liking that here was a woman who would accept no nonsense, not even from the Pope. I licked my lips, then asked, in a sudden burst of wine-fuelled audacity, "Is it true that the Duke threw you in the mud?"

Her eyes twinkled—green-blue, the hue of summer seas in Brittany. "Yes, it is true."

"And yet you chose to marry him even so?"

"Yes. My father was raging like a mad bull and I was so shocked and bruised that I had to take to my bed. But as I lay there, hating William, a sudden thought came to my mind. If he were so confident, so bold, as to strike me while in my sire's domain, this was a man afraid of *nothing*. A man who would reach out to take what he wants. A man who would be victorious in battle. Maybe even…a man who might one day become a King. And if I wed such a man, I could take my place beside him as his Queen! I would like to be Queen; after all, I am a descendant of Charles the Great myself."

"A King? How could William become King?" The hairs on the back of my neck prickled; I prayed she was not going to reveal some treasonous plot against Henry, King of France, or some other dark secret I'd be forced to bear like a cross.

"William is kin to Edward the Confessor, King of England. The English King's mother is William's great-aunt," Matilda's voice emerged in a breathless rush. "William fared over the sea to visit him once and…and…upon his death Edward promised him the throne." She crossed herself. "Do not misread my words, Lady Mabel, I do not wish the Confessor ill—but someday, in good time, when God decrees…"

"Someday I might kneel to you…" I muttered, awestruck. It seemed fantastical and yet an aura of power had always clung to William's broad frame; I had sensed it on our first meeting. And if he was King, how much higher could Roger and I climb; how much wealthier would we be? The sky was, perhaps, the limit.

"Someday it may come to pass, maybe. But for now, Lady Mabel, I am content just to remain Duchess. Will you accompany me back to the banqueting hall? The Matins bells have rung in the abbey beyond, and surely it is time for my husband to cease carousal and drinking...and retire to greater pleasures."

"Of course I shall walk with you, your Grace." She reached out her graceful arm, and I took it, eager to curry favour, and together, resplendent in our finery, we returned to the heat and noise of the Great Hall.

The next day William and his new Duchess fared on to Rouen, accompanied by Matilda's parents, who were to visit William's castle there. Roger and I began the long journey back to our own home at Montgomery.

On the way, I told Roger that I believed I was with child again; the sickness had raddled my belly, and there were other familiar signs. He laughed and shook his head. "We had best ask permission to build some castles as we will have so many sons who will need one each."

Then he glanced over at me in my travelling cart, suddenly grown serious. "While at Castle Eu, I talked to Duke William in private, Mabel. About your brother Arnulf and how he unlawfully holds Alencon and other Belleme possessions. He was not pleased to hear the whole story. I believe soon, Arnulf Talvas may find himself in the unenviable position of being opposed to the Duke."

Beaming, I sat upright in the cart, ignoring the bumps and lurches of the cart as it rolled down the rutted road. "Roger! This is the happiest news I have had for ever such a long time!"

CHAPTER TEN

I gave birth to another daughter, Maude, early in the winter, and a few months later we heard that Duchess Matilda had given William a healthy boy-child they named Robert, the same as my own eldest son. I wondered if the two Roberts would ever become good friends; I would have to see if I could make sure there was a good chance such bonds could be forged.

Still weakened from Maude's birth, I tried to divert my mind to the numerous dull duties of a noble lady, and not think overmuch about what Roger had told me of William's plan to drive Arnulf from Alencon. To consume my time, I petitioned Uncle Yves, still alive and thriving in Seez, to build a monastery on lands I held nearby—I had no interests in monks or nuns or spending overlong on my knees contemplating the divine, but such building to God's glory was expected of a woman of my rank. Best to do *something* for the good of my soul...

The abbey stones were no sooner laid than Roger was summoned to fight with William against a new threat, Geoffrey Martel, the Count of Anjou. Geoffrey was attempting to extend his power into the lands of Maine—which contained most of the Belleme holdings, including Alencon and Domfront, and Belleme itself upon the border.

I prayed fervently every night that this was the hour in which my prideful, sour brother would have his fall from power, whether at Martel's hands or Duke William's.

When Roger finally returned, with word of victory arriving before him, I raced out to the courtyard to greet him with a cup of mead in hand. "Drink, drink, my lord!" I cried. "And then tell me—is Alencon mine—I mean Father's—again. Has Arnulf been cast from its gates?"

Roger removed his helm, staring down seriously. "Mabel, we had best converse alone. There is much I would tell you and this is not the best place."

My heart fell. I began to fiddle nervously with one of my braids while Roger dismounted and the grooms took his horse. In silence, we hurried to the solar, decked in its painted cloths depicting kings and warriors and saints. I beckoned for a servant to light the two oil lamps and draw back the wooden grilles to admit extra light.

I sat on a stool and Roger did likewise, stretching out his legs, aching from the long ride, with a grimace.

"What has gone wrong?" I asked, abuzz with nerves.

"Your brother, Arnulf…" murmured Roger. "He is dead."

"Dead?" My eyes widened. "Roger, this is not evil news, this is-is *wonderful*! You know what he did to Father and me…"

"Be silent." Roger's tone was weary and sterner than I was used to. "I have more to tell you."

Inwardly, I seethed that he should silence me, but did not protest. An argument would avail nought.

Roger stared into the fire brazier. "When Duke William arrived in Alencon, he found the castle gates barred against him. He was angry, as you might imagine, since the lordship of the castle is ultimately held through the Duke of Normandy, as you know well."

"Yes, of course I know," I said, crossly. The Belleme holdings were uniquely placed—our overlords had been the Dukes of Normandy, the King of France, and the Count of Maine, leaving my family in the enviable position of being able to play each great lord against the other if necessary.

"William demanded passage into the town and brought his army before the castle. On the battlements were many defenders loyal to Arnulf, waving tanned hides like flags. *Tanned hides*, Mabel."

"Christ, they dared jeer at his mother, a tanner's daughter. Arnulf was a fool indeed."

"Aye, and you know how sensitive William is about his illegitimate birth, even though he often signs himself 'William Bastard.' He called to his captains to gather thirty-two men of the town and bring them before the castle walls. There, within sight of the defenders on the battlements, he hacked off his captives' hands and feet. He told Arnulf and his captains that next it would be heads, and he would send them over the walls as gifts via a trebuchet. The castle surrendered at once and lowered the drawbridge."

"And my brother? Did the Duke slay him? Did they fight hand to hand for mastery of Alencon?"

Roger shook his head. "There was no confrontation; they never even met. He attempted to escape by leaping from a tower near the poster gate, but fell awkwardly and broke his neck."

Sighing, I leaned back. "My brother Arnulf, ever the coward save for that one single time when he drove me and Father onto the road like beggars. Who is to deal with his burial? I suppose that task will fall to Father or Uncle Yves."

Roger shuffled his feet. "His head was smitten off and put on the town gates of Alencon as a warning. The rest of him…I am not sure what became of the body. William dragged it to the town centre and left it. Maybe local priests or monks have taken it for Christian burial."

I shrugged. "Oh well, as long as *someone* takes care of what must need be done. I shall pray for his soul—the treacherous rat will need my prayers! I will go to the chapel and light a candle; the smallest I can find, mind…"

My husband reached out and grasped my hand, holding me back. "Wait, Mabel. I have news that may displease you."

Perplexed, I tore my hand away. "What is it? You are toying with me and I do not like it."

William let out a long sigh. "It is…Alencon. William toured the castle and town, inspecting them thoroughly from the millpond to the privies. He has decided…to take the town back into his keeping."

My eyes widened and I leapt up, enraged. "He wants Alencon! But my family have held it for years."

"Only through the Duke of Normandy, and that is William. He has every right to take it."

"This is unjust, an outrage, a travesty!" Grabbing a pisspot hidden in the corner, I smashed it against the wall in fury. Fortunately, the servants had emptied it earlier in the day and it was only shards of earthenware that skittered across the floor. "He insults me and the House of Belleme! How could he do so, when he claims to be your friend?"

"Friendship plays no part in this," Roger said gruffly. "In this matter, he is our sworn lord, and you know it. It is no disgrace to you, and besides, did you truly think he would present it to you like a sweetmeat on a silver tray? You might do well to remember that although you are William Talvas's heir, the Belleme inheritance will not be fully yours till both he and your uncle Yves are dead."

"It sounds like you are on the Duke's side and not mine!" I screamed, hands clenched into fists at my sides, the nails eating into my palms.

"I am on your side...*our* side... but I am not a fool to battle out this matter with William. Give it time, Mabel; he is probably waiting till your Father dies. Talvas and William were never friends."

Exasperated noises tore from my throat. "I want that castle back! If it's my father's demise William wants, I'd be glad to send him to his eternal rest! From what I hear, he is ailing these days anyway, lying in his bed while Haberga de Beaumont tends him like an infant, spooning food into his mouth and wiping his arse!"

"Mabel!" Roger stared at me in horror. "What has come over you to speak so of your own sire?"

"Oh, Roger, stop it, stop it, you sound like a chiding priest. You know what kind of man my father was...is. But I am part of him too, born of his seed...I am him, as a female. Do you not see it in my mood as well as my face? I have nothing in me of my weak, wan mother. If he should be slain that we may prosper, let him be slain."

Roger's expression, rather than showing understanding, grew even more horrified. He shot from the stool, upending it on the floor. "I am going to call the physician. You are not in your right mind. Maybe you are in the grip of some illness..."

"How can you not understand?" I hurled myself at him, clutching his arm. "The honour of Belleme is everything to me. As important as life itself!"

He pulled away as if repulsed. "All this shouting and drama is unseemly, Mabel. Or healthy. I take my leave of you. I will come again when you cease acting like one of our children in a tantrum."

He swept from the room, slamming the door. I searched around the chamber for something to hurl in his wake but I'd already broken the pisspot. Furious, I leapt on my bed and wept tears of rage and humiliation.

When dawn came, I washed my sagging, pasty face in rosewater and stared gloomily at the red-eyed reflection in the piece of polished bronze my tiring-woman Erembourg held before my face. I had to regain my dignity; once my anger was spent, I realised how foolish my behaviour had been. William was within his rights to hold Alencon, and it was neither prudent nor possible to make war over it.

I must gather my composure, make sure my husband did not see me as a madwoman, and work on getting a firm date for the return of Alencon, or at very least, suitable compensation, from the Duke. I decided I would send a letter to him; not directly, as that would be considered impertinent, but to the Duchess Matilda. I had hopefully made a favourable impression there; I admired her, for beneath her beauty and piety, I sensed steely ambition. What woman would otherwise choose to marry a man who had beaten her and hurled her in the mud? She had seen something in William, perhaps the same power I sensed, and had grasped it, quite literally, with both lily-white hands…

But I could not write immediately; that would be too obvious, too crass. My head must cool first, so that I might devise pleasing and persuasive words.

"Erembourg, bring me the wheaten paste to smooth my face," I ordered. "And the ground Angelica leaves to redden my cheeks."

The maid scurried to do my bidding, and I sat on the bed while she did her ministrations with paste and crushed leaves. When I finally looked presentable, I had her affix my hood with a silver circlet over it, and I went forth into the castle to show my husband I was a good, docile wife and not a raging harridan.

When I happened upon him, he looked alarmed, as if he thought I was a fierce, clawed cat ready to pounce on him. For a moment, I felt a pang of disdain, but I fought it away. Such thoughts were unworthy; Roger was a good man and a good husband. It was I who was wicked, but if my wickedness benefitted my growing brood with lands and castles, then so be it, wicked I would remain.

"Roger, my lord," I said politely. "Would you attend Mass with me in the chapel? Let us pray to Lord God for all our worldly goods, for all that we should be thankful for."

"You are no longer angry about Alencon?"

I attempted to keep my countenance untroubled, my eyes modestly downcast. "It was my childhood home. I shed a few tears last night for I loved it dearly and was shocked by the Duke's decision. However, upon reflection, it is but stones and mortar. We have enough..." *I will never have enough...*Satan whispered in my ear. I gritted my teeth, chasing his malign presence away, at least for now.

"After Mass, the nurses can bring the children into the garden. Robert and Hugh want to see the new horses in the stables; you know how they love horses...." *No doubt they will also start trying to stab each other with pitchforks while we're there.* My boys, young as they were, showed incredible brotherly love...just like Cain and Abel...

A pleased expression brightened my husband's face. He was simpler than me in his likes and dislikes. He was war-like and yet content on his lands with his hawks and hounds. He spent far more time on his knees in the chapel, seeking forgiveness for his sins, and he doted on the children more than I, a doting and sometimes indulgent father. Truth be told, I had little interest in them other than seeing that the boys were active and strong and the girls skilled at many tasks. Children were for alliances, better than gold pieces for creating rich blood-ties.

Roger was reaching for my hand. "Yes, yes, we will go to Mass together, and then visit with the children. I am pleased you are no longer upset, Mab."

"I will never mention it to you again, Roger," I murmured.

But I will try to get Matilda of Flanders on my side...

My chance came a few months later. Robert had gone to Paris after word reached him that his father had died in exile there. He was going to arrange the burial and see the will proved. I had never met the old man but dearly hoped he had a few surprises up his treacherous sleeve and had left us something worthwhile...

Retiring to my solar, I had Erembourg summon a scribe. Shuffling in a long baggy robe, a little weedy man with a nose as red as the neat bowl of his hair arrived shortly. He seemed uncomfortable in my presence, reminding me of Brother Giso, my easily embarrassed childhood tutor, which amused me no end. A pity I could not tease him in the same way—it was such good sport!—but I had serious business on my mind.

The scribe bowed before me, clutching his goose quill, inkhorn, and parchment of goatskin to his heart as if he feared I might snatch them away. Indeed, I longed to do so, for my words would contain truths that were, well, slightly bent, and I'd rather no one saw them but me and the recipient. However, my Latin was only passable (despite my old tutor's best efforts) and my hand not steady enough to write such an important missive myself.

"What is your name?" I said to the man, gesturing to a bench

"Onfrey, my Lady" Beads of sweat gleamed on his shaven upper lip.

"Well, then, Onfrey, seat yourself and I will tell you what I want to say. Your very best hand is required—the missive is going to the Duchess Matilda."

I noted his Adam's apple bob nervously. "Yes, my Lady."

"Good." I cleared my throat. "I will begin. *Greetings, to the High and Mighty Duchess Matilda of Normandy. Long has it been since we met, your Grace, and I pray you might remember one so humble as Mabel de Montgomery de Belleme. I wish to express my happiest joy to hear that you have been delivered of a healthy son, Lord Robert. Long may you and his Grace be fruitful as our Lord commanded. I, too, have experienced the pangs of childbirth, but it was a daughter I bore, Matilda, after your eminence, although we call her Maude...*' I thought it best to mention my daughters, for William's son would need a wife of good blood some time in the future... *I trust we will meet again in the future as our husbands are almost as brothers, and we should be as sisters. One thing brings me sorrow and grieves my heart, though, your Grace. When the Duke liberated my father's castle of Alencon, he took it back into his protection, as is his right; I have no query about his occupation as he is our dearest lord. However, it grieves me to see wicked men such as Arnold d'Echafour flourish after they took my sire's lands, even as my brother took Alencon...*"

I went on at some length with flowery blandishments mixed with hints about what I desired, and finally finished with, '*Your faithful and loving servant, Mabel Talvas de Belleme. Christ send His Blessings to you, to his Grace the Duke and to the darling baby, Robert...'*

"There, I am done." I nodded toward Onfrey the Scribe. He continued to scribble for a bit, then rose, holding out his work for inspection. Letting my eyes glide across the neatly written words, I placed my wax seal upon the bottom of the parchment, then rolled it and sealed it again. "It is fine. You are dismissed."

He bowed and almost fled the room. I stroked the parchment with a finger, closing my eyes in silent prayer. If I could see Fitz Giroie's arrogant son Arnold displaced or disgraced, the loss of my dearest Alencon with its imposing turrets and walls would not cause such pain in my heart...

Some months passed before Roger returned from Paris. As he entered the solar, he seemed sadder, older, but I could not wait to tell him my happy news. "Husband," I said gaily, "I am so glad to have you home. Would you like to go hawking with me? The day is fine."

He rubbed a hand over his brow. "I am still a little saddle-sore from my travels, Mab, but yes...yes, I will. Perhaps the clean wind will blow away my weariness."

We had our horses saddled and bridled and together with the falconer and a party of brightly dressed men and women, we headed out to the long low fields between the castle and the river. I had a new falcon named Jezebel, a fine beast with a bright, cruel eye and fierce yellow beak curved into a hook. I delighted to see her rise on the sharp breezes, wings dark against the sun, before spiralling down to attack her prey. She reminded me of *myself*, watching and waiting for my enemy, my prey, and then descending like a lightning bolt... I laughed for pure joy at the thought of it—and suddenly Jezebel frighted and went soaring toward the nearest clump of trees.

"Jesu, damn the bird!" I cried, "And you, man, you have not trained her properly..."

I rounded on the falconer, a gangly, lugubrious fellow. "M-milady, the falcon became distressed when you laughed..."

"You are blaming me?" I spat, almost in his face.

"N-No, not at all, " he stammered. "But the bird is new; she's skittish…"!

"Get her back or else!" I threatened. I stared at the stand of oak and ash trees where Jezebel had vanished. I thought I caught a quick flash of her feathers amidst the tangled boughs. "There, she's *there*, in that great twisted oak, near the top…Get her out of from the tree, even if you have to climb it."

The falconer stomped away, shoulders slumped in weary determination. I glanced at Roger, sitting with his great gyrfalcon perched on his wrist. He did not look pleased.

Immediately I softened my expression. "Oh, Roger, forgive me my temper, but Jezebel is a new purchase who cost a pretty penny and I would hate to lose her."

"You know it often happens," he said. "Hawks and falcons gain their freedom and never return."

A strange tone lurked in his voice and a chill rippled down my spine. Did he refer to himself? Since his return from the burial in Paris, he had been glum and moody, which surprised me, since his father had not been close to him for years and had left no extras in his will, asking instead for rather many Masses and a fine stone effigy. The cheek of the man! But despite old Roger's failings as a father, my husband was clearly disturbed by his loss.

I pushed aside my discomfort at Roger's gloominess. He would surely be happy when I told him my news. I smiled winsomely. "While we wait for the falconer to retrieve Jezebel, I must let you know what occurred when you were away in Paris. I am sure it will please you."

"What is it?" He glanced at my middle as if expecting me to say I was with child again.

I was disappointed in him. I could do more than just produce babies.

"I have had a letter from the Duchess Matilda," I said, hoping that would pique his interest.

It did. He lifted his head and gazed at me quizzically, unspeaking, a thin little frown line across his brow. "The Duchess?"

"Yes, but in her missive, she brought word straight from the Duke…."

"For you? Not for me?" The frown line deepened.

"He knew you were away, did he not?" I sounded waspish even in my own ears, but I could not understand his wariness, his suspicion. Did he think me too witless to converse with the great and good when my husband was on other business?

"Aye, aye, I suppose. But I am surprised. What on God's green earth did he want with you?"

That dull embers of rage that always coiled deep in my heart ignited. I strove to keep my voice pleasant. "He has given me a gift. A wonderful gift. Because of Alencon."

"Alencon? I thought we had agreed to talk no more on that matter."

"I am *not* talking about it; William holds it; it is over and done." I waved my hand as if I cared nothing for the castle. "But William has seen that it was, perhaps, unjust to rob the Belleme family of a castle where they were domiciled for so long. So he has offered an alternative. Some lands and castles in exchange."

"Has he?" Roger looked incredulous. On his wrist, his gyrfalcon began to dance and scream, as irritated and anxious as I was becoming.

"Yes, he has. The grants have been made."

"And where have these lands and minor castles come from?"

"You would not believe it." I straightened my skirts. "My old enemy Arnold d'Eschafour."

A strange purplish colour rose into Roger's visage. His bright blue eyes blackened with wrath,

"I thought you would be pleased!"

"His lands border ours, Mabel. You know what kind of a man he is. You've already had dealings with him. He will not take this insult lightly. Christ, we will probably not sleep safe in our beds now!"

"You exaggerate. Those lands were my sire's anyway, through your aunt. Arnold d'Eschafour is nothing, as his father was nothing, and is less than nothing now, crawling around a monastery with his empty, blind eye sockets!"

Roger stared at me, and suddenly yanked on his horse's reins, causing the beast to spin away from me. "Sometimes I wonder what I married, the way you speak. I am returning to the castle. I should write to the Duke…"

"No, no," I interrupted. "Do not do that! I deserve recompense for Alencon. I want those lands!"

His lips were a taut, white line; his hands trembled with rage. "So you do, and I am guessing you have lied and manipulated behind my back to obtain your desire. I won't write; I'd look a fool to William, a man who cannot trust his wife. Damn you, Mabel!" He struck his heels to his mount's flanks and galloped towards Castle Montgomery, leaving the rest of the small company staring after him.

At the same time, the falconer returned from the grove, the knees of his hose torn, green and brown smudges on his garments, his hat askew and his hair full of twigs and leaves.

"Where's my falcon?" I asked, my voice harsh as the cry of a bird of prey.

He swallowed and took off his cap, holding tightly to it as if it gave him some kind of security. "My Lady…she flew away, as they sometimes do. She's gone. We've lost her."

I did not know whether to explode in rage or weep like a babe. It was not a good day for dealing with either hawks or husbands.

Roger's anger dwindled over the subsequent months, and Arnold d'Eschafour was pleasantly silent over the subject of his confiscated lands. I grew big with child and played the role of a contented lady of the castle, but I listened intently to any gossip that arrived at the gates in case it should prove relevant to my wants and needs.

A few months after my newest son, Philip, was born, I did my filial duty and visited my father William, whose litany of ailments had grown long indeed; long enough that it became clear he might not have long to live. My nose wrinkled in disgust as Haberga, her gown both dowdy and rather dirty, her body heavy with dropsy, led me to his bedchamber. Inside, Father lay against the bolster, eyed red and pouched, phlegmy and rheumy, body raddled with gout and goodness knows what other maladies. He had grown obese, with breasts like a woman's albeit covered in bristly grey hair. The sickroom reeked of piss and sweat. I never could bear foul odours and held a small pomander of dried herbs before my offended nose. Haberga glared at me but I ignored her, the repulsive old creature.

"Mabel..." He held out a hand; I did not take it and it flopped back like a limp fish to his side. "It has been long since I've seen you. I thought you might bring my newest grandson to bring gladness to my heart."

"I dared not; the child is frail," I lied. "I see you are not well."

"Just the afflictions of old age and a hard life," he said, heaving himself up then falling back with a groan. "All my limbs ache these days, God curse it."

"I will pray for you, Father," I said quickly.

He cast an eye suddenly grown cold upon me. "You were never a praying girl, Mab. Not for anyone, and I doubt you will make an exception in my case. But I thought you felt some slight affection for me, after all we shared in the past."

I gazed at him. Once a great warrior, now he was nothing, a bedridden fat man who already stunk of the grave. In truth, it would be better if he died in his sleep rather than linger on in further decline... "I do feel affection for you," I said, "but I am not a miracle worker and I have my own family to attend to."

He nodded, and let out a sigh heavy with despair. "I have heard Roger is even more firmly entrenched with William the Bastard..."

"Yes, he is...and you should not call him that."

"Why not. It's true and he even signs himself 'the Bastard.'"

"It's fine for him, not for you."

"And what's this about the lands the de Giroie whelps stole from me and Haberga?"

"Ah, you have heard of that." I played nervously with a silver bangle on my wrist.

"You might think me in my dotage, girl, but I am no man—or woman's—fool. I have heard William granted them to your keeping. I would ask you for them, as they should be mine, but the Duke, to my surprise, gave me something when Arnulf died."

I stared, frowning. "W-what?"

Father's eyes became wolfish and he looked fierce, less an invalid, more like the warlord of old. "Your spies and allies didn't tell you all then! William kept Alencon...but the lands surrounding it were placed back into my care."

I could not hide my shock—and my fury.

Father laughed at my clear dismay, pointing with a finger grown plump and gnarled. "Take care, Mabel, my daughter. I am not in my coffin as yet, and you grow overbold in your dealings, especially for a woman."

I knew he said those last words to taunt, and in silence, I turned around and departed, slamming the chamber door behind me. Through the stout oak-wood, I could hear his peals of hearty laughter.

In the Great Hall, I bumped into my half-brother Oliver. Frogspawn had now grown into a young man, standing several inches taller than me. He still had a wan, wavy face with goggling eyes and a broad froggish mouth, but his appearance was improved by a cap of waving brown hair and a loss of childhood weight.

"Father has been waiting to see you, Mabel," he said. He had a nasal voice as if he had a permanent cold.

"Yes, so he could taunt me and laugh," I said with bitterness."

Frog stared at me as if shocked. "Truly, that is not why..."

"Yes, it is," I interrupted. "And I am warning you, brother— when the old man goes to his final rest, don't you dare try to claim any of the Belleme lands just because you have a pizzle. Father promised them to me long ago, do you understand?"

His expression was, strangely, almost one of hurt. "I have no wish to claim them; I won't stand in your way. I...I want to become a knight and fight in far off lands for the glory of God, and then, when that is done—if I survive, that is—I think I might take holy orders."

"Truly?" Doubtful, I peered at him. His clothes were dour, his demeanour certainly monkish.

"Truly! he replied quite forcefully, as if surprised that I might doubt his ambitions. "I cannot think of anything more noble and honourable to do with my life!"

Filled with sudden joy, I leaned over and planted a quick, hard kiss on that frog-like face. "Then I wish you well with all your endeavours...*brother*. I will pray that all you desire comes to you..."

Startled by my sudden warmth, he stepped back, his cheeks florid. "Y-you too, sister. I hope you get what you desire most in this world too."

I left him, smiling, a warm glow inside. It was the first time I had ever felt any sisterly feelings towards Oliver. He had promised to stay out of my way in regards to my inheritance. This was good. It meant he would not have to be removed.

Such a sensible lad was my Frogspawn…

CHAPTER ELEVEN

Over the next few years, my life was quiet, almost irritatingly so. I bore one other daughter, a beautiful auburn-haired girl I called Sybil. I also birthed another son, whom I insisted be named Arnulf.

Roger glared at me in perplexity when I told him what I wanted to call the child. "But you always hated your brother," he said, crossing his arms over his chest. "You were pleased when he died. Why not call the boy William after the Duke, my older brother who died during the Duke's minority, and your father, William Talvas."

Shaking my head, I laughed and stared at the red-faced scrap that lay in my arms, tightly wrapped in swaddling. "No, Arnulf it must be, husband. It is an old and noble name, used often by members of the House of Belleme—but alas, my brother dragged the name into disrepute. I want my son to bear the same name so that one day he can rectify Arnulf's shame."

Roger sighed. He knew he could not win when I had made up my mind on a matter. "If it matters to you so much, Mabel, then let it be…"

"It *does* matter." I leant over, brought my lips to the soft fluff on the baby's brow. "You'll be a doughty knight, won't you, my little Arnulf. Not a nasty, craven traitor."

In the wider world beyond our castle walls, Duchess Matilda's family had grown even as mine—she now had Robert, Richard, William, Mathilda and Adeliza. The more the merrier, and it made a better chance of my children marrying into that family, or at least having strong allies in the future. The Duke had firm sway over the Duchy now, his enemies vanquished or withdrawn, unwilling to fight against his iron will and great military abilities. I admired him; he was, as Roger said, a brilliant warrior and strategist. He had defeated the fractious Bishop Mauger, and one wing of his army, led by Robert, Count of Eu, defeated Odo, the brother of the French King, at the Battle of Mortemer. King Henry, who had turned against William, fearing his growing power, had taken his brother's defeat badly and fled before William's oncoming mounted knights without a single blow being struck.

Now, Roger told me William's gaze turned ever toward the waters of the Little Sea and to mist-shrouded England beyond. The English crown had been promised him, or so he insisted with great passion, but there were other claimants, clustering like a flock of ravens...

"Think of it, Mab," Robert said, "if William should rule England—we, as his favourite and loyal supporters, would be in the forefront for great rewards. The united Houses of Montgomery and Belleme might well make their marks on English soil. Think of our sons, and what could be theirs one day in the future."

"What is England like?" I wondered out loud. I had seldom crossed the borders of Normandy, let alone sailed on a ship to foreign lands.

Roger shook his head. "I have not been there, but I have known men who traded with the thanes. It is a green, fertile land, although colder and wetter than Normandy. Grey clouds hang over it like a helm on most days."

"Sounds gloomy," I said. "What are the people like?"

He shrugged. "There are not Normans or even French, what more can I say? Uncouth people with a harsh tongue, sharp as lightning, who like to drink and boast and brawl."

"But are some of them not Danes? Do we not also have men of the north as ancestors?"

"Yes...and it is through the inheritances of the old North that William makes his claim to the English throne. His father's sister, Emma, was mother of Edward the Confessor, who has no offspring."

"And what of the other claimants?"

"They are only of half-blood. Their claims are lesser to my Lord's."

"I doubt they will feel so when the time comes. Swords shall be drawn and blood spilt."

"In all likelihood, this will be true...but when the day dawns, William shall be ready. If his right to the crown by blood is denied by the English Witangemot, he will take it by Right of Conquest."

I liked the sound of that very much, and a deep curiosity about England grew within me. I began to think of its green but rainy lands, rich and fertile—a wealthy plum perhaps soon ripe for the Duke's picking....

In 1170 my father William Talvas died, not altogether unexpectedly, as he had been ailing for years but rather *embarrassingly*. In my youth, I had always imagined he would die fighting some knight he had cuckolded or whose lands he had burned. At very least, I thought he might drink himself to death or collapse in the act of swiving a fat-bottomed chamber-maid. Instead, his end was quick and ignominious: he ate a heavy meal, banged on his chest then stumbled to the privy, where he was found dead, the cold air from the moat below turning his bare arse into a veritable lump of ice.

Haberga sniffled and snuffled at the burial; Oliver stood with grim, sorrowful countenance, while I pretended to wipe tears from my eyes. I was closer to receiving my full inheritance now, and Father had also left me a bed and some astonishing tapestries—much to Haberga's dismay by her purse-lipped scowl.

Merrily I returned home after Father's interment, the tapestries, deconstructed wooden bed and some plate and goblets I'd managed to take rattling around in vast wains. I had thought Horsey Haberga would explode as they were carried out the castle door, but in the end, she just retreated to her chambers and never emerged again.

I was not offended by the snub. The sooner I could forget her and Frogspawn, the happier I would be. She would not have dared try to stop me anyway, for as Roger's powers had increased, so too did our personal army. Everywhere I rode, I journeyed with a retinue of at least a hundred armed men, ready to pillage or kill at my command.

I was Dame Belleme, de Seez and, best of all, Alencon. Duke William had returned my favourite fortress to the Belleme family upon my sire's demise. Even Matilda of Flanders did not fare about Normandy in such style as I did, banners flying, horns blaring, driving lesser men before my passage as leaves are driven by the rising storm.

My journeys through my new lands took me, at one point, to the Benedictine Abbey of Evroul which Roger and I had endowed. I was nowhere near an ardent churchgoer—Roger attended more regular than I—but it was good policy to show one's face to the religious, and besides, I was on my way to Alencon after visiting Duchess Matilda in Caen and the monastery was on the way, sitting grey-stoned and tall-pinnacled amidst green fields and forest, an open invitation to weary travellers.

The Abbot there was named Theodoric, and he was one of the few churchmen I could abide, although he did not fear to chastise me. Perhaps that is why I occasionally listened to his sermons; he could look me straight in the eye and speak his mind, no bowing or toadying or sour-faced but silent disapproval.

The Abbot looked less than pleased as my entourage rolled into the abbey precinct. Carts were everywhere and my ladies were shrieking about the mud in the courtyard ruining their gowns. Some had brought their children, who ran about screeching, playing with their mother's yapping lapdogs. Men-at-arms and knights were stomping hither and yon, casting the reins of their horses towards passing monks and demanding they be watered and fed.

"This is an unexpected...*pleasure*." Abbot Theodoric fixed me with a beady-eyed stare. "Would that you had sent me notice before arriving, Lady Mabel, so that I could be prepared to receive your party."

"Ah, Theodoric, I could not pass by without a greeting," I said with a smirk. "Surely you know how much I love the good Lord Creator, and most of all the monks and abbots that serve his gracious goodness."

He waggled a bony, arthritic finger beneath my nose. "I have told you before, my Lady, you must temper your tongue, even if you merely jest. It is not..."

"...seemly in a woman," I finished with a sigh. "You tell me that every time we meet. Now, how about meat and drink and beds for my entourage? The women are weary..."

"They are shrieking like fishwives! They are not weary at all. They're upsetting my monks with their lewd attire! Brother Cellarer and Brother Hosteller are both unprepared for an onslaught of..."

I folded my arms. Theodoric was bristlier than I had remembered. "Make them *get* prepared then, Abbot. I am here and I do not like standing outside in the wind." I glanced up at the grey hurrying skies. Damp splotches darkened my lamb's wool mantle. "It's starting to rain."

"You truly presume, my Lady Mabel. You and the Lord Montgomery and a reasonable guard are no problem to accommodate, but this...this circus!" He waved an agitated hand in the direction of my followers.

"Oh, stop complaining, Theodoric," I snapped, "or next time I pass by, I will bring twice as many to your door."

The Abbot's jaw went rigid. Ignoring me, he whirled about on his heel and barked orders to some of the passing monks. "Get the Cellarer and the Kitchener. Tell them to prepare a meal for many. The Hosteller too—put the ladies and their children in the guest house, while the men can sleep in the outbuildings near the fires."

"And me?" I asked.

"You, my Lady, shall come with me and we will talk."

He led me into his quarters, oppressive with the glowering carvings of saints, lit by cressets and candles and smelling of tallow. In his private office, where parchments lay sprawled haphazardly across a table, he gestured to the elderly monk tending the brazier to leave, then sat upon a stout wooden chair. I had only a stool to sit upon, which placed me below him in an awkward position. That was intentional and I did not like it one bit.

"Where am I to sleep?" I snapped. "In here with you? What would the His Holiness the Pope say?"

"You will indeed have my chamber as the guesthouse is stuffed to the brim with your women and their offspring," he said. "I shall spend the night with the monks in the dormitory, or on my knees in prayer. I would ask you to join me in that, for I dare say you have need of guidance, but I surmise you will say no."

I stared at the garish crucifix hanging on the wall behind Abbot Theodoric's head; Christ with his head lolling, the wound in his side gushing red paint. "I am weary, Abbot..." I began. "I have been on business..."

"Riding around the country terrifying the locals and asserting your power."

"It has to be done. My Lord Montgomery and I want no more rebellions. Remember how my brother Arnulf treated my sire!"

"And he had some cause, Lady Mabel. I remember your mother, Hildeburg, a most saintly and pious woman. Her fate was most lamentable, was it not?" His eyes were two icy lances, stabbing me

"Peasants killed her!" I barked, almost toppling off my stool. "You know that. ..."

"I heard differently, from Arnulf himself, when he lived."

"He would say that, wouldn't he? I'll swear on your Bible that she died as I told you."

"Hmmm." The Abbot stroked his chin. "Strange as it seems, I have a soft spot for you, Lady Mabel...because of Hildeburg. I think you have become the way you are because of the unhealthy influence of Lord Talvas upon an impressionable young maid."

"That is my father you're insulting," I muttered.

"Even so. I do not speak to hurt you; I speak only the truth. I fear for you, my child."

"Fear for me? But why? Look at the men I have, all well-armed. I have many castles with sturdy walls. My husband is a close advisor and friend to the Duke of Normandy himself."

"I fear because I hear what you let those soldiers do when you inspect your lands. I fear because you have made enemies along the paths of your short life. Enemies who will not forget."

"You mean Arnold d'Eschafour and his allies. They have not bothered us for some years now."

"But I assure you, they have not forgotten and things change." Theodoric's brow grew furrowed. "Mabel, you are a mother of ten children. They need your guidance...good guidance. You have young, innocent daughters. What would befall them if anything happened to you and Lord Roger?"

"Nothing will happen to us!" I fairly shouted. "Abbot Theodoric, either give me a room and be done with it or tell me to go on my way. I did not come to the Abbey for a lecture, and invented tales of some future disaster!"

Bowing his head, he rose from his chair. "I will leave you to your own devices, Lady Mabel, but I beg you, forget not my words. I do not mean to hurt, nor even to cause you to fear—I just want you to *think*. May God shed light on you, child, and keep you and yours from wickedness. Otherwise, you may suffer what is terribly painful to you in this world or the next."

He exited the chamber and I got up, scowling as I straightened my crumpled skirts. Who did he think he was to lecture me? Yet a little fear niggled at me, like the pain in a tooth gone rotten. What *was* Arnold up to these days? Were my children safe? My lands and castles?

A knock sounded on the old, smoke-stained door, a feeble, tentative rapping. "Enter!" I said, tone imperious. I had no more wish to talk.

A small, wizened monk scuttled in bearing a tray full of food and drink, which he thrust onto the nearby table before he rushed away as if he feared I was a malevolent witch about to cast a spell on him.

I sat down and examined the food—simple fare, the usual type eaten by monks—a little smoked fish, its taste pungent; a handful of ripe cheese curds, a salad full of turnip. Filled with hunger after my long ride, I wolfed it all down, then finished with the modest pitcher of ale, throwing it back with unladylike haste to assuage the dustiness of my throat.

It was not long after, shortly after the sun had set, that the pains came. They started high in my gut, ran up near my heart, then began a niggling cramp in my side. A rank sweat began to moisten my brow. Groaning, I glanced around for the Abbot's chamber pot, which I found in the ante-chamber, tucked away behind the bed-hangings.

How humiliating! I thought, holding the chill earthenware in my moist, shaking hands.

The pains grew worse, rhythmic. I could not understand it. I had felt fine all day long if a little wearier than normal. I sank to my knees, trying to suppress thoughts of fatal bloody fluxes and other serious illnesses.

But still those unwholesome thoughts came, and darker ones besides... Abbot Theodoric's words thundered through my fevered brain— *You may suffer what is terribly painful to you.*

Had...had he *poisoned* me? Sought to teach me a final, bitter lesson? Theodoric did not seem the murderous type, but one never knew what shadows lurked behind a pious exterior...

Another pain lanced through me, and I clutched the edge of the bed in agony, fingers gripping the quilt till my knuckles turned bone-white. I had to get out of there...*now*.

Stumbling and falling, hand pressed to my gurgling belly, I made my way through the monastery, scandalised monks staring and pointing before flittering away into the gloom like dark moths. No one came to my aid; Theodoric was notable by his absence. He was doubtless praying in seclusion...or laughing behind his hand.

I ran to the guesthouse, bowling over the monk who appeared, lamp swinging, his face a white, sleepy moon. Flinging the door open, I screamed for my women to attend their mistress without delay. Many of them were dicing or playing other games; their play ceased at once, with most rushing to my side like fluttering hens while the remainder woke the children.

"We are leaving!" I cried to Eremboug, who as my chief tiring woman, was at my side trying to steady me. "I-I do not know if I have been poisoned!!"

"B-but should you not tell the Abbot, my Lady?" she stammered.

"No! He most likely did it!" I cried. "Now go—go forth and summon the men. Have them mount at once. I will lie in one of the wagons rather than ride my mount."

She hoisted her bliaut and rushed out of the guesthouse into the darkness of the courtyard, tripping in her haste. Before the hour was up, I was in the cart, wrapped in sheepskins, still feeling as if knives were slicing into my belly. Theodoric had turned up, seemingly full of concern—was it real concern or feigned? In my weakened, pain-wracked state I could not tell.

"You should not leave, Lady Mabel," the Abbot said, staring down at my supine form. "You need the help of Brother Infirmarer; he is very skilled in medical arts."

"I want nought more of you, Abbot," I gasped, as further pains rippled through my bowels. "You never wanted me to stay...If I live, I swear I will never darken your door again. Never!"

The abbey gates were creaking open, the monks rushing about with torches. I lay back and shut my eyes against the pain as my entourage lurched off into the night.

I gave instructions that we make for Domfront as soon as possible. The horses' hooves made a sharp clipping noise on the packed surface of the road. The wagon was rolling and veering as it struck deep ruts; a hard ride indeed when one is gravely ill. Erembourg squatted next to me, aiding me to clean myself, for now my belly was purging itself of whatever it was, poison or spoilt food, that I had ingested. I felt utterly humiliated, and then, to add insult to injury, it began to rain, a fine drizzle at first that soon became an incessant torrent.

After a while, I could bear no more of the rollicking cart and the rain which poured through gaps in the overhead canvas and drenched me to the skin. I wanted no more than to crawl into some dark space and despair of my life—but I managed to sit up, weak and wobbling, and shout to my captain, "Next dwelling along the road, be it hovel or castle—I must stop there to rest!"

Soon a rambling old farmhouse appeared out of the thunderous spray. It was quite ramshackle but its size implied that the owners were perhaps not completely impoverished. I gestured towards it with a wet and dripping hand, and the entourage veered down the winding track toward the building, guided by the light of a primitive stone lantern hanging under the thatch overhanging the door.

As the party approached, the door swung open and a goodwife appeared, looking as most goodwives seemed to—portly with a red, round, shiny face and a wide dirty apron that flapped in the night-wind. She gave a shriek when she saw us and flung up her hands to her face; at the same time, the farmer joined her, holding a rusty sword from some ancient long-forgotten battle in his gnarled hand.

"Peace!" I called out wearily from the cart. "I mean you no harm. I merely seek rest for the night, for I am sorely afflicted…"

The man stepped from under the thatching out into the rain. It bounced off his bald head, ran into his matted beard. He peered at me with a suspicious brown eye. "And who are ye, and these men with swords and arrows at the ready."

"I am the Lady Mabel of Montgomery," I answered. I decided not to mention the name of Belleme or Talvas, owing to the family's reputation. It was fine to be feared by nobles and peasants alike…but not when you lay ill, helpless as a babe, in the back of a cart

"And what be the problem?" His tone was not very respectful.

"I am ill. I must rest or I will surely never reach my home alive."

The man glanced at his fat wife. She was sucking on her lip in consternation, then gave an almost imperceptible nod. The farmer tottered over to the edge of his cart. "You can come inside by the fire with your women. The men must stay in the barns. It will be a tight fit, mind; they may have to take turns sitting out in the rain. Oh, and I want their swords piled up near the door so's I can keep a watch on them. We want no trouble here. Do you agree, madam?"

"Yes, yes, I agree, "I gasped. "Now, get me inside." I struggled up, with Erembourg and another maid called Maynild supporting my weight, and they dragged me between them through the puddles into the farmer's smoky cottage.

The farmhouse was larger than I thought, maybe having once belonged to someone wealthier than its present tenant. If so, it had fallen on hard times; the white-washed walls peeled and puffed with green mould while green wood on the central fire cast up a pungent smoke that clung to everything. There was a black iron cauldron, much dented, filled with the remains of a stew whose odour made my offended belly churn even more, half a dozen slinking brindled dogs, and a gaggle of the couple's sons and grandchildren, who were all rushed out of the room by the frantic flapping of Goodwife Fatty.

Eremboug and Maynild laid me on the ground and the Goodwife brought a huge sheepskin that smelt, to my horror, very much like a live sheep. Still, it was warm and the convulsive shivers that had gripped my body began to ease. The pain and spasms in my gut did not, however, and soon my maids were busy at their embarrassing cleaning task. The farmer glanced away, as well he might. The woman looked terrified, as if she was afraid I might expire and my soldiers kill her in misguided vengeance.

"Do you think we should call someone, Goubert?" she asked her husband. "She's poorly and may need, you know, special help."

Farmer Goubert pulled a face. "She might not go for that, Denice, her being a highborn lady and all."

"But-but what if we don't help and she *dies*..." the Goodwife tried to whisper but her voice reached my ears like a thunderous roar.

The man scratched his damp beard. "Well, go on then, call for *them*, if you think it will help. You know more than I do about such matters."

"Who is *them*?" I gasped as Maynild wiped the sweat from my brow.

Denice the Goodwife glanced at me, licking her lips nervously. "The wisewomen of the village, milady. They know how to cure many ailments; well...they're the best we got around here anyway."

She shuffled out of the door, grappling with its wooden weight as the wind tried to blew it open wide. Mercifully, she banged it shut a moment later, vanishing into the storm beyond.

Chilled by the sudden blast from the door, I huddled closer to the fire, the pain washing over me in waves yet again. Erembourg grabbed a bucket as I spewed, while Goubert made a face and turned toward the firepit, stabbing the logs with a poker.

It did not take long for Denice to return with the healers. A mother and daughter, it seemed—the elder wizened like dried apple and as foul as if the mark of Satan lay upon her, with a huge wen on her chin, bristling hair, and a purple stain across half her cheek. Some were born with such marred countenances and never lived within normal society, but someone must have lain with her at least one, for the gangling woman at her side, her dark hair in messy grey-flecked braids, had the same jutting chin that almost met the downwards curve of her hooked nose. Their eyes were similar too, a pale blue, greedy and calculating. I felt immediate dislike and suspicion, but what could I do? I was desperate.

"So, what ails you, mistress..." cackled the old woman, bending over me. She smelt of her last dinner—onions. I gagged.

"It is 'my lady' to you—and I think I've been poisoned. Or cursed. By the Abbot Theodoric, no less."

In the corner, Goodwife Denice gasped loudly and wrung her hands before crossing herself.

The hags squatted next to me, hands prodding my belly, smelling my breath, asking what I had eaten and drank at the monastery. "I do not think you're dying, lady. You've probably just had sommat that's gone off. It will hurt like the Devil's pitchfork was in ye, but you'll shit it all out in the end. Just drink lots of water, bucket's full—Denice will bring you some—and then I'll tell her how to brew a tea to settle your guts."

I banged the floor with my fist. "You come here to tell me I merely ate a bad piece of fish? Fie on you, woman. I've never been so sick in all my years on this earth and I've eaten worse than the Abbot's fare! Do something *useful* for me, you pair of charlatans. I am Mabel Talvas...Mabel de Belleme. You, crone, must be able to remember my father. If you do not aid me to recover, I can make things go bad for you!"

The two wisewomen glanced at each other, clearly alarmed as they realised my identity. The hag cleared her throat, mashing her toothless mouth with a horrid smacking noise; I thought she might spit on me but fortunately the phlegm hit the fire, where it hissed as it was consumed. "A curse it must be, then, Lady, if you're so sure it ain't just a flux from rotten food. Me and my girl, Ib, will go away for a while...and confer. We'll come back when we have decided what we can do about this 'curse' that afflicts ye."

She shuffled from the room with the great gawky horse called Ib stalking behind, and I rolled my eyes and groaned, calling for a bucket yet again. Goodwife Fatty Denice got me some water which I guzzled down. I had to admit, the nausea lightened a little soon after.

It seemed ages had passed before the farmhouse door creaked back open and the two healer women returned carrying a large basket. The older woman knelt beside me again, peering into my face with her sharp, wrinkle-encased gaze.

"Feeling any better, milady?"

"No! Well, maybe...I do not know." I pressed my hand to my side as my innards twisted like serpents, making a ferocious and embarrassing roar.

"Then I am guessing you want to go ahead with the removal...of the *curse*." She bent down low, so close her dangling, verminous grey locks brushed my cheek. I could see straight up her hairy nostrils. "It is a dark way, though, milady, I warn you. Not for the faint-hearted."

I stared straight up into those pale, rheumy eyes, the eyelashes missing, fringed instead by red, hot boils. "You mean...*witchcraft*?"

She scratched her pointed chin, her dirty nail making a grating noise on rough skin and bristles. "No, I wouldn't call it that exactly. It's an old remedy from the time afore..."

"Before what?"

"Before this land worshipped the Christ, o' course...."

So, the 'cure' for the curse *was* witchcraft...or close enough to it. The thought was enough to make my blood run cold for a second. But only a second. If this cure would save my life, so be it. I could do penance later, wear a hair shirt for a few months if I felt the need. I doubted I would, and only if anyone found out. None of these slack-jawed peasants would dare talk, especially the witch herself, and no one would believe them if they came out with such a story. My tiring women would stay silent; they might be gossipy about goings-on in the household but never told tales about me—they knew I'd have their tongues if they did.

"Well?" The woman leaning even closer, far too close. A louse ran into her collar and a dot of spittle landed on my lip.

"Do it...just do it. Whatever it takes."

The hag's paw appeared before my nose. "I—I hate to ask it, milady, but what we do here tonight could have serious consequences for me and Ib. I need a little something extra, this ain't just herbs and the like."

"You want money?"

She nodded vigorously. "Tis only fair."

"So be it," I said with resignation. "I should have expected as much from the start."

"Then we can begin. Ib?" She gestured to the tall woman, who was holding the basket. Ib strode over and thumped her burden down; from inside the basket came a mewling sound like that of a kitten. I frowned. They had brought me a cat?

But Ib then reached into the basket and pulled out...a baby. Or was it? It was smaller than any babe I'd ever birthed and its face seemed *wrong*. Almost like an old man or woman but not in the usual, amusing way a babe may resemble its elders. It was liverish in hue, and as it waved a feeble arm, I noted it was deformed—it had an extra finger.

"What...what is that creature?" I cried, squirming away.

"'Tis a changeling-child," said the hag, "left in a normal babe's cradle by the wicked fays. The true babe has been carried off to the realm of the Goodly People."

"And what am I supposed to do with this monster? How can it help me in my time of need?"

"It's come from Faerie. It can suck the poison from you, taking it into itself."

"Suck out the poison? I do not understand, woman..."

"Eh...you're a mother, aren't you?"

My face began to burn even hotter as I deduced what she wanted me to do. It was monstrous! Like most noblewomen I had never given the pap to my children; that was the duty of the wetnurses. Freed from the constant needs of an infant, a nurse left me able to perform my duties as chatelaine—and return, after the proscribed time had passed and the Churching was done, to the marital bed...

"What you ask is repulsive and demeaning. It is too much!" I struggled into a sitting position.

"Well, we can go home then." Ib went to return the unholy infant to its basket.

I almost shouted at her to get from my sight with the imp, but another wave of cramps rippled through me, twisting and stitching. *Oh God, this was terrible...*Was my pride, my modesty, more important than my life?

"No, wait, bring it here," I croaked. "I will do it. Maynild, hold up a cloak so that no one can look. Erembourg, my laces."

Maynild removed her cloak and held it over me as Erembourg undid my gown and Ib passed the monstrous babe to me. It was hungry and scrabbled at my skin like some monster. Its lips latched onto my breast, and I swallowed my nausea as it attempted to suckle—I had been dry of mother's milk for a long time now.

Above the little tent Maynild had made with the cloak, I could hear the hag and her daughter chanting, "*As Blessed Mary with her Holy Milk enchanted her Son against the bite of elves and the bite of men, so we join this flesh to flesh, and this blood to blood, and so the sick shall recover and the curse disperse....*"

Filled with revulsion, I stared ahead, keeping my eyes averted from the creature on my lap. If this mummery did not work, the two 'wisewomen' would find their heads on spikes, even if the command for their executions was made with my dying breath...

"How much longer must I endure this torment?" I called out.

"That should be enough." The hag snatched the creature, whisking it away. Hastily, I pulled my kirtle over myself. "You've done good, milady. Now drink this, it will calm you; it's been a harrowing experience for you, I know." She passed me a flagon, filled with a greyish unsavoury liquid that had a minty scent, and I gulped it down. "Now, about that payment."

I nodded to Eremboug. "Go out to the wains and get money for this woman and her daughter." I glared up at the ragged pair and their bundle. "But do not think you have my leave to go. You stay the night, and if my health does not improve or gets worse—you will pay for it."

The hag looked uneasy at that but nodded her head; again, giving a meaningful glance at Ib. "As you wish, milady."

I lay back down. Whatever was in it, the crone's potion began to take effect; my eyelid began to drift closed. I still had to haul myself up now and then to squat in the corner and relieve myself, but the violent cramping seemed to have receded and the sweat dried on my skin and did not burst forth again. Beyond all hope, I eventually fell into a fitful, exhausted slumber.

In the morning I woke with a pounding head and a sense of disorientation. Then mouldy thatching above came into view and remembered where I was and what I endured. I pressed my hand to my belly. The swelling...it had gone down. I no longer felt like a horse had planted its hoof in the pit of my stomach. I was sore and achy...but alive! The witch's foul remedy had worked!

I staggered up, still weak and lurching. My head pounded at the temples but the sickness in the pit of my belly had departed. The hag and Ib were crouched by the hearth, mooning over the basket.

"I hate to admit it, but your spell or whatever it was, worked," I said. "You saved me, and for that I am grateful—but I swear if either of you ever speaks of what transpired…"

"We won't, milady," said the hag hurriedly. "Cross my heart and hope to die…"

"You will die if you prove a liar. Now…what will you do with the creature…the changeling?" I nodded toward the basket. A blanket lay over it, I presumed to give the ghastly being warmth.

"Take it to the churchyard, I reckon," said Ib, with an unwholesome grin that showed her worn yellow teeth, big as a horse's. "It's dead, milady. It sucked all the poison and wickedness out of your teat, and then it died from that foul brew."

Horror filled me at her words. I stared at the shrouded basket.

"Do you want to see?" asked Ib slyly, reaching for the corner of the blanket.

"No, don't you dare move!"

Whirling around, my heart drumming crazily, I gestured for my maids. "We must leave! We must leave this place at once!"

"Are you well enough, my Lady?" asked Erembourg, doubtful. "You are still weak…"

"Just obey me, as is your duty!" I screamed into her face, and I reeled towards the farmhouse door and staggered out into the pale, drizzling morning.

Within the hour, I was in my cart on the road toward a safe haven. I would never visit Abbot Theodoric again. If I could have proved he was a poisoner I'd have sent men to take him prisoner and cast him in a dungeon, but I could not and he was well thought of throughout Normandy. Besides, if it came out what I had done to be healed…

I shuddered, imagining Roger annulling our marriage and taking my children far away, having shut me in a remote convent.

No one must ever know what I had done. It would forever be my secret.

CHAPTER TWELVE

Days, months and years passed, like leaves blown from the trees. My children were growing, each one strong of body and strong of will. Robert, my eldest, was an arrow-straight young man, lean and dark like his father, but with the smoother planes of my face and the eyes of my sire William, though a pale green. Some of my father's bellicosity burned in Robert's blood too, and he was in frequent scraps with local lads both noble and of lowly birth. Sometimes he was cruel—I saw him whip a horse once when he fell from the saddle after showing off to the squires—I had him dragged before me and birched, a stroke for every time he hit the horse.

"Horses are valuable beasts, Robert," I told him sternly as he glowered after his thrashing by the Master of Horse. "You must learn to contain your anger."

"Would you prefer I beat a peasant instead?" he asked with impudence. "Those churls laughed at me as I rolled in the mud, my lip bloody. At *me*, the son of Roger de Montgomery and the heir of the House of Belleme after you."

"When you are a lord over your own demesne, you may beat who you like. But for now, no, you may strike neither horses nor peasants. Your father and I do not want revolts upon our lands caused by your hot-temper."

He sulked, his lip outthrust. "I wish I could go from here. I am confined like a weak maiden."

"Yes, it *is* time for you to leave home," I said. "You need to continue your knightly training in another household. It might help you to kerb your temper and hopefully advance future alliances. I have given it much thought."

Excitement crossed his eager young face, replacing his sullen pique. "With who, madam? I beg you, tell me!"

I smiled. "You are going to Duke William in Rouen and will receive training alongside his sons. It is the wish of your father and me that you try to befriend Robert, the Duke's eldest son."

Robert's lip curled contemptuously, excitement waning. "Is he not the one his father calls 'Curthose' because his legs are mere stumps? From what I have heard, he is scarce bigger than a dwarf!"

"Well, you heard wrong, Robert, and you are not to repeat that lie in my hearing—and certainly not when you are in Duke William's household. Young Lord Robert lacks height, it is true, but so does his mother the Duchess. He is formed normally in all ways and he is young yet and may grow. You *will* be courteous."

My son looked mutinous, but at the same time, I could tell he was eager to be away learning battle-craft and horsemanship, as expected in any noble young man of war-like stock.

"You will make me proud." Walking over to him, I placed my hand on his back, where beneath his linen shirt the stripes from the birch-rob still stung and wept. He flinched with pain. "Promise me. Friendship with Lord Robert could bring great honour to our family."

"I-I promise. I would go just to witness the Duke's court anyway and hear his tales of battle!"

"Good. I will have your passage to Rouen arranged. Just remember—no intimidating your inferiors, no chasing serving wenches when you are gone. I have seen how the laundresses and village girls fear you. William and Matilda are pious; they will not put up with lewd behaviour. So, no striking horses, wenches, peasants— and most certainly, no striking Robert Curthose."

"I will keep my anger in check unless someone attacks me first. But then you must expect me to defend myself, with my fists if not a blade."

"Yes, that would be natural and expected." I inclined my head.

As he walked away, wincing slightly in pain from his birching, I thought how, with any luck, he would reach the highest echelons when he was a man grown. I would accept nought less for a scion of the House of Belleme.

So Robert left Montgomery Castle, and over the months that followed, news reached us that he fitted well within the Duke's household, and that he and Robert Curthose had become fast friends despite the difference in their ages. I was pleased my son had seen the wisdom in befriending William's boy and had not risen to the temptation of calling him 'dwarf' or other insulting names.

One day, however, as I arrived home from a day at the market with my ladies, I saw the ducal messenger's pennants and felt a sensation of unease. Robert sent his own missives, paid for by Roger—why was an official messenger at the castle? A stab of terror jolted me, as I envisioned my eldest son dead—slain by some brutish serf in a brawl or accidentally slashed in training. Slipping clumsily off my mount, I dragged up my heavy skirts and shoved my way into the castle door, hastening for the solar, where I expected the messenger would be confined with Roger.

I found him there, before my husband's seat. Roger looked grim, his lips pinched, his hands splayed out on his knees. Both men jumped in alarm as I crashed rather inelegantly into the chamber, headdress askew, veil twisted like a mourning shroud over my face.

"Roger, is something amiss?" My gaze fell on the startled messenger. "Is it…is it Robert?"

Roger beckoned the man to leave. He scurried past me with a perfunctory bow. "Roger," I gasped. "Tell me our son is not harmed."

"Robert? Why would you think he is harmed? He is in good hands," said Roger with a frown. "But be seated, wife, there is something you should know. Something that will not please you."

Heavily I slumped upon a bench, relieved that my son was hale but concerned by Roger's countenance. Had war broken out in Normandy? The barons and counts were ever fractious and grasping. No, no it had to be something more personal to make my husband so grim.

"So," I said, "tell me this unpleasant news."

"It is de Giroie's son, Arnold d'Eschafour."

My mouth pursed with dislike. "*Him*. Is he causing problems again? I wondered at his long absence. Well, he can go to Hell. If I catch him on the lands the Duke granted me, I will have the bastard strung up…"

"Mab, listen to me." Roger's voice was harsh, insistent. "The Duke's letter—it is about those very lands."

Sickness clawed at me, nigh as strongly as when I feared my boy was slain. "The lands? What about them?"

He cleared his throat, reached out to clasp my hands; but it was not a reassuring clasp—rather one that held me prisoner. "Mabel, I hate to inform you, but d'Eschafour has petitioned William for the return of some of his lands. Over the last few years, he has served the Duke well on many excursions into the field and William feels it is appropriate to reward him…"

Spluttering with rage and indignation, I pulled away from my husband. His fingers left red marks on my wrists. "They are *MY* lands!" I screamed. "This is ridiculous, it's an insult. I won't have it."

"The lands were only yours as long as William willed it," Roger snapped, annoyance in his eyes. "Stop screeching—you sound like some fishwife on a seaside quay!"

"How dare you!" I roared, flinging myself back in his direction. "Those lands are mine…*mine*. I must go to William at once and beg that I retain them. You are his friend; he'll listen, surely."

Roger caught my wrists again, even tighter this time—I thought the fragile bones might snap. "Mabel. *No*. You are not going to the Duke. The transfer of rights has already been made a fortnight ago; Arnold d'Eschafour has lawful possession of any castles or fortifications therein. You must accept this, Mabel. It is the way of things. You did not need those lands and manors. We have enough."

I tore from him again and fell at his feet. I pounded the rushes with my fists, almost enjoying the shocks that went up my arms from the hard wooden boards below. "Curse Arnold d'Eschafour! Curse the faithless Duke! But I will get my revenge on that whelp of Fitz Giroie, I swear it. Roger, *I will get my revenge….*"

The final surrender of the disputed properties to d'Eschafour was to take place in a month's time. Roger was on the Duke's business, so he did not realise I had my scribe write to my old enemy, using Roger's seal, telling Arnold that Roger's brother, Gilbert, who was steward at Saint Ceneri Castle, would meet him to assist his reclamation of the fortress. I poured cheerful lies onto the paper, how bygones were bygones and the past was now buried, and how we must move forward in amity.

Merrily I sent the letter on its way and then hastened, hidden by the shadows of early eventide, to the herbalist who dwelt on the edge of Montgomery town. Boldly, I went alone, hooded and cloaked, the long dagger my sire had given me long ago belted at my thigh. I rode astride, which was not the best for secrecy, but if I ran into any trouble on my mission, a horse would enable me to flee.

The herbalist lived beyond the stout timber-framed houses, her abode lying in the marshy ground down by the river where it was hidden from prying eyes by a hedge decked with blood-red berries. As I fought my way through a gap in the hedge, I saw a hovel rather than a house, its flimsy frame covered with loosely bound river-reeds and a skin hanging in the doorway. A pig grunted in a rickety pen and an open smoke-hole billowed strong-smelling blue smoke.

Dismounting, I let my steed's reins dangled and inched towards the entrance. "Hello? "I called. "Herbalist! I would see you!"

A swishing and scuttling sounded inside the hovel. Several cats, one black, one striped dashed out and vanished into the purple twilight, their eyes gleaming yellow-green. They were followed by what seemed a bundle of stinking rags. On legs. As the bundle unfolded, I saw a small, ugly old woman staring at me. She reminded me of the hag who had tormented me with the changeling on my night of shame, which did not fill me with confidence. Short and bent, she had similar pointed features, baleful eyes and a visibly bristling chin.

"What is it? What do y' want?" she slurred. "I'm busy!"

"You're the herbalist, aren't you? Rotrude?"

"I am. What of it?"

"I need your help, obviously."

"Oh, it's like that, is it? She looked me up and down. "Pennyroyal, is it?"

I flushed; pennyroyal opened the womb early so women could rid themselves of an unwanted child. I had never needed such a thing but I had heard the servants' gossip.

"No, nothing like that." I approached Rotrude. "Do you know who I am?" I flicked back a flap of my hood.

The whiskered lips parted to emit a little gasp. "Milady Montgomery! What brings you to a humble herbalist like old Rotrude?"

There was no way I could skirt the issue. "Poison. I need a good, strong poison."

"To…ah…kill rats or the like?" She eyed me blearily.

I gave a short, harsh laugh. "You could say that Rotrude. Oh, do not look so shocked; I've heard the stories. You've advised the local women on putting poisons in stews to get rid of unwanted husbands—just as you dole out pennyroyal for their unwanted babies."

"Oh, no, madam, I just do cures and poultices, nothing wicked!" she stammered. "That mention of pennyroyal—it was but a jest. Not a very fitting one…"

I drew my dagger, gleaming cold in the moonlight. "Please do not play the innocent. It doesn't suit you and it's a lie anyway. You are not innocent—but you will remain alive if you do as I ask. Do you understand?"

Her tangled head bobbed on its skinny neck.

"Poison it is then, potent and not easily detected. Easiest if it can be put in drink."

"Nightshade is good…but if the victim takes too little he will just sleep," murmured Rotrude, looking thoughtful. "A poisonous toad squeezed inside a cup is another good way, but there's no guarantee I can find a suitable toad…"

"Let's forget the toad, too difficult." I said with impatience. "What about hemlock?"

"Ah, yes, yes," she nodded. "Scabby-hands, the Devil's Own Flower. Her Ladyship is learned in these matters. What a surprise for old Rotrude."

"I hear things, crone. Everything that goes on in the village eventually reaches me up at the castle."

The white, wrinkly old face became even paler. "Uh…your diligence is appreciated, milady. Another good choice for what you require is Tyr's Helm."

"Tyr's Helm?" I frowned, fingering my bright blade. "What is that?"

"They also call it Monk's Hood or Wolf's Bane. The old ones from the North used it; Tyr was one of their gods, one-handed, who fought the deadly wolf of the Great Winter. Hence the name Wolf's Bane."

"Is it potent?"

"Yes, milady. The, er, ah, witches use it in the ointments that make them *fly*."

"Fly. Well, I could make my enemy just fly away—but I'd prefer him dead and buried to make certain he never bothers me again. So, you think this Wolf's Bane will work?"

"I can make it potent enough so that there will be no question."

"Do that, then, old woman."

"When would you need it, milady?"

"Now…this night…"

"B-but I…" Rotrude began to argue, the hairs on her chin vibrating in agitation. "That is a tall order! I have other brews in the making, poultices and unguents that need delivering."

"Those are not important. Put them aside. My wants are paramount." I fixed her with a hard gaze. "I will wait for you, all night if needs be."

She let out a hard, pained groan.

"Mayhap this will sweeten the task." Opening my belt-purse, I drew out two coins. They gleamed in the half-light. I saw Rotrude's eyes suddenly light up, two watery moons.

"And if that doesn't convince you," I said, with a tight little smile, "I am sure *this* will…" I extended my blade, cold as a finger of ice. "It's rather useful, especially for popping eyes…"

"Milady, I'll do your bidding, I'll do it!" Rotrude wailed and she dived into her foetid hut. The sound of banging pots and cursing ensued. A torch was lit and the hearth fire stoked, making the crooked doorway gleam red like the mouth of hell.

Satisfied, I spread my skirts and sat on the ground to wait. My mare trundled over, nudging my shoulder, looking for treats. I plaited her mane with wild Day's Eye flowers from the unkempt grass. Overhead, the Moon watched, a pitted face, spying on dark deeds done within night's fold.

My heart was light and joyful. If all went well, Arnold d' Eschafour would soon be no more, and as his less hot-headed brother was fighting in foreign wars, hopefully the Duke could be persuaded to return the contentious lands to my worthy hands…

Saint Ceneri, the castle Arnold wanted back so desperately was small and mean compared to the vast, towered fortresses of Domfront, Alencon or Montgomery. It was mainly wrought of wood, with some feeble stonework shoring up the defences. I almost felt sorry for the man, desiring such a weak castle so badly. Almost. It had been given to *me*, and I intended to keep it.

"I am surprised to see you here...sister." Roger's younger brother Gilbert was fluttering about, ill at ease at my arrival, especially as I had brought, amongst labourers, a choice selection of hard-bitten soldiers and had them gathered in the stables, still armed. "I expected Sir d'Eschafour..."

"Yes, I know who you expect," I said. "Well, now you have me too. I have business with Arnold d'Eschafour. For one thing, I want all my furnishings...the beds...the hangings. Those are not his; they are mine. The trestle table and benches can stay—ha, that table looks like a butcher's chopping block in a market!"

"Does Roger know you are at Saint Ceneri?" Gilbert asked warily, shuffling from one foot to the next.

"Of course not," I snapped. "This is *my* business, not his..." I waved to my servants, clustered anxiously in the doorway into the castle hall. They entered in a flurry and began to strip it of its meagre goods. A candelabra was carried out, and two moth-eaten tapestries depicting Noah's Ark and Jonah and the Whale.

"But you are Roger's wife..." murmured Gilbert, running his hand nervously through his unkempt red hair.

"Not his slave, and the truth is—friend of Count William though he may be, I *am* the great land-holder of the two of us—or will be when Uncle Yves goes to his final rest. And Saint Ceneri and its lands belonged to me...before the Duke handed it back to Arnold on a foolish whim."

Gilbert looked even more uneasy. "I am to hand over the keys of the castle to d'Eschafour. You won't create a fuss, will you, Mabel? I know you are a woman of strong passions."

"I won't stop you, and no, I shan't try and snatch the keys back from that wretch's paws. I want my goods, that's all, though I dare say I am displeased by the castle's unrighteous seizure. Why does d'

Eschafour even want it? Has he not been away in Apulia, where he made a fortune? Surely he could do better than this somewhere, somewhere far away."

"I doubt *he* will see it that way," mumbled Gilbert, jingling the contentious keys in his hand. "I wish Roger was here to advise…."

Outside the narrow slit of the window, a horn sounded, a harsh bleat that echoed about the walls. "I think Arnold has arrived," I said, my heartbeat becoming loud in my ears. "As steward, you must see to him. I shall prepare myself for my meeting with my old foe."

I raced to the bedchamber I had earlier chosen for myself—although the best one, the lord's chamber, it was damp and chill, with soot from torches on walls and ceilings and the scuttling of mice in the walls. I had thrown off the sheets and covers and demanded the washerwomen clean them immediately upon my arrival. Reaching into the cedar chest carted in by my servants, I took out the stoppered jug filled with Wolf's Bane and slid it into the pouch attached to my girdle. Then I summoned my maids; I had brought them along, plus some extra females from the castle household who all looked rather mystified and a bit frightened.

"I have a task for you," I told them, "you are to go and entertain Arnold d'Eschafour and his men. And get them, very, very drunk."

The women glanced uneasily at one another; they did not like my words one bit, and truth be told, I did not blame them—but they had no choice. It was my will. "Jesu's Nails, I am not asking you to sleep with these oafs," I said peevishly. "Just ply them with drink and promises until they are falling from their benches in a stupor."

The women looked a little more relieved but still apprehensive.

"You and your families will be meetly rewarded," I soothed. "Now, go, down to the hall."

They went, timid as little sheep. I waited, beautifying my own hair in a mirror made of brass and rubbing unguents on my cheeks to redden them. Down below, I smelt the aroma of food emerging from the kitchens, and then the sound of a shawm and the banging of a drum. Roars of laughter drifted to my ears—a sweet sound. Arnold's men already sounded half-drunk. They had ridden many a mile and now were making the most of Gilbert's hospitality in their lord's evilly-gotten stronghold.

I waited a little longer, my hand drifting every now and then to the flagon tucked in my pouch. Arnold must not drink it too soon; Rotrude had said the effects overwhelmed the victim several hours after consumption, so I must make certain I was well out of reach before death occurred.

Just after midnight—I heard the abbey bells chime for Matins in the nearby village—I drew my cloak around my shoulders and approached Saint Ceneri's Great Hall. For a moment I paused in the outside corridor, wrapped in smoke and darkness, gazing in at my enemy, Arnold d'Eschafour.

Arnold had taken over the dais, the lord's position. The candelabras were gone—I had made sure of that—but the spacious chamber was lit by several sputtering torches. Arnold was talking animatedly to some of her fellows—great, loutish men in boiled leather, while others writhed and rolled on the benches below. My ladies, their faces wearing rictus-like smiles, were plying them with drink and other blandishments. I felt a swell of pride at how well they played their parts after their initial reluctance—I would reward them with gowns and coin when we returned to Castle Montgomery.

Taking a deep breath, I stepped into the hall. The music died and from the dais Arnold stared, eyes hot and furious, cheeks flaming from the drink. "Oh ho!" he shouted, banging his goblet on the table, "the Lady de Montgomery has come to welcome me here herself. I must say this is a surprise, Lady Mabel."

"I have come to retrieve my goods." I strolled towards the dais, "You surely did not think I would leave my valuables for the likes of you to ruin."

"Ah," he said. "I saw a bed on a cart outside. So you would have me and mine sleep on the cold hard floor?"

"That is the most fitting place for dogs."

"Ah, maybe one of those trulls flirting with my men will come upstairs to warm me up. Or better yet, two or three of them."

"No, do not dare think it. They are my women. I sent them to make you welcome, but a welcome does not mean they will share your bed. They do not generally appreciate…pigs."

He roared with laughter; drops of liquor trailed down his chin and dripped onto his tunic. "You try to provoke me, do you not,

Mabel de Belleme? Ah, come, after all these years surely our enmity is not so strong. Your husband accepted a fine cloak off me when I returned from Apulia in return for free passage over his lands."

"My husband can be too trusting and too giving at times," I said icily. "You will find I am neither."

He waved a hand in front of his inflamed face. "I am sure…but come, sit up here at my side. After all, we are going to be neighbours whether we like it or not."

Daintily I ascended the steps to the dais. Arnold's brutes were howling and roaring as if this meant I had somehow submitted to their boorish lord. A bench was dragged up, below the sloppy canopy Arnold's minions had raised on poles and I sat under it as proud as any queen. The music started again, and the carousal. The main courses had already been served and the last was brought—wafers and wine with small sweet pastries.

"So sweet and delicate," said Arnold, examining one before popping it into his mouth. Ginger coated his thick lips. "Just like you, Lady Mabel." Wobbling, he stood up, holding his goblet aloft as drink slopped over the rim. "A toast to the incomparable Lady Mabel de Belleme, a lady of high spirits known for her wit, charm…and the dagger she always carries. Beware of your eyes, my friends, and other parts too."

More raucous laughter echoed in the great chamber. I kept my composure. The less I responded, the more I hoped d'Eschafour would believe I had mellowed with age and motherhood.

At last, the torches set about the walls had burnt low. Men started staggering out of the Hall, arms around each other's shoulders as they sang bawdy songs. My ladies flew like birds from the Hall, expressions filled with relief; now they could barricade themselves safely into their rooms.

Arnold slammed his empty goblet down on the nearest table and began to reel after his men. I snatched the cup up and hid it in my lap, trying to keep my eyes on my adversary's back as I poured the Wolf's Bane into it and then righted it on the table again.

"Lord Arnold," I called after him. He halted, stumbling around to face me, a dull lust filling his eyes.

"You wouldn't care for a little night-ride, would you?" he slurred. "Then we could truly let bygones be bygones..."

"And you'd have something to hold over me for the rest of our lives," I said with a wry smile. "I do not think so, Arnold, but I think we *should* drink together, toasting new amity between our Houses. I am a mother and a good wife to my lord Roger; it is time to give up the feuds of the past. I am sorry for your father's plight, but it was not my doing, no matter what you have heard. Blame my sire, who was, as men say, an evil man."

Arnold came staggering back in my direction, finger pointing, growing slightly aggressive. "In his monastery, my father said you put out his eyes yourself. Do you say he lies?"

"I was there, I admit." I schooled my face to solemnity. "However, I did not harm him. My sire forced me to watch. Your father, stricken by terror and feverish afterwards was mistaken..."

"*Mistaken...*" growled Arnold, and he pressed his hands to his head as if seeking to shake up his drink-fuddled mind.

"Yes, mistaken, and who could blame him in such circumstances?" I said with cool finality. "Now, let us drink to a new beginning, without hostility...Gilbert, where are you?"

Gilbert, as steward, was hovering near one of the exits where he had been directing the servants to carry out voiders full of scraps and animal bones. Looking a little out of sorts, for this was his last night in his position and he would have to vacate the castle the next day, he strode toward the dais. "My Lady?"

"Refill Lord Arnold's goblet and mine as well," I ordered. "We are to drink to peace."

Gilbert dutifully obtained a flagon of wine and filled my goblet and then Arnold's. I watched the blood-red wine mix with the poison. Pleased, I handed Arnold's cup to him. "Drink, my Lord, to a new friendship..."

He lifted the goblet on high, wine showering. "To—to, ah...ah Christ..." His eyes suddenly crossed and he let out a foul, malodorous belch. Banging down the goblet with its precious, lethal contents, he slumped back into his vacated seat before vomiting then falling forward with his head in his hands. He made groaning noises. "My head..."

"He's had too much to drink," said Gilbert.

I was vexed—and nervous now, my plans unravelling in a way I had not foreseen.

"Gilbert, let's get him to his chamber," I said. "I'll bring the wine along."

"The wine?"

"Yes, it's the best from the cellars. *My* cellars! If he's going to get drunk on my wine, he better bloody well not waste it!" I lied quickly.

Gilbert grabbed Arnold beneath the arms and dragged him from his seat. My foe moaned and mumbled, eyelids fluttering. I picked up the cup of poison as Gilbert hauled d'Eschafour bodily down the hallways to the lord's chambers. There was no bed—I had taken it and Arnold had not yet brought in his furnishings, but some of the servants had dumped some moth-eaten curtains and dirty linens in a heap.

"He can lie on those," I said, and Gilbert, straining, dragged d'Eschafour the last few feet and deposited his dead-weight atop the heap. Arnold uttered a muffled roar and grabbed at the linens, drawing them over his head. I set the goblet down near him—near but not so close he might knock it over with a thrashing, drunken foot or arm.

I hurried for the door, not best pleased by this turn of events. I had wanted to see Arnold down the poison—and laugh inwardly as I did. But it was not to be. However... "Gilbert," I said in a wheedling voice. "There is something I would ask of you. I fear you will not like it overmuch, though."

His brow wrinkled. "What is it, Mabel?"

"Will you stay the night with Arnold?"

"Why?" he choked. "I dislike the man near as much as you do, and I am not his body servant. He must have a squire or two lurking around who can attend him."

"His men are all drunk, drunk and carousing out in the bailey. I would not trust any of them inside, even the youngest, and I know my maids are terrified. I need you to watch over him, and make sure he does not choke on his own spew, as drunkards sometimes do. I would no doubt be blamed if he should come to any harm in the night. Or *you* would, as steward…"

I saw his face blanch at that thought and my heart lifted. He would do as I desired, I knew it.

"I will stay then," he said, folding his arms, "although I had not thought to act as a nursemaid on my last night in this castle."

Gratefully I kissed him on the cheek, watching him redden. "My thanks," I said, "you are a good, loyal friend Gilbert. Roger and I will reward you handsomely, I swear, and find you a choicer position, maybe even one with the Duke of Normandy."

I wanted to remind him about the goblet but decided to hold my tongue—my intent would be too obvious if I kept bringing up the subject. But if Arnold awoke in the night or at dawn, he would no doubt want to quell his thirst with more wine, as such men often did. Or maybe he would want sops to break his fast in the morn, and Gilbert could fetch him stale bread to dip in his deadly drink…

I could think no more on my endeavour, which had gone a little awry. Wishing Gilbert farewell and goodnight, I flitted down the unlit corridors to my chamber, where I spent the night fitfully tossing and turning, wondering when and if my intended victim had consumed the deadly draught…

I woke before dawn and called the women to dress me for the journey back to Castle Montgomery. Outside in the courtyard, I could hear the household springing to life—men whistling, dogs barking, chickens clucking, women singing as they hauled garments down to the river to wash.

I did not bother to break my fast—I sent the ladies out of the apartments to go find places in the wains. Then I went in search of Gilbert, who I expected to be preparing for his own departure.

I could not find him—not in the kitchen, or the hall, or the bailey. As a frisson of fear rushed through me, I managed, at last, to corner a solitary pot-boy cleaning out the ovens in the kitchens.

"Boy," I snapped, grabbing his collar and hauling him towards me, "where is the Lord Gilbert this morning? I am eager to set off upon the road."

His eyes became round globes in the grease-smeared circle of his face. "He's not well, milady. Some kind of ague. He's still in bed."

The cold wave turned to a sensation of ice on the back of my neck. Dropping the boy, who fell on the flagstones in a heap like a fallen marionette, I raced for Gilbert's quarters. I arrived just as a black-clad, long-bearded man was exiting—I knew him for a doctor by his funereal garb. He harumphed angrily as I shoved past him and into the presence of my husband's brother.

Gilbert was lying on his bed, white and pale, a fine sheen of sweat on his brow. He did not even attempt to rise as I drew near. "Gilbert, what ails you?" My voice was a hoarse rasp.

"I-I do not know. It must have been something I ate last night; I have great pains in the gut and bowels but there is more besides. My heart beats like a drum and skips like a child at play! I am weak as a kitten; even the doctor is perplexed."

The physician might be, but I was not. I leant over the bed, lips close to his ear. "Gilbert, you must tell me—did you touch the wine I poured for Arnold d'Eschafour?"

He gazed up at me, pupil wide, distended, swallowing light. An expression of horror and terror crossed his countenance. "Mabel, you did not…No, *no!*"

I sprang back and ran from the chamber, slamming the door behind me with a resounding crash. Seeking the stares, I passed the doctor who had paused upon hearing the commotion from his patient's chamber. "My Lady," he began, "what has happened…"

"He…he…Gilbert raves, he has gone mad!" I blurted. "He blames me, his sister-by-marriage, for his ills! Go to him, I bid you; give him potions to calm him down… I-I am going to call for a priest."

Soon I found the castle chaplain, a small man with a long bony neck and a hairless head. Gabbling that Gilbert's life was in great danger and he must go to him immediately, I sent him running for Gilbert's chamber, Bible clutched in hand. As he disappeared up the stairs, I ran from the wooden tower of Saint Ceneri Castle and out into the bailey. Mercifully, my entourage was ready and waiting, the horses stamping in their traces, eager to be away, the guards armed and at attention.

As I rushed for the covered cart in which I travelled, I heard a shout from behind. I froze. Glancing over my shoulder, I saw Arnold d'Eschafour, bleary-eyed, his hair in knotted spikes, stumbling from the castle door. "You leave so soon, Lady—without a farewell?" he bawled. He appeared to still be drunk, his shirt dank from where he'd spewed upon himself.

"Go, go!" I shouted to my men, hoisting up my skirts and leaping into the safety of my cart. "It's after curfew, the gates will be open. Go, and do not hesitate for anyone! If anyone tries to stop the entourage—ride them down!"

The lead riders spurred their horses onwards and the carts began to roll. Mounted mail-clad men gathered on either side of my wain, encircling me in a ring of steel. The rest of the waggons trundled after, groaning under the weight of the castle furnishings and bouncing over the rough cobbles in the courtyard.

Arnold d'Eschafour ceased to bellow and halted, swaying in his tracks, glaring in my direction. I glared back, full of hatred.

It was all *his* fault, the bastard.

He should have drunk the wine, not Gilbert. The poison was meant for *him*, not my husband's hapless brother.

Full of rage, I thought on what I would do next to get revenge. Arnold would never escape my wrath.

Never.

CHAPTER THIRTEEN

"My brother is dead…" A strangled sob tore from Roger's throat as the news arrived from Saint Ceneri. "Poor Gilbert! Mabel, did anything seem amiss when you left Arnold's castle?"

The picture of innocence, I shook my head. "Gilbert was not well that morn, hence he did not travel on the road with us. I assumed he had overeaten at the banquet…or over-drank. You—you do not think he died of other than natural causes, do you?"

"I do not know." Roger sank onto a bench, holding his head in his hands. "He was young and healthy, never ill, but we all know how swiftly death may strike one down even so. A cold draught, food that overheats or chills the humours, an evil miasma off the surface of water…"

"God's will," I said firmly.

"Aye, God's Will," muttered Roger cheerlessly.

In silence I stood gazing upon my husband's misery, hiding my fury beneath a calm exterior. Inside I raged—at Arnold d'Eschafour and at the dead Gilbert himself. Why had Gilbert been such a greedy fool he felt the need to drink the wine while on watch? It is his own fault he was dead! It was certainly not *MY* fault he had drunk the poison. He had ruined all my plans and died to make things even worse.

Roger glanced up and I cringed to see tears glistening in the eyes of such a strong warrior. *Oh, stop, stop, Roger*! "W-was de Eschavour in the castle when Arnold died? I cannot imagine he might have done this, as he had held out a hand in reconciliation…"

"You know what a liar he is," I snapped, eager to heap the blame onto my hated foe. "He insulted me while I was there, jeered about taking back the castle. He treated Gilbert like a menial, not a steward. Who knows what might have occurred when I lay abed, the door barred, in fear for my own life?"

Roger grunted and put his head back in his hands. I sulked; I had hoped my embroidered tale might have goaded him into gathering the levies and riding to Arnold's castle to make an end. But I should have known better—the Duke had allowed d'Eschafour to have the lands back and Roger would not contest his friend's will.

"It is not impossible Gilbert was slain by foul means." Roger raised his head an inch or two. The torchlight gleamed on his damp, reddened eyes. "But there is no proof. As much as it pains me, I must let the matter lie and carry on."

"I will light candles for Gilbert's soul," I said brusquely.

Roger reached out and clasped my hand; his fingers were cold, mine damp with a warm, guilty sweat.

It was not my fault...Gilbert was a fool...and d'Eschafour a lucky drunk...

But Arnold's luck would run out one day. No man made a fool of me.

I made inquiries, lots of them. I found out that Arnold's new Chamberlain was a knight called Roger Goulafre. Goulafre's sire had once served my father and I remembered him as a fellow who would do anything to advance himself or make money, preferably both. The son seemed cast in the same mould, hence his current service with Arnold d'Eschafour. I plied him with cheerful letters detailing my memories of his father; at first, I think the dolt believed I was mysteriously enamoured of him, but soon he came to realise my only desire was to kill his present employer.

We met at a ruined castle between Castle Montgomery and Arnold's fortress at Saint Ceneri; a sombre, lonely place where stark fangs of stone thrust from greenery like the bones of its owner, who had died in some fray deep in time, so long ago no one remembered his name or those who died for his cause.

Clad in black leather, tall and sallow-complected, Roger Goulafre was waiting in the shadow of a vast holly tree that poked through the tumbled ruins. "My Lady Mabel," he said as he spotted me, giving a slight bow, "you have come."

"You thought I wouldn't?" I walked slowly in his direction, picking my way around fallen masonry. A few hundred yards away, a guard stood with my horse, alert to trouble from any quarter.

"What you propose is dangerous business," said Goulafre. He grinned; his teeth were brown-stained ruins, craggy as the shattered castle.

"Life is a dangerous business, is it not?" I said. "You met my sire, did you not, when your sire served him? You know how he thought about such things."

"Ah, William Talvas...yes. God rest his soul."

"God? I doubt it. Father always said he'd have a better time in the company of the Devil."

"That is not a thing to jest about."

"Isn't it? Life, death...the afterlife? Why not jest? Sometimes it all seems a great jest to me. But that aside, I have brought enticement..."

"Besides yourself?" His grin became a sickening leer; I fought to keep my disgust from showing. So, he still had the nonsense in his head that I might lie with him.

"Oh, I would be too much for you, Roger Golafre," I said. "You would be better off with *this*..." I yanked out a purse from beneath my cloak; it clinked noisily as I shook it. "If you do my bidding and *dispose* of Arnold, murderer of my husband's dear brother Gilbert, you can have not only this purse now but another when the deed is complete. You will be a rich man."

As if entranced, his hand reached out. I dropped the bag into it. "Do not fail me, Roger Golafre," I said, my lips drawn tightly over my upper teeth in a smile one might have described as vulpine. "If Arnold d'Eschafour still walks this earth within the next three turnings of the moon, I will want this money back. And I will send some doughty men with swords to get it."

"You can count on me, my Lady." A nervous note hung in his voice now, which brought me much pleasure. He must learn to fear; I was not to be trifled with just because I was a woman of small stature and harmless appearance.

"Go then." I stepped back over the fallen stones and tangled briars that clawed at the hem of my gown. "Go, and make it quick!"

I returned to Montgomery Castle and flung myself into a flurry of the gentle arts that bored me so, needlework and accounts, overseeing the tutoring of the children, dance lessons for my pack of daughters.

Roger walked about, swathed in a dark mood, his face long and sorrowful. He prayed for his brother every day, which irked me to the core. I no longer wanted to hear his laments about Gilbert. The man was dead; unless Christ raised him like Lazarus, and there was no reason why the Saviour would favour Gilbert so, he was gone forever, cold bones in a tomb.

Christmas came and went in a flurry of ice, mud and freezing rain. I grew bored and morose, my hopes of hearing news from Roger Goulafre beginning to wither. I would have to go after him if he did not come through with what he promised; he was not keeping that coin without killing Arnold d'Eschafour.

In bleakest January, snow began to fall outside the castle, turning the green rises of the surrounding landscape into waves of white. The nearby river was frozen, as was our shallow moat; local children skated on them both. I laughed to watch the ones on the moat fall through the ice; the waters of course were full of frozen chunks of dung expelled from the castle garderobes. The horrified screams and the angry shouts of the brats' wretched mothers brought great amusement to my heart. My own children, watching from the walls, hurled snowballs down upon the peasant's heads, shrieking in mirth. I watched with glad heart, remembering how I had done the same in my childhood at Alencon.

And then I spotted a lone rider in the distance, a black blot, like an ant, against the wintry starkness. Leaning over the battlements, eyes narrowed against the brightness of the snow as the weak sun caressed it, I watched the horseman trot past the humble grey church and proceed down a track claggy with mud from where the locals hauled their wagons.

I held my breath, fearing he was just some passer-by seeking sustenance and shelter in the nearest inn. But no, no, he was passing the taverns at town's edge and started riding up the hill toward the gates. As he drew closer, I noted that he wore no visible badge.

Not daring to hope, I backed away, tapping my knuckles nervously against an ice-caked crenel until they grew red and sore. After what seemed an interminable wait, one of my ladies appeared on the wall, her breath a puff of smoke before her lips as she hurried in my direction.

"Lady Mabel, a messenger awaits your pleasure."

I followed her down into the Great Hall, where a ragged-looking man, features rosy from the heat of the fire, stood warming his hands before the blaze. My heart sank when I saw it was not Roger Goulafre. "Who are you?" I said curtly.

"Can we speak alone, my Lady? It is important."

I would not have such a churl in my private solar, so I said, "To the chapel, then." That would surely keep suspicions away, and if he had criminal intentions, it was less likely he would try to perpetrate them in a holy place.

The chaplain was not there when I arrived, the stranger following like a dark shadow, and I beckoned the newcomer into a corner behind the screen. "Who are you?" I asked. "Who sent you?"

"I am Walter de Mauley, and bring you this." He reached with gloved hands to his belt and pulled out a little box. He opened it. I gazed upon a lock of tangled hair.

"What is this you bring?" Perplexed, I stared at the matted lock.

"This comes from the head of Arnold d'Eschafour," de Mauley said. "My master Roger Goulafre sends it hence as a token of his fidelity."

I leaned closer to this Walter. "And Arnold?"

"Dead, my Lady. Upon the first of January just gone. He had fared to Courville to spend the Christmas season there with his kinsmen Lord Giroie and William Gouet of Montmirail. Alas, all three men became *sick*..." He gazed at me meaningfully. "Lord Giroie and Gouet recovered slowly after several days but Arnold was not so fortunate."

"Ah," I said, "it is the time of the year for great sicknesses to descend, is it not?"

"It is, my Lady. So many ailments that might carry a man off. Especially if he overindulged like Lord Arnold. Late nights, excessive drink, found lying in a stupor out in the snow..."

"What of his family?" I said breezily. I felt almost light-headed with joy, there in the gloom betwixt the long beeswax candles with their heavy smell. "He had a wife, did he not?"

"Aye, she was there, and never had I seen a woman so possessed by grief when he died. She tore her hair like a mad thing."

"Where is she now?"

"Still at Courville in mourning. She had two small infants with her."

"Well…" I took a deep breath. "I have no doubt the Duke of Normandy will grant my Lord Roger and I possession of d'Eschafour's lands once more. The widow and her offspring cannot return to any of them. Bear this message to Sir Roger Goulafre and see that she does not try to enter any village or castle in the debatable areas." I paused, thoughtful. "I am not entirely a hard woman, though. Let her also be told that I will have any goods she owns returned as soon as I may—minus a fee for their transport to wherever she might find lodgings."

"It will be done, Lady." Walter gave a slight bow.

"Excellent. Now I will pay you for your services and give you the rest of Goulafre's payment to bear to him. You will not mind riding out again on the morrow at dawn? I am eager that this transaction is complete."

"No, my Lady," he said with a wry smile. "Master Goulafre expected you would demand punctuality. That is why he sent me here. I was once a mercenary and expect no niceties from town or castle."

"How thoughtful of Goulafre," I mused. "Maybe he is more intelligent than I thought. Now go, I will have the payments sent to the stable. Keep out of the way of Lord Montgomery if he is about." My eyes narrowed fiercely. "He must know nought of what has occurred."

As I had guessed, the contentious lands and manors claimed by Arnold soon reverted to me. Roger suspected nothing, muttering that Arnold drank too much and that likely brought on his premature demise.

Yes, he drank too much indeed. It was just a pity he had not done so before hapless Gilbert drained the cup ready and waiting for Arnold to awaken...

News came that Arnold's wife Gundrada had given up her children to become wards of various barons, and that she, nigh penniless, had gone to live on the charity of her brother Eudo, who was Duke William's steward. As his children were both girls, I had no fear that the Giroie family would ever disturb me again, William de Giroie the Younger having left for Italy, where he had married a powerful nobleman's daughter and rejoiced in the nickname of 'the Good Norman.'

I now turned my hand to collecting even more property—after all, I had many children who would one day need inheritances worthy of their stature. It was far easier than I thought. Duke William was concerned about uprisings and he was a close friend of my Roger. I listened intently for any rumours about dissent, and if I heard any, I pounced. Messages flew to William's court by swiftest messenger. Through my diligence—and slivers of exaggeration here and there—I soon managed to obtain the lands and manors of Roger's greatest rivals, Eudulf de Tosni and Hugh de Grandmesnil.

As for Roger, he grew ever higher in William's esteem, and there was talk of arranging a marriage between my prettiest daughter, Maude, with William's young half-brother, Robert, son of Arlette and her husband Herluin de Conteville. My own son Robert remained high in William's favour too, and Hugh, my second son, had also joined his brother at the Duke's court.

Roger and I were invited to join the Christmas festivities in the citadel of Rouen in the year of Our Lord 1065. Splendid were the banquets in the great fortress of the Dukes of Normandy as the snow whirled around outside. Beef was served and haunches of venison; eels and tench in rich sauce slid on trenchers of the best-quality bread. Cheese wheels were rolled into the Hall, moon-like and pungent, followed by a *dragee* of imported sugar lumps dipped in golden honey gleaned from the castle beehives.

Each night of feasting, William would dress in red silks and a coronet; Matilda wore cloth of gold and a headdress clattering with pearls. Roger and I would recline on benches near the high table alongside the most puissant of lords and barons, wearing our finest raiment, flaunting gaudy cabochons and other jewels to show our wealth to the throng.

The weather across France turned fierce, blocking many roadways with deep, impassable drifts. Even after the Christmas festivities were officially over, we stayed on in Rouen as guests of William and Matilda, waiting for the roads to clear. With our patrons, we journeyed along the frozen banks of the Seine to view the town and visit the cathedral recently rebuilt and re-consecrated by Archbishop Maurille. It was a fabulous building with rounded arches of Roman style, replacing the earlier church damaged a century ago by the incoming Norsemen. Rollo, the first Duke of Normandy, had received baptism in the cathedral after giving up his gods of fire and thunder and converting to Christianity.

Late one night, as I lingered with my husband in our quarters in Rouen Castle, listening to a troubadour sing and hearing our eldest sons tell in excited voices of the horses, hounds and hawks that had they had hunted with at William's court, the solar door, firmly shut, was thrown open with an almighty crash.

The boys fell silent and Roger and Robert grabbed the hilts of their swords.

To everyone's surprise, Duke William stormed in, inelegantly dressed in a nightrobe, his face suffused and angry, eyes crackling rage.

"Out!" he roared at the troubadour who dropped his lute in terror before gathering it into his arms and fleeing. "And you two also!" He pointed a shaking finger at Robert and Hugh, who bowed hastily and rushed out into the corridor. I made to rise, expecting that my presence, as a woman, might not be welcome, but William gestured me to keep my seat.

"You may stay, madam." His voice was flat, harsh.

"W-what ails you, William, my lord," stammered Roger. "I hope I have done nought to offend…"

"No, no, not you," said the Duke irritably. "Don't be a fool, Roger. A messenger has come from England."

"Ah," said Roger, visibly relieved that he was not the focus of William's wrath, "the Confessor. He has been ill, has he not? I pray the news is not bad."

William's lips were taut, bloodless. "He is dead."

Roger and I glanced at each other. We had heard many times how Edward, William's childless cousin, had named William as his heir. Well we knew how his eyes ofttimes turned toward the grey waves of the Narrow Sea and the shores beyond.

"God rest his soul," said Roger quietly. He crossed himself, then glanced up at his friend, eyes quizzical. What should we do? Kneel? Were we in the presence of a new King?

William's visage grew even redder and he began to tremble, not with fear but pure rage, hot and terrible. "God *curse* him, not rest his soul!" he roared, spittle flying from his mouth. "May he burn in Hell!"

Both Roger and I were aghast by his disrespect toward his newly-dead kinsman. "What—what has happened, my lord?" asked Roger.

"He betrayed me! Years ago, when I visited England, Edward told me that one day the country would be mine to rule! But on his deathbed, the dithering dotard gave my inheritance to the Saxon, Harold Godwine. The English have already proclaimed him Harold the Second. And in accepting England's crown, he, too, is a traitor, for when visited me in Normandy, an honoured guest, he fought at my side and swore an oath to me as his future sovereign. So Godwine is an oath-breaker as well as a traitor."

"My lord Duke, this is evil news indeed," said Roger in a hushed voice. "What will you do?"

"What do you think I will do?" William began to pace, his long robe swishing across the rushes, bristling with an all-consuming passion. "I will contest Godwine's claim first of all."

"And if that does not work? The Saxons will no doubt favour one of their own."

"If the Saxon clergy and nobles are such treacherous dogs and do not accept my rightful claim," spat William, his fists clenching and unclenching as if he yearned to grasp a sword or battle-axe and swing it, "then there is only one thing left for me to do…"

"My lord?"

"I will invade. England will be mine, even if I must make its rivers run crimson with blood."

CHAPTER FOURTEEN

Duke William, aided loyally by Roger, began to amass a great army. Men arrived to join him from far and wide, eager to gain the riches they heard lay across the Narrow Sea. The Duke wrote to Pope Alexander, outlining his complaint against Harold and asking him to 'urge the justice of his campaign.' The Pope agreed with William's claim to the crown and sent him a gleaming white banner lined with blue silk and displaying a cross of gold.

I stayed in Rouen, leaving our castle in the safe hands of the Constable and other members of the household. Excitement grew in my breast as the wheels of William's war-machine began to turn and Normandy sprang to attention. Duchess Matilda played her part too, adding the grand spectacle needed to help convince all men that William's claim was just and right.

In the Abbey La Trinite in Caen, which Matilda had founded, she and William gave their little seven-year-old daughter, Cecilia, to be a novice of the Order. The Duke himself led the child to the Abbey's high altar, lifting her in his strong, muscular arms, almost as if he would place her on the altar-top as a sacrifice—Cecilia's youth and maidenhood given unto God so that, in return, her sire could possess England and its bounty. On the same day, many other great lords offered up their daughters to the nunnery of La Trinite as well. I saw Roger glance at me as many stepped forward, but I could not make such a decision for any of our girls, not yet. For my brood, I preferred marriage and alliances to alliances with God, and for the one chosen for the church, I planned to see her in a convent where she might rise to greatness, not just one of many maidens in La Trinite.

William decided to leave Duchess Matilda as regent of Normandy in his absence, a high-standing role for a woman. Assisting her would be my Roger, wise old Lord de Beaumont and Hugh d'Avranches. In my secret heart of hearts, this news pleased me, for it meant my husband would remain in Normandy not engage in any dangerous fighting overseas.

As Roger took control of amassing troops, commissioning the forging of spears, arrows and longswords, and supplying the flotilla preparing to cross the Channel, I turned to Duchess Matilda for company. I had always admired her spirit and intellect; like me, she was no ordinary female—and maybe soon she would be Queen, someone whose favour I desperately would want.

"I am going to build a special ship for my husband," she told me, "but you must speak of it to no one, Mabel, not even your Roger. Do you understand?"

She gazed at me in such a way I knew she had commanded my silence, not merely asked for it. I nodded. I would not dare betray her wish.

"Then you may come with me and my ladies to the shipyard and witness my endeavours."

Sailing vessels were of little interest to me and I had never set foot on one, but the ship Matilda was building in secret was truly awe-inspiring. Larger than most cogs and other vessels, it resembled the ships used by our northern forebears—sleek and dragon-like, painted in stripes of burnt red and yellow-gold. She had named it *Mora*, the Great Mansion, and so it was—a wave-buoyed mansion for her lord that would sail across the stormy seas to victory. A lion's head roared from the prow, teeth bared to meet the rolling breakers, and the figurehead was of a golden boy-child holding an ivory horn to his lips.

"Is the child meant to be one of your sons?" I asked as I examined the handsome carving.

The Duchess nodded. "For me, it will always represent Robert, my eldest, although he is well past that age now. However, to my husband, in his mind, it will no doubt be his namesake, William, whom he loves the most."

She drew closer to the exquisite gilded figure, gesturing to one of its hands—the carefully crafted forefinger was outstretched. "When *Mora* glides over the waves, this child, the symbol of William's dynasty, will be pointing towards England where our bloodline shall, if God wills it, reign forevermore."

I was moved by her words and began myself to dream of that green island across the waves—dreams of vast tracts of land rewarded to Roger for his loyalty and good counsel, which would, in time, be passed on to our children. Normandy, France and Maine, the main seats of power for Roger and me were fair enough, and profitable if one could hold them—but they were crowded, full of constantly warring petty nobles. England; it would be different there...*if William won*....

A few weeks after my visit to the shipyard, Roger and I travelled from Rouen to Caen, where William planned to build a mighty citadel if his efforts in England proved fruitful. We had visited Matilda's abbey of La Trinite and were riding back to our accommodation when we heard people in the distance shouting in mingled wonder and fear. Night had fallen, the dome of the firmament strewn with stars, and the alleys and lanes of Caen were full of creeping shadows and who knew what else. Roger loosened his sword in its sheath.

"I do not like the sound of those cries," he said grimly, nodding to our guards to draw closer. "I wonder if there is rioting, although I have not heard tales of any unrest."

As we rounded a corner into the torch-lit market square, we saw groups of peasants, soldiers and merchants gathered together around the central stone cross, pointing up at the sky. Some wept, some sank to their knees on the grimy cobbles and prayed. There were tears, there were exhortations to God and the Virgin. It was no riot.

Apprehensive, I turned my gaze to the heavens and a gasp tore from my lips. I clutched at my husband's cold hand. Above us, clear against the heavens, raged a comet, its three-forked tail streaking away into the southern sky.

"It-it is an omen!" I heard men cry, and in my heart, I too felt it was, though an omen of good or evil I could not say.

"What do you think it means, Roger?" I murmured.

"Only God Almighty can say," he murmured. "But such heavenly events often betoken great change, it is said. Change—as in a new King come to claim his rightful Kingdom."

Shortly after Roger and I witnessed the bright-tailed comet, I returned home to Castle Montgomery, leaving my husband and the

Duchess to continue to prepare for William's invasion of England. Part of me would have preferred to stay in that atmosphere of tense excitement, but Roger convinced me that a firm hand was needed to control our numerous lands. Both of us away from our domains was not to be borne overlong; there were always greedy petty lords out to make trouble and unlawfully loot villages and even seize minor castles.

"I will call for you as soon as I can." He kissed my cheek as I climbed into a litter to bear me in haste to Montgomery. "And mayhap, if all goes as planned for William, we will sail together to England one day."

"I will pray for a victorious outcome every night." I clutched his forearm and gave him a hard kiss on the cheek in return. "I will pray that winds are fair in the Narrow Sea and that Norman swords and Norman horses will prevail against the long-haired barbarians of England."

With that, I climbed into the litter, my ladies circling me in their rich clothes, and I gave the signal for the entourage to depart. After several days of travel, familiar towers appeared through a haze of pink cherry blossoms drifting in the warm breezes of late Spring, and I knew I was home again, ready to slip into my usual job of chatelaine and mother.

But not for long…

In late September, William sailed out of St Valery on *Mora* with an immense army that consisted of Normans, Bretons and Frenchmen. He managed to leave just in time, for talk of desertion amongst the troops had run rife—they had grumbled, stewing in their tents, that the wait for departure was too long, that God frowned on William's enterprise because He did not send ample winds to drive on the ships.

Yet at last, near dusk on a clear, cool night, those blessed winds had risen, filling the great painted sails of *Mora*, and without a moment's hesitation, William had called for the ships to depart, ignoring the approaching nightfall. A horn was blown from *Mora*'s prow, its lonely call echoing across the harbour from wall to wall, and a lantern was hung on the mast to cut into the growing gloom and signal to the other vessels in the Duke's flotilla.

The race to claim England was on.

After the departure of the fleet, I knew nought more for a long while. Even Roger, aiding Matilda in the regency, had little knowledge of what was taking place over the Narrow Sea. Then on a stormy, leaf-strewn October eve, he arrived unexpectedly at Castle Montgomery late at night, slathered with mud from a hard ride from Caen.

"Why are you here, with no warning?" I cried, as I pulled a mantle around my shoulders and ran into the bailey to greet him. "Is it joy or evil news you bring? I am terrified to hear…and yet I must listen!"

Dismounting, Roger flung his arms around me and lifted me off my feet, whirling me around like a young maid, not a matron who was the mother of many children. "I want to be the first to bring you the joyous news, Mabel. The Duke has been successful. England is won!"

"Tell me all!" I dragged him up the stairs to the solar, where I shouted to the servants to stoke the fire and bring warm spiced wine for their master. Divesting himself of his rain-splattered travelling cloak and muddy boots, Roger sat before the fire, stretching out his legs, looking happy and content.

"So…" I knelt at his feet. "What news has come to Normandy"

"It is a great tale," said Roger. "Troubadours shall sing of it for a thousand years or more."

"Well, sing it or speak it—do not keep me in suspense!"

Roger's fingers danced on the stem of his golden wine goblet. "After leaving Normandy, William sailed to a place called Pevensey in England, where stood the ruins of an old Roman fort. The Duke said he would use the old castrum for a base. Some men did not fancy dwelling near the old Roman dead and muttered that using such a place would bring bad luck. When William disembarked the *Mora* and stumbled on the rough terrain, falling to his knees with hands splayed upon the earth many muttered that the ancient dead had spoken, that it was an evil omen, warding our forces off…"

"Evil omen," I sneered. "A simple fall that could happen to anyone on damp ground."

"Indeed, and the wiser soldiers knew his stumble was of no consequence. One stalwart knight cried out to the Duke, whose hands were all muddy with earth, "*My lord, England is in your hands—and so you shall be King!*" His words calmed some of the fearful rumours and gave men new heart."

"Was King Harold waiting with his army? Did he quail to see the Duke and his great host?"

Roger smiled but shook his head. "No one was there at first. The English army had been engaged with the Northmen and had defeated Harald Hardrada at Stamford Bridge."

"A victory! That must have filled him with foolish pride."

"It did, and foolish confidence too. But most of all, it made the English army weary. The Duke, eager to engage before Harold recruited fresh soldiers, marched without delay from Hastings to a place called Senlac Hill—and there my Lord and the usurper Harold clashed. The battle lasted almost from dawn to dusk, the Saxons fighting with their axes, on foot behind their shield walls, while William's mounted knight charged with lances after the archers and crossbowmen had wreaked as much carnage as possible."

"And in the end?"

"To finish it, William played a ruse on his foe. He pretended he was beaten and in retreat…then turned on his advancing enemies and slaughtered them. Harold was struck in the face by an arrow, and then the Duke's mounted knights surrounded him. He was hacked to death on the spot, his corpse so mangled it is said his mistress, Edith Swansneck, identified him only by the tattoos upon his skin."

I laughed; the fire crackled.

"England had never seen such slaughter, it is said. The fields gleamed blood-red and corpses lay strewn from east to west as far as the eye could see. William ordered all his fallen to be promptly buried with the priest speaking words over them, but the Saxons…" He shook his head again. "He left them for the wolves and the worms owing to their support of a usurper."

"That is harsh," I said, then smiled, "but just, and I dare say, as they deserved."

"He would not even allow Harold's mother to take his body for burial—not even for the dead king's weight in gold."

"Harold was half a heathen with his long hair and tattooed flesh," I said. "Let the wolves have him or let him be burnt on a pyre as the heathens did long ago." I reached up to drape my arm across my husband's knees. "Roger, you have been a good servant to the Duke, a trusted one; what gains do you think will come to us?"

Reaching down, he stroked my chin. His deep blue eyes glittered in the smoky gloom. "I do not know yet. William will be crowned upon Christmas Day in an Abbey in the city of London. It is known as Westminster, and the Confessor is buried therein. A crown has been commissioned, like to that of wise Solomon, wrought of gold and set with a ruby and other precious gemstones."

"Christmas Day! That is not so far off. I fear the weather will be too dire to attempt a late crossing. We will have to miss the event, which displeases me. Why could he have not waited a little longer?"

"William wanted to be crowned with Matilda at his side, but his English advisors said no, he must consolidate his position as king without delay. Otherwise, great unrest will break out. The English, what remains of them, are not happy, Mabel. They call him tyrant and...bastard."

I veiled my eyes with downcast lashes, amused to think of William's anger at hearing his birth mocked. "Oh, he will hate that. The barbarians daring to name him 'Bastard.' He will punish them..."

"He will if they do not come to heel, "agreed Roger. "I expect he will return to Normandy next year when and if it is safe to do so. Then we will know what else he requires from us, and what, if any, rewards might come our way."

"There had better be rewards. You worked hard for his cause, even if you did not wield a sword in battle. You have counselled Duchess Matilda well, have you not?"

"I have...or at least I think so. She is a strong woman, though, and I never know exactly what goes through her head. Rather like you, my sweet Mabel!"

Filled with mirth, I threw back my head, and Roger drank the last dregs of his wine and drew me up from the floor onto his lap, where we soon forgot about bloody battles and kings raised and unworthy kings trampled into the dust.

Duke William returned to Normandy in spring of the next year, the crown of England sitting uneasily on his brow—but still there, uncontested by any English prince.

CHAPTER FIFTEEN

I joined Roger to welcome William in Caen, which he had sworn to make a new capital. He was not in a good mood when he arrived; not only did he look older, harder, the stubble rough on his face, there was a cruelness in his mouth and the set of his jaw. His struggles in England against those who loathed him had taken their toll. He reminded me of a more intelligent version of my sire Talvas—the hard, unyielding shield.

The first thing William did as he entered the hall of the half-built new castle was stare around him, clenching and unclenching his sword-hardened hands. His hair was mussed, his face dark with stubble, and his eyes bloodshot, the irises almost black with anger.

"M-my Lord Duke. My Lord King." Recognising his friend's rage, Roger stepped towards him in concern.

"*Where is she!*" William bellowed, his face turning a dark, unhealthy purple. "Where is that bitch!"

"My Lord?" Roger asked again, perplexed.

William reached out and grasped the front of my husband's tunic, yanking him close. My hand flew to my mouth, stifling a gasp, afraid the newly-crowned king would strike his old boon companion.

"Matilda! Where is Matilda…the whore!"

Had he gone mad? Silence fell in the hall and all the courtiers stared, appalled. Matilda, of all women, was no harlot; she was deeply pious, and her morals were impeccable. The worst ever said about her was that she pined for an English noble called Brihtric years ago, but he had rejected her long looks and blandishments, earning her lifelong enmity. In William's absence, she had done nought to shame herself and had worked as hard as any man to keep the duchy peaceful and prosperous.

"I have heard rumours, Roger," William growled, pacing the floor like a beast ready to pounce. "When I reached the dock in *Mora*, a knight was waiting to tell me a tale…a terrible tale. He wept and cringed as he said the awful words; words that have stabbed me to the heart! This knight told me that Matilda has sullied our marriage bed with another!"

"And you believe this slanderous knight?" cried Roger, disbelieving. "William, your Grace, whatever you have been told, it is nonsense! I have been in her Grace's presence for most of your absence, and when I was not, de Beaumont or Hugh d'Avranches were there. She would never betray you anyway; she is the most virtuous of women!"

"You could not have been there every hour, every minute of every day!" William smashed his fist against the wall, cracking a wooden strut. He was quite terrifying, his jealousy consuming him like a flame. I found it oddly…arousing. "The knight had no reason to lie and took his life into his own hands when he bore me such news…Where is my faithless wife?"

"I am here, and you do me wrong in front of this high company." Ashen-faced, Matilda appeared in a door arch, obviously astounded by her husband's accusations. Rumours had always run rife that their marriage was a tempestuous one, even sometimes coming to blows…but never had a dispute become as public and damaging as this. Not since their early meeting where William grabbed her braids and dragged her from her horse.

Matilda stepped over the threshold, shimmering pale, her steps surprisingly confident despite the angry man who stood, bull-like, glowering at her, the veins standing out like twisted cords on neck and brow.

In anticipation of her lord's return, the Duchess had been preparing for bed. She had thrown a robe over her shift and her hair hung free, silver-gold to past her hips. She was past her mid-thirties now but looked younger than her age, still beautiful and desirable.

The sight of her standing thus, tinged by torchlight, seemed to inflame the Duke even further. Grasping her by the wrist, he yanked her towards him. "You will pay for this outrage, woman! I swear, by God, you will not play me false!"

"Name my accuser!" she cried as William dragged her down the hall. "Do that at least, my husband! Let me know who has spread these outrageous lies!"

"Grimoult de Plessis, who stayed behind with the garrison. He wept as he told me."

"Grimoult!" she laughed bitterly. "That ill-favoured churl! He loves you not, William. He fought against you at Val-es-Dunes, do you not remember? He seeks to make trouble between us! He has ever borne a grudge despite his pretty words of loyalty! Tears—they were tears of laughter to see you fall for his falsehoods!"

William was not listening, however. Eyes fixed and glassy like those of a madman, he dragged her from the hall, across the expanse of the bailey and into the streets of Caen. Desperate, Roger and his fellow counsellors rushed after him, begging him to calm down, to see sense, but it was as if his all-consuming rage had blocked his ears. I ran alongside too, amongst Matilda's women, who were begging him to have mercy and proclaiming her innocence.

In the busy street the Duke halted, shouting for a squire to bring a horse. My stomach churned and one of the ladies fainted. Surely, he was not going to have Matilda torn apart by horses, a barbaric custom even if she was guilty—which everyone except the Duke knew she was not.

But fortunately, only a single horse was brought, a swaybacked nag who had hauled barrels and crates to the castle pantry. With a sneer, William grabbed his wife's long fair tresses and tied them to the horse's unkempt tail.

The gathering crowd, at first shocked and perplexed, was beginning to turn ugly. I had noted from time in my father's company that when violence began, some men, who were otherwise docile as lambs, would turn into wolves baying for blood and destruction.

And so it was on this ill-starred day.

The men and women filtering amidst the houses, churches and little alleys of Caen began to hiss and boo—not at William but at the innocent Matilda. Screeches of 'whore' and even 'witch' rang out, cruel and full of threat. It seemed almost unbelievable for only a few days before William's return from England, the very same folk had hurled flowers and shouted blessings when Matilda rode past with her entourage.

Face still purple, a vein throbbing dangerously on his temple, now grabbed hold of Matilda's loose robe. A knife appeared in his hand and the crowd gasped, fearing blood might be shed. Instead, he slashed and hacked at her garments, leaving her standing near-naked in her ripped and torn under-kirtle. The rent bed robe was tossed into the mob, who tore it apart, trying to get pieces for keepsakes.

William smacked the waiting nag on its dirty, fly-bitten rump. "Off you go; a pair of old jades to be paraded!"

The horse ambled forward, dragging Duchess Matilda behind it in her rent kirtle. "My lord...your Grace, you must not do this thing!" Roger cried desperately, trying to grasp at the mare's bridle and halt the shameful procession, but William thrust out at him with a burly arm, shoving him so hard he careered into me.

"Out of my way, Montgomery!" the Duke shouted at Roger. "Do not presume on our friendship!"

Whirling away, he thundered up the road behind his shamed wife, calling down curses on her supposed harlotry. As for Matilda, she gritted her teeth and did not weep, which made my admiration of the woman grow. She was small and delicate to behold, yet her will was iron. She was not guilty of any wrongdoing and would never admit to it, even if such an admission and a plea for clemency might mean her release.

Up to the old High Cross with its broken head the sickening procession trundled. Flung stones skittered across the cobbles and obscenities were shouted. By the time the steps of the cross were reached, William's visage was beginning to gain some normality; he now looked merely weary, perhaps even a trifle contrite and doubtful. Reaching out, he untangled his wife's hair from the horse's tail. Matilda stumbled up the base of the cross, her feet black from mud and bleeding. She clung to the pillar, staring heavenward. "I swear before God Almighty that I have never done wrong to my lord and husband! If I speak falsehood may God smite me down!"

The crowd fell silent, hoping for some divine action. Angels...demons...lightning bolts from on high. The sky remained blue. A loud gasp, the sound of a mass of held breaths exhaled, filled the air.

Matilda turned to William. Reaching down, she ripped away the remains of her ruined kirtle and stood unclad save for her long, wind-tangled hair. "I came to you a virgin bride, and I stand before you now as I did then—innocent. No hands save yours have touched this body you see before you. If you still believe lies about my chastity, smite me down now for God has not...and He will not for God knows I have done no wrong."

William's lips began to move and suddenly he looked as if he might weep. "Wife...Matilda...What possessed me?"

Roger dashed up the steps of the cross and flung his cloak around Matilda just as her knees began to buckle as the horror of her situation overwhelmed her at last. William put his hands to his brow. "Get a cart for the Duchess!" he roared to his men. "Now, *now*!"

A cart was brought and Matilda placed inside. Roger beckoned for me to ride alongside the Duchess and care for her. I sat there in silence as we all returned to the castle and the crowds slipped away into the side streets—*like rats*, I thought.

Once in the castle, Matilda was taken to her bed and a physician called. A priest arrived too and closeted himself in her chamber. William was pacing in the Great Hall, looking half-mad, tearing at his hair, shouting, "God should punish me! I am the wicked one, the one who should be shamed! I should walk out unclad in the streets with paupers and beggars hurling waste at me as I pass! Christ! Christ! What have I done?"

"What is it that ails him?" I asked Roger as we watched, horrified, from the shadows at the back of the hall. "Has he gone mad? Did some Saxon bash his helm with his axe during his battles?"

"It has not been easy for him in England," said Roger gruffly. "Even at his Coronation, it is said he trembled halfway through, fearing an attack even in that holy place. William *trembling*—it is hard to imagine, is it not? Every day he fears the assassin's knife, the loss of his crown. The English are fractious and bloodthirsty; long-haired, hard-bitten northern men who have the courage of ten lions when the drink is in them—and they love to drink! Worry and uncertainty have taken their toll, and hence he did not even trust his own wife and was inclined to listen to foul lies."

"Surely he no longer believes Matilda put the cuckold's horns on him."

"No, his senses have returned in regards to that falsehood. He has sent out a party to find the treacherous knight, Grimoult du Plessis—and skin him alive for his perfidy."

I nodded, understanding the Duke's desire for vengeance well. I had taken my own revenge on Arnold d'Eschafour and his father. But still I was worried, not for the Duke and his Duchess, but for the families of Montgomery and Belleme. "Out in the town, he pushed you aside, Roger, and spoke harsh words. You—you do think you are still in favour, don't you? I have been so looking forward to any rewards…"

Roger cast me an unexpectedly glacial stare and I closed my mouth with a snap. "Be silent, wife. This is not the time for you to prattle about obtaining more wealth! A terrible thing has happened today and who knows what its consequences may be. Go to your chamber and stay there till I call you—sometimes I loathe the way you seem to savour mischief and unseemly behaviour."

My face flushed and I wanted to rail at him for being so blunt, so censorious—but at that moment, my attention was drawn to William, who had kicked his chair of estate halfway across the room. "What have I done!" he roared again to no one, ripping down a wall-hanging and stabbing it with his dagger.

Roger's fingers bit into my soft upper arm. "Out of here, Mabel. Now!"

Grasping my heavy skirts, I rushed to my quarters as William, Duke of Normandy, new King of England, ranted and raged like a madman in the hall that had become more like Hell.

The following days in Caen were strange. The Duke and Matilda were reconciled, appearing together to sit on a dais side by side in their jewels and finery. Matilda was peaked and pale but her expression bland and emotionless as that of a marble statue. William had regained his composure and his anger had burnt out; around his sword hilt was wrapped what appeared to be a dusky reddish cloth— the courtiers whispered that it was the flayed skin of the poison-tongued du Plessis.

I became nervous and ill at ease for all the reasons I had vainly tried to explain to Roger—until, at last, after a long council meeting my husband sent a message asking me to meet him in the castle's herb gardens. Under a drizzling grey sky I waited, my red cloak damp, the scent of lavender, of rosemary, of mint pungent around me. I was expecting the worst, for I had scarcely seen Roger since he had sent me from the Great Hall during William's fit of anguished insanity. I had spent the days in boredom with my women, or sometimes with my son, Robert, who was still close friends with the younger Robert Curthose, William's eldest son.

Indeed, earlier that day, I had sat and watched them spar with blunted swords, grunting and heaving as they bashed at each other. Young Robert had taken a scratch; my Robert had mocked him for grimacing and the boy leapt up and smacked him in the face, bloodying his nose.

Robert's face had frozen and he lunged at his opponent with murderous eyes. I leapt up and dragged him back. "You forget yourself, my son. You do not strike your Lord's son in anger."

"But he hit me!" Robert was wiping his nose on his sleeve.

"And you cut his arm."

"That was his fault…He was too slow, mother!"

"Be quiet." I cast him my kerchief to mop up the red flow from his nose. "Your bawling is unseemly. *Lord* Robert…" I made sure to emphasise the words 'lord', to both please the lad and hopefully curb the excesses of my hot-headed son. "Are you hurt?"

The scratch on young Curthose's arm was but little, a few red drops oozing from it like jewels, and he had looked embarrassed. "No, madam, it is nought. I apologise to Robert for hitting him, and to you for being so uncouth in front of a high-born lady."

"I will live," I chuckled. "I am the daughter of a man they called 'the shield' for his hardness, and I am much like him, despite my weak sex."

"I hit out in anger, that was why I was clumsy," Robert Curthose suddenly blurted out. "I was pretending Robert was my sire… I wish he had stayed in England and not come home. He hates me because I am short while he dotes on my sisters and my brother William. That makes Will feel disdain towards me…And then there is my mother. I heard how he shamed her as if she were a harlot. And she's not— she's *not*."

"I believe you. I do." I had patted his shoulder, knowing with a strange prescience that this one of Matilda's brood, beloved of his mother, a scapegoat for the Duke's cruel japes, would one day bring his father grief...

I was shaken from my musings about the Duke's son as Roger trudged, heavy-eyed, into the garden, crushing tender plants beneath his boots. He was unshaven; the scent of old wine clung to him. Male deliberations, I'd found, were driven by much strong drink.

"Mabel," he began. "I have important news...."

"Bad news?" Raindrops stuck to my brows and lashes, dripped from my nose. The rain was coming down harder now; drizzle turning to downpour.

"That depends on if you like lots of rain—*this* accursed weather, nearly every day!" He held his arms up and stared skyward as the rain descended in sheets, hissing onto the grass, soaking his hair and jewelling on his brows.

"I do not know what you mean, Roger? Speak clearly...unless you cannot because you are still drunk." I eyed him suspiciously, ignoring the fact that I was getting as wet as he. In the distance, thunder boomed.

"Mabel, shortly we shall be called to depart for England. Duchess Matilda has asked for you to be amongst her women at her Coronation in Westminster Abbey. And for my efforts in keeping Normandy peaceful during William's absence, I have been granted the Rape of Arundel, which is a rich land in England's south. He also wishes our daughter Maude should wed his brother, Robert of Mortain without further delay. I have given my final agreement to the match and I know you will have no objections. Mabel, we have what you always dreamed of—we now truly walk in the circles of the great."

CHAPTER SIXTEEN

"They must learn to love me," said Matilda. "I am their Queen." A rock flew, hurled by some grimy-faced brat on the roadside. It bounced off the axle of the wagon's wheel and plopped into a deep pool of rainwater.

We were in England for Matilda's Coronation.

It was, of course, as we had been warned by our husbands, raining heavily.

"You should have those little savages whipped for their insult." I glared at the Saxon children as they scuttled away into the thick hedgerows.

"I would not be seen as overly harsh." Matilda cradled her growing belly; the strife between her and William had ended and their marriage had borne fruit once more, a child of reconciliation and hope. "My babe will be born on English soil and, if it is a boy, the folk of this land will hopefully look to him as their prince. If not and they continue to rebel, then William shall deal with them and he will not show the gentleness and mercy I have."

I harumphed, sitting miserably in the wagon with its damp-soaked cover. My son Hugh, who, as Roger's second son, would one day inherit his sire's English lands, was snivelling away as he lay on a pillow, his expression one of crushing boredom. Across from him, one of William and Matilda's sons, Richard, looked equally ill-tempered as he toyed with dice made from rock crystal. We were on our way to Westminster at Whitsuntide, there to prepare for the Matilda's Coronation.

"I do not like it here," Richard opined sulkily, throwing the dice from one hand to the other. One fell into the hay strewn around to soften the ride; Matilda's little lap-dog snapped at it and received a clout on its nose.

"You are a prince here, do not forget that." Matilda's picked up her dog, cradled it. It bared its teeth at Richard.

"I don't care about my being a prince. Neither do they..." The boy gestured out a flap of the sheltering canvas at a group of peasants congregating on the roadside, the man scowling, uncouth and barbarous, his wife like a great red-faced ox with a swaddled babe in arms and three more babes snatching at filthy skirts. "They hate us, mother; they hate what father did. They call him a usurper. And, you...they call you..."

Matilda's eyes glittered and she grasped her son's shoulder, pulling him towards her. Griffon sprang away, still growling at Richard. "They call me *what*...and how would you know?"

Richard's cheeks filled with vivid colour and the second crystal dice clattered to the floorboards. "Yesterday I heard some Englishmen on the roadside laughing and pointing. I asked the Abbot of St Edmondsbury, who knew some of their tongue, what they were muttering. He did not want to tell me at first, but I nagged at him until he relented. Mother, they call you 'that strange woman...'"

Embarrassed, he hung his head.

"Well, it could have been worse." I tried to inject some light cheer.

Matilda pushed her son away. "No more tittle-tattle from you, Richard. You are worse than your sisters. It is unseemly for a boy to spread such silly talk, especially one of your rank."

As Richard resumed grizzling in the corner, I peered out from the canvas covering through the curtain of rain; I could see walls now, poorly kept, fragments of broken stone that may have been Roman they looked so eroded and ancient. Church bells rang fitfully in the distance and the air was rank with smoke, dung and the scent of murky water. Many soldiers were tramping about, the rain sliding down their conical helmets. They looked so cold and ridiculous I stifled a laugh with my sleeve.

"I think we must be at the place they called London," I said to the Duchess. "Thank God in heaven; I could use a hot bath before my fingers and toes freeze off..." I hesitated and then, horrified, craned my head around to stare at Matilda. "Your Grace...they will have baths and hot water here, won't they?"

She pursed her lips, ill concealing her amusement. "I am sure something can be found for your ease, Lady Mabel."

At Westminster I was reunited with Roger, who had sailed for England in King William's company some months before I departed with Matilda. "What do you think, wife?" he asked as he stood before me arrayed in the richest cloth—damson colour, fringed with gold.

"You look a popinjay," I retorted "And if it is England you ask me about—does the rain *never* stop?"

I glared out the narrow little window in our temporary lodgings; the rain beat on the horn casements. We were in old King Edward's Palace near the Abbey, both crammed together on a muddy little islet named Thorney Island. Everything seemed old and dim, smelling of damp and the river, and the fading paintings on the walls were of saints and apostles—but all done with a Saxon flare, making them look heathenish and strange to my Norman eyes.

"You are homesick already?" asked Roger. "I am rather enjoying myself here."

"I can see that," I said, nodding towards his lavish outfit, "but I feel…I felt it all along as I rode here with the Queen, that the land itself broods, hating our kind, hating *me*…As soon as the Coronation is over, I wish to return to Normandy."

"You know I will often be required to attend my lord King here," Roger warned. "He wishes it."

"Sacrifices must be made. It is not safe for us both to tarry here too long. Our children are back home, save for Hugh, and many men would happily steal our daughters and our lands."

"Ah, of course, the children." He rubbed his chin. "Our Maud is settled with Mortain, but we have been somewhat remiss with matches for the others. Yes, perhaps, it is wise if you return home and begin work on finding suitable mates—oh, and mayhap give one to the church. It might do well for you to keep an eye on our Rob as well; William's Robert has been granted his first taste of power looking after Normandy in his parents' absence, but Rob is that bit older, and he has, at times, an almost malicious streak…"

"I have no idea where he gets that from," I said meekly. "But fear you not, he will bow to his mother if he knows what is good for him. But let us not ponder on these matters—it is a time for us to see a Queen made!"

Leaving our quarters in the Palace, we proceeded under heavy guard to the nearby Abbey of Westminster. Folk gathered in the alleys, craning, many openly hostile in demeanour; the banks of the boggy little island were three deep and boats scudded all over the flat brown water beyond. Some of the nearest onlookers spat. "Filthy curs," Roger grumbled as our guards formed a ring of steel around us.

In the dim, smoky confines of the Abbey of St Peter, a Saxon bishop, Ealdred of York, stood waiting for Matilda. As the congregation took its place around the fat pillars, she was led into the church and up the long nave to the high altar where she prostrated herself before God, her golden robes burning bright against the dark flagstones. When at last she rose from prayer, the Bishop anointed her with the Holy Oil and set a ring upon her finger, symbolising her union not only with the King but with the land over which she now ruled. The old Matilda was forgotten and gone, no one would dare mention the day William slung her in the mud before their marriage or stripped her before the eyes of all men upon his return from victory at Senlac Hill. She was now chosen and sanctified by God himself.

Slowly, reverently, her new crown was brought up to the altar on a tasselled cushion; its gems burned like lambent flames amidst coils of candle smoke. Bishop Ealdred raised it in both hands, holding it aloft, then placed it firmly upon Matilda's brow, all the while chanting the holy words of *laudes*.

Laetatur gens Anglica domini imperio regenda et regina... The English are blessed by the rule of their Queen.

The words boomed through the forest of pillars. I wondered if those self-same English could hear them all across Thorney Island, and if there was even one amongst them that agreed with the sentiment.

The banquet that followed in the nearby hall was lavish. William and Matilda sat on the dais, both wearing their crowns. As the company took its place at the benches, a trumpet blared and into the chamber galloped a mounted knight, full dressed in helm and mail coat, holding a sword aloft like a silver flame.

Rising in his stirrups, he cried, "My name, my lords and ladies, is Marmion, and I am the Champion of our gracious King and Queen! If any man denies our mighty sovereign William and his wife Matilda are not the rightful rulers of England, I proclaim him a false traitor and a speaker of lies, and I, as Champion, do challenge him to a fight to the death!"

A hush fell over Westminster's Great Hall. The few Englishmen in attendance looked astonished and perplexed by Marmion's challenge, the likes of which they had never seen before at a Coronation feast. No one spoke out against the monarchs, and no one had expected they would. The invited English might have held their grudges, but they were sorely outnumbered and so remained silent—sombre, pinch-faced clergymen like Ealdred and Stigand, Archbishop of Canterbury, and the remaining English Earls, Edwin, Morcar and Waltheof, all strange, uncouth fellows with streaming hair and moustaches and eyes like sharp spears.

William's brother, Bishop Odo, who was seated at the table next to Roger, gave a throaty chuckle as he saw me inspecting the sullen, out-of-place English nobles. "I see you gaze upon the wildmen of the woods," he laughed. "Just wait till the wine really starts flowing. They will eat until they spew and imbibe mead till they fall on the floor in a stupor."

"Normans and Frenchmen both have similar habits," I said. "I suspect it is a man's failing rather than solely an English vice."

"Oh, but these...these *men* are very much worse," said Odo. "However, this much is true—most of William's army has adopted their dissolute ways after observing them. It's extraordinary! No discipline, and can you imagine eschewing good Norman wine to binge on sour English ale?"

I smiled at Odo without much warmth, dabbing at my lips with a bleached linen napkin. The Bishop was hardly one to talk of a lack of discipline—a man of God known for his harsh punishments and numerous mistresses. Still, I could scarcely blame him for his follies. He was a young man who had been chosen for the church against his natural inclination, and he was a warrior who fought at Senlac with a steal-bound club since a Bishop was not permitted to kill with the sword.

At the end of the hall, a group of minstrels started to play a lively air. Cries of delight came from the tables as servers emerged from the kitchens carrying the salt cellar for the royal table, followed by loaves of bread, pottage and a rich white soup called *dillegrout*. This first course was followed by wild boar, venison pie and wild salmon in sauce, then kid, fawn, capons and samplings of wild birds. Lastly, there was a pie shaped into a crown and a sea of tarts and pastries on gilt dishes.

After the dining was over and the candles burnt to stub dripping pale yellow wax, William and Matilda rose in regal splendour and left the Great Hall together. The Norman nobility, the Bishops and other clergy processed behind them, leaving the English nobles to follow in the rear.

As Roger and I walked across the torch and lantern-lit courtyard beyond, the crowds began to separate as celebrants headed for their lodgings. As we exited the ring of torchlight, I became aware of footsteps loud on the stones behind us and glanced uneasily over my shoulder.

Drawing close, were two of the English Earls, Edwin and Morcar, who had, at least purportedly, bent the knee to William. Their sister had been dead King Harold's wife; Roger had informed me that both men had clamoured to be elected king when Harold was slain but their claims were unanimously rejected. So, seeking to make the best of a bad situation, they swore loyalty to the Conqueror at Barking, once the crown was firmly on his head.

The one named Morcar, darker-visaged than the majority of his Saxon kin with his straggling raven-black hair blowing out in greasy wings, gave me a grin I deemed disrespectful. Immediately I disliked him and put my nose in the air. Shivering, I yanked my cloak a little closer around my shoulders and strode on with what I hoped was bold dignity.

The two Saxons, swift on their long, lanky legs, moved past us, Morcar bowing his head in a cocky acknowledgement that reeked of insolence rather than any kind of respect. A wave of fear swelled over me, even with Roger at my side, and I wished my pretty little dagger was bound to my leg, but weapons had been forbidden for the attendees of both coronation and feast.

Fortunately, the Saxons kept on moving and disappeared into the night fog that had risen from the great turgid River Thames, coiling like a serpent around Thorney Island and cutting it off from the main body of London, that the Saxons called Lundenwic.

"Beware of those two," I murmured to Roger, nodding in the direction the Englishman had vanished. "I would bet my life they are fomenting trouble."

"All is settled now; they have sworn allegiance," said Roger. "They know what punishments will befall if they break faith with their new King."

"Oh, I have heard about William's punishments—gouging out traitor's eyes, cutting off their hands, raping their women... But when have such punishments ever truly deterred men who might seek a throne for themselves?"

By my shoulder, Roger sighed, his breath a misty cloud before his mouth. "You speak truth. I did not like the looks they gave either, and look, they have left the palace compound, heading for the bridge over the river into London. I wonder where they are heading with such haste. On the morrow, I will speak with the King."

Sure enough, my suspicions proved correct and before many months had passed, troubles broke out in the north, fomented by oath-breaking Morcar and Edwin who were joined by Edgar the Atheling and Gospatrick of Northumbria. William marched away in haste to deal with the uprising, pausing to command that great castles be built at Nottingham, Exeter and Lincoln. Once he reached the walls of York, he decreed that two castles would be erected to defend the city. The rebellion against him soon failed, and Edwin and Morcar submitted to William once more—miraculously keeping both hands and their heads.

Despite her advanced state of pregnancy, Queen Matilda had insisted on travelling north to meet up with her victorious husband. However, babies heed not the actions of kings, and she ended up lying-in near Selby, where she produced a lusty boy who was named Henry.

Fortunately, I had not been asked to travel north with Matilda's entourage. Roger had sent me to his new lands at Arundel, to oversee the beginning stages of building a great castle there—his castle, *our* castle, while he rode against the treacherous earls with William. In my care, I had my son Hugh and Matilda and William's son Richard, who was in a perpetual sulk because his mother had refused permission for him to ride out at his sire's side.

It was a dangerous and fraught time, even for me; many Saxon hovels and halls need to be cleared before the castle-building could commence, and the little town below the hill was full of displaced peasants who glowered and murmured threats under their breath. One was caught calling me *"hore"* in his harsh, cawing tongue; my Chamberlain, when pressed, told me it was a word for a *putain*, harlot, prostitute. I had the insolent sot whipped and threatened worse, but my threats seemed to fan the flames and at last I retreated behind the rising wooden walls of the castle and let my soldiers fend off the angry English raging up the hillside.

Grudgingly I had to admit England was as fair a land as Normandy—green and fertile, full of rolling downs dotted with the shepherds' flocks, but it also had a dark undertone, as if within the earthy bosom of the Land itself there dwelt ancient spirits, nameless and faceless, that loved not the tread of foreign feet. The English were very superstitious and had many strange rites as if they were still pagans, wearing masks on certain feast days and dancing coarse, rustic dances while twining straw into dollies which they dropped into the furrows of their fields or slashed with honed sickles. Their forests were eerie, huge stands of oak, alder and birch lit by green-tinged light, overrun by bloodthirsty outlaws and, according to local lore, fey creatures, elves, who shot at men with flint-tipped arrows. I had even seen such an arrowhead, brought to me by my son, who had found one while digging for 'treasure' in a mound upon our lands. It was beautiful, smooth to the touch as if newly wrought, and holding it up to the wan light the sun shone through its translucent heart. I would not let him keep it, of course, and buried it beneath a stone marked with a cross; the arrowhead made me shudder, despite its beauty—it was a fell object, not of the normal world. It was a heathen thing. An *English* thing...

How I longed for the civility of Norman life away from the endless mist and rain, the haunted woods and hollow hills, the glaring and fractious peasantry!

At the end of the year, I got my wish. Having put down the northern uprising to his satisfaction, King William announced his intention to hold his Christmas Court back in Caen.

In early December Roger and I departed with the King and Queen and the new little Prince, Henry. The crossing of the Narrow Sea was rough and I spent most of my time spilling my guts into a copper bowl, but I did not care.

I almost kissed the ground of the grubby quay when I reached the shores of Normandy.

I would never travel to England again.

Let Roger use the country to increase his wealth and to occasionally exercise his sword-arm. I had my own pleasures to attend to at home.

CHAPTER SEVENTEEN

In 1070 Uncle Yves finally shuffled out of this mortal world and went to heaven…or wherever it was men like Yves went. I would not like to speculate. At long last, the entire Belleme inheritance was mine. *Mine.* I was the wealthiest woman in Normandy, excepting Queen Matilda herself.

I set about making brilliant matches for my children, to ensure they lived the lifestyle to which they were born. Robert was betrothed to young Agnes of Ponthieu, but she was just a child and many years would pass before she was ripe for the marriage bed. Robert cared not, and went about merrily wenching and whoring with his companion, Lord Robert. Roger, my third son, wed Almodis, daughter of Count Aldebert II of Poitou, a wealthy girl who was the heir to her childless brother, Count Boso. Her countenance reminded me a little of a rat, but no matter—the money was the main thing. Hugh, Arnulf and Phillip I left unwed since Roger had written to say they might benefit by marrying English heiresses, which would increase their possessions as younger sons. He would send me the details of potential brides when he had them. Sybil was betrothed to Robert Fitzhamon, Lord of Cruelly, and Mabel to Gervaise de Châteauneuf. Emma, ever the quiet, biddable one, went to a convent as had always been her destiny.

Across the Narrow Sea, Roger remained in high favour with King William, spending much of his time in England. As time passed, we grew apart somewhat, but so it often happens in a marriage when age replaced youthful lusts, and I, growing older and more ambitious for my children, did not mourn that distancing overmuch. He did return home occasionally to tell of the foreign wealth he now possessed and how large Arundel Castle had grown, its keep one of the mightiest in England. William had made him Earl of Shrewsbury so now I was *Countess* Mabel de Belleme de Montgomery, not just 'Lady.' The King had also granted him manors all through south and middle England, making him among the richest of William's supporters. Ah, yes, it was good to have friends in very high places…

Not all was good for my family, however. The alliance between my son Robert of Belleme and Robert Curthose, which I had tried so hard to foster, blossomed indeed, but not in a good way. The nasty little man, for so Curthose had become, had his own separate court full of lechery and vice, where the young Normans wore hair long like the Saxons and cavorted with harlots of both sexes. There, he jealously brooded over the Duchy, which he thought Willian should grant him without delay. "You already have a crown, sire!" he whined.

It all ended terribly when Curthose got into a fight with his two younger brothers, William and Henry, who emptied a piss-pot on his head from an upstairs window of their lodgings. This childish tussle had resulted in an inflamed Robert Curthose riding to Rouen with our Rob and his other close companions—where they tried, vainly, to storm the castle.

This action was, of course, high treason, and could have seen my son imprisoned or worse. However, he managed to flee into exile alongside the unworthy little swine Robert Curthose who from then on I called by his other insulting nickname—*Gambaron*. Fat Legs.

Despite worry about the whereabouts and future of my eldest, I continued to manage the Belleme and Montgomery lands, almost ruling like a queen from the fastness of either Domfront or Alencon. However, peace was not to last for me, either. Reports reached my ears that looting and pillaging had taken place around the castles of Eschafour and Montreuil. Villages had been burnt, goodwives outraged, cattle and other livestock stolen. Deer and other animals were poached from the forests, while the streams and rivers were stripped of fish. Monks and nuns travelling from surrounding abbeys were accosted and robbed and church plate was ripped from the altars.

Uneasiness filled my heart that it should be those particular two castles were involved—for they had once been in the possession of my old, dead enemy Arnold d'Eschafour. Arnold's scattered kinsmen had recently set petitions to King William in an attempt to regain their strongholds, but William, favouring Roger more than ever before, refused to even consider their pleas.

So I sent out a band of well-trusted men to visit these unruly areas and report back on their findings.

What came back...were their severed heads, thrust into a sack and left at the gates of Domfront under the cover of darkness. They were brought into the hall by the captain of the guard, still wrapped in the bloody, dripping bag they had arrived in.

"My Lady Countess?" The captain, a brutish oaf with a bristly, unshaven face gazed uneasily at me.

"Open the bag...I *want* to see," I said in a sharp voice.

Reluctantly he opened the sack. The heads rolled onto the floor in front of my high seat.

At my side, my son Hugh, who was visiting from England, gasped in horror and grasped my shoulder. He was a gentle youth, the gentlest of my brood, known jokingly as Red Hugh for his flaming hair. It was time he toughened up, especially as he would inherit his lands in ever-rebellious England and would one day be lord over a conquered people.

"Look at this outrage, my son," I said, gesturing to the gaping grey heads. "These servants of mine must be avenged. I know not who has committed these crimes but I swear to God Almighty I will find out." Then I gestured to the captain of the guard and the terrified, whispering servants gathered on the periphery of the chamber. "Take the heads to the families for decent burial, captain. And the rest of you lurking in the shadows—get to cleaning the blood off my floor."

Angered to the point of distraction by this insult against my authority, I now sent out spies rather than soldiers to find out what was happening in the vicinity of Eschafour and Montreuil. Soon they returned, fortunately with their heads still on their shoulders, to recount their findings.

It was indeed no ordinary outlaws that ravaged the bounty of my forests and raided the villages and monasteries. "My Lady," said my chief spy, one Godfroi of Alencon, "the one who seeks to wound you and yours is Hugh Bunel, son of Robert de La Roche."

Making a face, I shook my head. "The name is not familiar to me. Who is his family?"

Godfroi cast me a wan smile. "I think you will not be surprised when I tell you that this Bunel is a cousin to Arnold d'Eschafour."

I took a deep breath; noisily let it out. "It is as I feared, but I am glad to know my fears, no matter how unpalatable, are confirmed. An enemy can be dealt with when one knows who he is."

"Bunel wishes to speak to you, my Lady."

Surprised, I leaned forward in my chair. "You *spoke* to the miscreant?"

"At much risk to my life..." he said dramatically, clearly angling for great reward.

"You will have your pay...and more," I muttered between taut lips. "Go on, sir."

"He said he would meet with you at the little chapel of St Austreberthe a mile or so outside Montreuil—in God's House where he knows he will be safe, and where you will also be safe."

Mocking laughter tore from my lips. "I think Bunel will find there has been more than one man dragged to his doom from 'God's House'."

"Even so...that is what he said, my Lady Countess. He asks that you come to Montreuil with only a small entourage and meet him alone within the church. He will do the same."

"Is he mad? How dare he make such demands when he has attacked my lands and the serfs and villeins dwelling upon them. His attacks on my properties are like an attack on me!"

"Yes, my Lady, that is true..." Godfroi's narrow yellowish little eyes swivelled away, "but those are the terms he set. He also said he doubted you would trust him but that you must rely on his honour as a knight."

"His honour!" I jeered, but inside I was seething. What could I do but meet the damned man? I could not take an army against him...for I knew not where he lived. I could seek out his father's lands and lay waste to them, but that would not help my situation. It could inflame it further as I would have attacked a man who had no part of my feud. No, like it or not, I had to speak to this Hugh Bunel myself, to impress upon the fool that as soon as Roger and the Duke returned to Normandy, he would suffer great penalties, including attainting and even death, if he should continue to harass my tenants and raid my woods and streams.

"I will meet him then," I said at length to Godfroi. "At Austreberthe's Chapel in ten days. Tell him I will leave my men in the woods near this church and he must do the same."

The spy bowed. "I will do as you bid, my Lady."

St Austreberthe's Chapel was small and partly ruinous, standing on a small hillock a few miles outside bustling Montreuil, where the Abbey bore the same saint's name and carried her relics. A solitary old priest still gave the occasional Mass to passers-by, but he was half a hermit, living in a little hut built into a slumped and fern-strewn wall. My emissaries had prepared the priest for my coming; ragged in dirty vestments, he appeared briefly, made the sign of the Cross over me, then rushed into his humble dwelling. I heard the sound of the door being barred from within…

Silently I slipped into the church nave. Cold and damp walls rose about me, rimed with worn, fragmented paintings—St Christopher carrying Christ, The Three Living standing in horror of the Three Dead, The Wheel of Five Senses with Reason standing predominant in the form of a crowned King.

I wondered if I had lost *my* reason coming here and leaving my men in the nearby woods.

Outside, the noise of boots on the gravel reached my ears. Then the church door creaked open, admitting a sharp blade of light that shot across the grimy tiles and touched the hem of my dress. A shadow stood in the door, black and tall; I shaded my eyes against the brightness and moved my legs a little—feeling the comforting coolness of my hidden favourite dagger, my long-term friend, ever faithful.

The door closed again, a muffled sound. The shadows returned and dust eddied. As my eyes adjusted, I saw a man, cowled and hooded, standing with booted feet spread wide apart in a defiant manner.

"Sir, remove your hood," I ordered in my most commanding tone.

A gloved hand reached up to flip the hood back. I stifled a gasp. It was like gazing upon my old enemy, my dead enemy, Arnold d'Eschafour all over again. The same arrogant jut of jaw and beady, watchful eyes, the same dull, rat's-tail coloured hair.

"I am Hugh de Bunel," he said. "Cousin to Arnold d'Eschafour, God assoil him." He folded his arms. "I do not need to ask who *you* are—you, my Lady, are infamous."

"Am I? I am glad to hear it," I said. "But I did not come all this way for silly chatter. Why do you keep attacking my lands? What is it you want?"

"Oh, I think you know. Those lands are mine, mine by right."

"I think you will find they are not—and that the Duke of Normandy, who is also King of England, would agree with me."

"Only because you have deceived him, you…you sorceress! I know how Arnold died, and what happened to his sire before he retreated to the Abbey at Bec! *I know what you did…*"

I went cold. "How…how dare you," I sputtered. "If you would accuse me of murder, take it to the justices, take it to the Duke! But I did nought wrong; your ruffian kinsman Arnold glutted himself on spoilt meat and imbibed too much drink, that is all. As for his sire, I was just a girl at the time, scarcely more than a child. If you want to lay blame for his grievous wounds, lay it at the feet of my sire, William Talvas—but you will have to dig him up first. He has lain mouldering in his grave many a year."

Hugh grinned unpleasantly, his eyes holding a dangerous, knowing gleam. "Do not play the innocent with me about Cousin Arnold, madam. The truth about your involvement in his demise was long whispered but it now known…"

"And how did such special knowledge come to a nobody like you?" I said haughtily. "Do tell." I kept my composure, but a small droplet of sweat trailed down my spine.

His grin widened; his mouth looked like a dark slash, a cut throat. He had lost most of his teeth, no doubt in some bygone skirmish. "Goulafre…Roger Goulafre. You should have killed him too, madam, or thrown him in a lightless dungeon somewhere. What he knew was far too dangerous. You silly little bitch; you have made a terrible mistake."

Goulafre! Curse him to Hell! I had indeed considering removing him but he had disappeared in the weeks after Arnold d'Eschafour's demise.

"So...Lady Montgomery, do you have a change of heart and, as a token of your newfound generousness, hand Montreuil and Eschafour back to my family? Or do I continue raiding your lands and killing your beasts and your servants—until, of course, Duke William is available and I can bring Roger Goulafre to bear witness against you?"

"Goulafre is only one man and a nobody at that!" I spat. "What makes you think William would listen to such a lowly churl!"

"He might not...but Goulafre's servant, also known to you, madam, is willing to testify as well. Many across Normandy have grievances against you; peasants near the Abbey of Evroul even speak of you killing a child with sorcery, letting it suck poison from your teat."

I flushed crimson, horrified that this man was aware of even my darkest secrets. My hands clenched until my rings bit into the skin.

"Hah—you do not deny it!" Hugh Bunel flashed. "I swear I will see you put to death for your crimes, hung as a witch..."

I had taken enough of his tongue. "Stand aside!" I ordered. "I will listen no more to these idle threats and lies! This meeting is over!" I took a long stride forward, skimming the block grey font and heading for the door.

Hugh Bunel looked startled and then with a shout lunged in my direction, hands outstretched. A moment later, my poniard was in my hand. And then it pierced his shoulder.

Bunel gave a shrill shriek that sounded almost womanish in my ears and made nervous laughter tumble from my lips. "Get back, you coward...and let me pass. You can be sure I will speak to William before ever you get the chance—for I have the ear of Duchess Matilda!"

I yanked my dagger from his flesh and fled towards the door, leaving Hugh howling and clutching his shoulder, redness dripping through his clawed fingers. As I grasped the door-ring and raced out into the murk of a cold, rainy afternoon, I heard him roar after me, "You won't escape justice, witch! Not this time! I will track you down! If the Duke will help me not, then I will do what I must to rid the world of your filth!"

Pressing my hands over my ears against his curses, I stumbled through the churchyard, tripping over leaning dead men's markers while the wind shrieked around me like a mocking ghoul.

The walls of the Castle of Bure-sur-Dives reared up before me, stony, implacable, the Black Tower of Belleme flying from the topmost tower. Dusk was falling, the stars hard shards of ice in the sky, frost crisp on the ground. Wrapped in a dark blue mantle, I rode alongside my son Hugh, our breath hanging white before our faces. Our entourage was few and cloaks furled their mail; we had travelled from Seez as swiftly and unobtrusively as we could so as not to attract unwelcome attention.

Hugh Bunel and his threats had frightened me, although I had heard nought more of him since our fateful meeting in the ruined chapel. At one time I would have stood up to him gladly, but I was no longer young and the fire had waned within my heart. I had my sons and daughters to look out for, lands to administer. I was Countess of Shrewsbury, even if England was but a distant memory. I no longer wished to engage in petty squabbles, especially since Roger was still away. I wanted the past to stay in the past and remain there, deeply buried.

Other troubles clouded my mind, too—Rob and Fat Legs Curthose had continued in their disloyal madness, aided by Hugh de Chateauneuf, who was husband to my daughter Mabille. He loaned them use of his castle and the two young hotheads embarked from there on raids throughout Normandy. If that was not wicked and provocative enough, they also appealed for aid to the French King and he gave Curthose the fortress of Gerberoy, from which he mounted further assaults on his own people.

The groans and cries of his subjects had brought William to the field, Roger at his side although in great grief at our son's perfidy. The Duke had pounded the walls of Gerberoy with great engines and catapults until at last father and son met in armed conflict outside the gate—where William's horse was shot from under him and he was wounded upon the hand by Robert Curthose himself.

It was the first defeat the Conqueror had ever known, but it seemed even his wayward son was appalled at the thought. Rather than crowing of victory, Curthose fled in the night and again, my foolish, war-mad Rob followed on his heels.

In the wake of Robert's betrayal of his oaths to William, I no longer felt quite so confident that the Duke would support me against Hugh Bunel, especially if he indeed dragged Goulafre out as a witness, and that caused me many nights of restless slumber. Hence, I decided to progress through all my domains, hopefully foiling any attempt to pin down my movements by either Bunel or, should it come to it, Duke William.

And so in the dark heart of unwelcoming December, I came to Bure-sur-Dives.

Riding side by side, Hugh and I entered the castle bailey. Bures was not a large castle; in fact, it was minuscule compared to Alencon and Domfront, but it had sound stonework—two blocky round towers with a stout gate and murder holes, and a thrusting donjon whose firelit windows gazed out like red eyes in the dusky gloom. No one would suspect I was here, or so I hoped—I had put out false messages saying that I was on my way to Caen.

Once my horse had been taken, I bade Hugh goodnight and told him not to worry. "This running about throughout Normandy is only temporary, Hugh. Bunel will lose interest soon enough, I am sure...."

"I think we should have fared to Caen," said Hugh, face pinched and pale within the folds of his hood. "There are many there who are friends and comrades of Father. They would have protected us amply; surely we would have had accommodation in Duke William's castle."

"I would not be so sure of that anymore, Hugh, thanks to your brother's folly," I murmured, head bowed, "and there have always been many who do not love the Belleme Clan."

"Nevertheless, I do not feel safe *here*." Hugh glanced up at the turrets, where nightbirds were wheeling, their shrieks faint and eerie in the descending night. "I wish we had more men. An *army*..."

I reached out and caught his wrist; his skin was ice-cold. So soft, my little Hugh, so unlike his brother Rob, all fire and steel. "Come, calm yourself," I said. "All shall be well. I will have meat and bread and wine sent to your quarters and once you have rested, the world will not seem such a fearsome place."

He attempted a smile but it did not quite reach his eyes. "As you wish, Lady Mother," he said, and he gestured the Steward to lead him to the apartments.

I was led to mine by the Chamberlain, a tall man with a pronounced hump to his back that made his head protrude at an odd forward angle; with his scrawny neck and large hooked nose, I was reminded of a hungry vulture. Normally such a thought would have amused me, but tonight all I could think of was how vultures picked at the bones of the dead.

In silence, I followed the Chamberlain to the lord's apartments, a series of dim chambers with a musty scent. At the door, he bowed. "I will send women to attend you as we agreed, Lady Mabel."

I nodded and he limped away into the poorly lit passageways beyond. I moved to the window, unlocking the narrow shutter. Down below, a striped cat slunk by on the moon-silvered flagstones; in the distance, over the jagged walls, lights from distant cottages glowed. Far away, a woman was singing, a sweet sad song…I slammed the shutter closed, waves of emotion I did not quite understand running through me.

Outside the heavy bedchamber door, I could hear women's voices, muffled but not so quiet that I could not make out some of the words. I was adept at eavesdropping on hidden conversations behind curtains and wooden walls—and I was horrified by what I heard: '…they say she kills and eats babies…bathes in blood…murdered her husband's brother…mates with Satan himself …"

The door swung open, giving an ear-splitting creak. Three drabs gathered from the household staff to attend me leapt back in fright, not realising I was so near at hand. Their whey, common faces flushed guiltily. At one time I would have had them stripped naked and chased through the courtyard with flails…but I had no stomach for such antics now.

"M-my Lady," stammered one, her hair as red as her guilty visage. "I've brought you some food." With shaking hands, she passed me a platter laden with chunks of badly cut barley bread, a rind of cheese, a pie that reeked like offal, a handful of slimy overripe grapes about to burst their skins.

"So this is what you bring your mistress?" I said, staring at the tray. "Fare fit for the pigs?"

"We did not have much time to prepare for your arrival, my Lady," muttered the ginger-haired wench, somewhat mutinously. "It's secret, isn't it?"

"I did not ask you for comments, girl," I snapped, sitting on the edge of the bed and tearing into the bread. "Now...I bid you prepare a bath for me. My bones ache and I am chilled to the bone from riding in the winter weather."

As I ate my meagre, insulting meal (save for the revolting pie, which I flung down to the cat in the courtyard), the three sullen trulls dragged in a huge wooden tub and began the arduous task of retrieving boiled water from the kitchens to fill it. It took what seemed an eternity, but at last the tub was halfway full, the steam rising in coils to the ceiling beams.

I rose and held out my arms and the three girls, smelling of damp and onions and sweat, began to unlace my gown. Such an everyday action seldom brought any sense of shame or embarrassment but tonight...it was different. I was sure these three dullards with their dim eyes and spotty faces were half-expecting to see a serpent-woman with a snake's tail below the waist, like a figure in some vile old legend. Instead, all they would see an ageing woman, her belly lined with white stripes from umpteen pregnancies. And they would hate her just as much.

If they were disappointed at no tail, they managed to keep their disappointment well-hidden; their wan faces were blank slates as they took my gown and kirtle, folded them neatly and draped them over a painted screen. I climbed the small wooden steps leaning against the side of the tub and lowered myself into the waters, fragrant with herbs. At least they wenches had not forgotten that nicety.

"Go!" I pointed to the door. "I do not want your company. I will call you if and when I need you."

The three creatures filed out obediently. I heard a giggle from the corridor and then nought more.

Sinking into the hot water with a sigh, I closed my weary eyes. I wished Roger was with me in this drear castle—but he was far away, trying to make amends to William for our faithless son. When we met again, I would have to tell him of the lack of hospitality and deference at Bures. Maybe he would drive the whole household out and get in a new one…

As the bathwater began to cool, I started to feel sleepy. My bones ached after my long ride from Seez. I debated calling the serving wenches to help me out of the tub, but promptly decided I had no wish to see their impertinent faces again. Climbing from the bath unaided, I wiped myself dry with a linen towel lying on the bed before slipping on the loose bed-robe I found beside it.

My bones ached and I let out a huge unladylike yawn. Tying my hair into a tight plait, I then slipped under the coverlet atop the bed. Soon I drifted into an uncomfortable, uneasy sleep. I dreamed…dreamed of someone I had not thought of for years—Gilbert, Roger's brother, whose greed had led him to down the poison meant for Arnold d'Eschavour.

Gilbert was gazing at me sadly, eyes hollow in his sunken, dead face. In his hands, he held a jewel-encrusted cup with noisome vapours coiling from its rim. "Mabel, my sister-by-marriage," he moaned, his voice the shake of old fleshless bones. "It did not have to be this way. All the evils that befell me and will soon befall you could have been averted if only you had repented of your wickedness…"

"I regret nought!" I snapped back, caught in the web of this foul nightmare.

"You slew me, who had done you no wrong…who had tried to help you. *You murdered me*."

"It was your own folly that killed you! You took the drink meant for d'Eschafour…."

"That day doomed you, Mabel…" He shook his head sadly; worms were dripping through his hair, his cheeks were greying and decaying, the teeth shining through like sharp spears. He held the gem-encrusted cup out toward me; blood bubbled within. "This is the Poisoned Chalice that you too drank from, Mabel de Belleme…You have drunk from it all your days and now it will slay you…"

"No, get away from me!" I struck out at the vile lich of Gilbert de Montgomery and the dream ended, and I sat bolt upright, gasping for air.

I glanced around. The candles in the solitary candelabra had burnt to stubs; the light had grown orange, dim, shadows springing across walls and ceiling.

Outside, in the passageway, footsteps sounded. Loud, growing louder. Heavy male footsteps, not the light, shuffling tread of the serving girls. I leapt from the bed, heart hammering but seemingly unable to move. It was as if a spell was upon me, maybe laid on me by Gilbert's ghost, if ghost it was and not just foolish imaginings and guilty thoughts. Distantly, I could hear my son's voice, rising, screaming...but it was far away and I could not make out the words.

A heavy boot struck the door and it crashed inward, tearing the flimsy latch away and sending it spinning across the floor.

In the confusion and the wavering light, I could not see Hugh Bunel's face but I recognised his sneering laugh. And then I spied a sea of swords, bright as morning, cold as moonlight, sharp as a wolf's hungry fangs.

I laughed wildly, crazily, as Bunel and his henchmen surged towards me. The draught from the poisoned chalice I had wrought for myself tasted bitter in my mouth as those blades lifted to heaven and then flashed towards my head like a hundred falling stars...

MABEL'S EPITAPH in TROARN ABBEY (tomb sadly no longer extant)

> Sprung from the noble and the brave,
> Here Mabel finds a narrow grave.
> But, above all woman's glory,
> Fills a page in famous story.
> Commanding, eloquent, and wise,
> And prompt to daring enterprise;
> Though slight her form, her soul was great,
> And, proudly swelling in her state,
> Rich dress, and pomp, and retinue,
> Lent it their grace and honours due.
> The border's guard, the country's shield,
> Both love and fear her might revealed,
> Till Hugh, revengeful, gained her bower,
> In dark December's midnight hour.
> Then saw the Dive's o'erflowing stream
> The ruthless murderer's poignard gleam.
> Now friends, some moments kindly spare,
> For her soul's rest to breathe a prayer!

Ordericus Vitalis, The Ecclesiastical History of England and Normandy, Trans. Thomas Forester, Vol. II (Henry G. Bohn, London, 1854), pp. 194-5

AUTHOR'S NOTES

Orderic Vitalis's description of Mabel de Belleme: *"small, very talkative, ready enough to do evil, shrewd and jocular, extremely cruel and daring."*

In common with the other subjects of my MEDIEVAL BABES series, Mabel de Belleme was a real person, and yes, an infamous one (showing that, without a doubt, medieval women were not all shrinking violets.) She is the furthest back in time of the ladies I have written about, was born several decades before the Norman Conquest. Due to this, records of her life are even scantier than those I usually work with and often more contradictory. Her exact dates of birth and marriage are unknown but can be guessed by events such as the birth of her children. It is true that Mabel's father, William Talvas murdered her mother, Hildeburg—and that Mabel decided to stick with her father through thick and thin, even when her brother rose in rebellion and William had to go forth, a penniless exile. I did bump up the time scale of Arnulf's rebellion, which may have taken place *after* his second marriage to one of the de Beaumont women (I placed it before, shortly after Hildeburg's murder). The second marriage is also hazy with no first name for his new bride given in most sources, although a few name her as Haberge or Haberga. Some appear to conflate her with the first wife, who has a similar name, so in reality, the second wife's name may have been much different.

Mabel ended up marrying Roger de Montgomery, who was a close friend of the youthful Duke William of Normandy—the future Conqueror. They had ten children, 9 of whom made it to adulthood.

Mabel's aggressive and often shocking behaviour was noted quite early on. She would turn up at abbeys unannounced with a huge entourage and then ate them out of house and home. The story of how an Abbot cursed her and she fell ill and had to suckle a child (which later died) to remove the curse is a traditional legend. However, Mabel's main 'talent' seemed to be for using poison on her enemies. She even poisoned her husband's brother but Roger seems to have forgiven her since it was an 'accident.'

Roger may or may not have accompanied Duke William on his invasion of England, but most modern historians believe he stayed behind to help the Duke's wife, Matilda of Flanders, who was regent in William's absence. I do not know how often Mabel met the Duke and Duchess but as Roger was a close friend, it was probably fairly often. William and Matilda's appearance in POISONED CHALICE is based on events recorded at the time—including the tales of William throwing his wife-to-be into the mud and making her do the 'walk of shame' like Cersei in Game of Thrones after believing she had cuckolded him. While some elements of these stories are almost certainly prurient monkish tales, there are enough mentions of marital violence by different authors to make one think there may have been a grain of truth.

After Mabel was murdered by Hugh Bunel at Bures, Roger soon married again—to a lady said to be pious and gentle. I guess he was eager for a quiet life.

However, Mabel and Roger's son, Robert de Belleme, decided to uphold the family tradition for nastiness, and ended up known as 'Robert the Devil.' He became the 3rd Earl of Shrewsbury, and illegally built a mighty castle at Bridgnorth, which today has a striking tower that looks about ready to fall. Orderic Vitalis said this of Robert—"*Grasping and cruel, an implacable persecutor of the Church of God and the poor... unequalled for his iniquity in the whole Christian era.*" Nice guy.

Robert married the heiress Agnes of Ponthieu and treated her poorly, shutting her up for years in the Castle of Belleme. Eventually, she escaped, retired to Ponthieu, and never returned to her husband's side. They had one son, William.

Interestingly, Robert de Belleme was the inspiration for the villainous sorcerer, Simon de Belleme, in the TV series Robin of Sherwood…

Today there are thousands and probably millions of living descendants of Roger Montgomery and Mabel de Belleme, including the Montgomery Clan of Scotland.

For Further Reading—
Matilda-Queen of the Conqueror by Tracy Borman

Chibnall, Marjorie (ed. and trans.), The Ecclesiastical History of Orderic Vitalis, 6 volumes (Oxford, 1968–1980) (Oxford Medieval Texts), ISBN 0-19-820220-2.

Chibnall, Marjorie, The World of Orderic Vitalis (Oxford, 1987).

OTHER WORKS BY J.P. REEDMAN

STONEHENGE and prehistory:

THE STONEHENGE SAGA. Huge epic of the Bronze Age. Ritual, war, love and death. A prehistoric GAME OF STONES roughly based on the Arthurian legends but set in the British Bronze Age.

THE SWORD OF TULKAR-Collection of prehistoric-based short stories

The Barrow Woman's Bones—short ghost story set around a real archaeological find.

THE GODS OF STONEHENGE-Short booklet about myths and legends associated with Stonehenge and about other possible mythological meanings.

MEDIEVAL BABES SERIES:

MY FAIR LADY: ELEANOR OF PROVENCE, HENRY III'S LOST QUEEN

MISTRESS OF THE MAZE: Rosamund Clifford, Mistress of Henry II

THE CAPTIVE PRINCESS: Eleanor of Brittany, sister of the murdered Arthur, a prisoner of King John.

THE WHITE ROSE RENT: The short life of Katherine, illegitimate daughter of Richard III

THE PRINCESS NUN. Mary of Woodstock, Daughter of Edward I, the nun who liked fun!

MY FATHER, MY ENEMY. Juliane, illegitimate daughter of Henry I, seeks to kill her father with a crossbow.

LONGSWORD'S LADY- Ela of Salisbury, married to William Longespee, half-brother to Richard I and King John. Found of Salisbury cathedral, female sheriff and powerful abbess.

RICHARD III and THE WARS OF THE ROSES:

I, RICHARD PLANTAGENET I: TANTE LE DESIREE. Richard in his own first-person perspective, as Duke of Gloucester

I, RICHARD PLANTAGENET II: LOYAULTE ME LIE. Second part of Richard's story, told in 1st person. The mystery of the Princes, the tragedy of Bosworth

A MAN WHO WOULD BE KING. First person account of Henry Stafford, Duke of Buckingham suspect in the murder of the Princes

THE ROAD FROM FOTHERINGHAY—Richard III's childhood to his time in Warwick's household.

SACRED KING—Historical fantasy in which Richard III enters a fantastical afterlife and is 'returned to the world' in a Leicester carpark

WHITE ROSES, GOLDEN SUNNES. Collection of short stories about Richard III and his family.

SECRET MARRIAGES. Edward IV's romantic entanglements with Eleanor Talbot and Elizabeth Woodville

BLOOD OF ROSES. Edward IV defeats the Lancastrians at Mortimer's Cross and Towton.

RING OF WHITE ROSES. Two short stories featuring Richard III, including a time-travel tale about a lost traveller in the town of Bridport.

THE MISTLETOE BRIDE OF MINSTER LOVELL. Retelling of the folkloric tale featuring Francis Lovell, his wife and his friend the Duke of Gloucester.

COMING SOON—AVOUS ME LIE. The youth of Richard III part 2 told from his first-person perspective.

Printed in Great Britain
by Amazon